Pirates of Mars

Chris Gerrib

To my parents

Special Thanks

A special thank you goes out to Jackie Powers, Literary Midwife and all-around good egg, for her efforts in bringing this novel to the world. Thanks also go out to Ron Miller, who did the cover for this book, and for his kind words about my "practice novel" *The Mars Run.* His validation of my efforts went a long way towards making this book happen. I would be remiss if I didn't thank Jeff Duntemann, Jim C. Hines and Richard Chwedyk, authors who provided valuable workshop assistance, albeit not on this novel. I would also like to thank Dr. Jerry Pournelle for letting me use his Iron Law of Bureaucracy.

A Word About Names and Concepts

The character Rachel in this book and the character "J. R." in my practice novel *The Mars Run* are the same people. The real ship *Charles S. Price* rolled over in a storm on Lake Huron in 1913, taking her crew of 28 with her.

Luidas "Lu Can Do" Volodka was a friend of mine and a damned good Rotarian. He wasn't the guy up front handing out the big check, rather he was the guy taking the picture. Lu did the unglamorous jobs that, if done right got a line in the program and if done wrong made your name Mudd. I served with a short, "black Irish" fireplug of a man named Kelly. We served on the *USS Jack Williams*, a ship named for a corpsman who went ashore on Iwo Jima and came off the beach in a box. They gave Jack's Medal of Honor to his family. Tony Chen is a professor at the College of DuPage.

Janet Pilgrim is the stage name of the second woman to appear naked in Playboy magazine. Marilyn Monroe was the first, of course, and that wasn't her real name either. I read of some celebrity naming her daughter "Arminta" and shortening it to "Minty." Since it led to one of those Ian Fleming-inspired double entendres, I borrowed it immediately.

The "Somali Rules" for piracy was taken from real-world research as reported on the blog Lawyers, Guns and Money (lawyersgunsmoneyblog.com). Marty Mackovic is my grandfather, and appears in the book because my mother bought Tuckerization rights at a Rotary charity auction. Roger McNally is Rand's cousin, while Penny Sharpe is my neighbor, and the realtor who found me my house.

In a previous draft of this book, I needed a private detective. Since a Rotarian of my acquaintance was a PI, Mike Slevnik made the book. When circumstances changed, the character became a Colonel. I went to school with twins named Scott and Todd, so that was an easy call to make.

Jim C. Hines you've met in the Special Thanks section. His friend, the writer Tobias Buckell, was born and raised in the Caribbean, and if I recall correctly named a spaceship the *Dread Ayatollah* in one of his books.

Contents

Chapter 1

Thursday, 30 Virgo Year 52 15:30 Martian Zulu Time (local) (March 1, 2074, 15:30 GMT)

Container Cargo Ship *Charles S. Price*, approaching Mars

I GOT A DEGREE IN ART HISTORY FOR THIS? Rachel Storey wondered, shivering in the cold and dark mid-deck of the *Charles S. Price*. One of the ship's officers had cut the power, rendering the *Price* a death-trap.

If we don't get power on, this ship's gonna crater into Mars. Rachel winced at the thought. The last failed attempt at piracy had nearly cost her life.

Get a move on!" Rachel barked at one of her fellow pirates. "I'm not going down with this ship."

"Movin' these Mex-cans all trussed up ain't easy," came the reply. "And besides, I don't work for you. You're just the damn bus driver."

Rachel glared at the speaker, his hair and features bleached by too much contact with Martian sand. Regarding her role in this attack, he was right. But she was damned if she was going to take crap from some sand-blonde scavenger. "Dave Eggman, if I wanted to hear your shit I'd have asked for it. Now get the lead out!"

Eggman pushed the bound and hooded prisoner, formerly a crewmember of the *Price*, up into the zero-gee environment of the mid-deck. He pushed too hard, of course, and the man bounced helplessly off of the far side of the corridor, smashing into a purple color-coded pipe. This elicited a stream of curses in Spanish. Rachel ignored the words and, bracing off of a stanchion, shoved the man down the tube-like corridor.

"Incoming!" she shouted, alerting the pirate at the other end of the corridor. *Pirates! Hah. Bunch of incompetent, trigger-happy mouth-breathing boobs.*

"Got him, boss," the crewman shouted.

"That's the last of them," Eggman said.

The last one alive, he meant. The Price's Master and Chief Engineer were dead. How had Eggman put it? "They had elected to shoot it out. They lost the election."

Rachel smiled at that. Eggman did occasionally have a way with words.

Chuckles, their leader, poked his head in the corridor. His face was flushed despite the cold, and his strawberry blonde hair was matted with sweat.

"What in the fuck are you doing?"

"Evacuating the hostages," Rachel replied. You idiot, she added mentally. *If only he was half as smart as his dad.* "You coming?"

"Hell no. Who gives a shit about the crew?"

"The insurance company does," Rachel said. "Remember? The plan was to ransom them back."

"Your plan," Chuckles said. "All we want is the special cargo."

The special cargo, Rachel thought. The mysterious container that their investors, presumably representing the Martian branch of some criminal gang, were paying extra for them to hijack. *All I want is enough cash to get out of Bensonville.*

"Have any luck finding it?" Rachel asked.

Chuckle's scowl deepened. "No, and you moving the crew means I can't question them."

"Charles Benson Junior," Rachel said, using his full name, "you can question them all you want. They don't know. Hell, if Bam Bam doesn't know, how would some Able Spacer?"

Chuckles scowled some more at that. Brenda "Bam Bam" Lords, Third Mate on the *Price*, had been their inside person, and instrumental in getting them onboard. Now she was trying to get ship's power restored before they literally cratered into Mars. Unsuccessfully, so far.

"Don't matter. Why don't you look at the computer?"

Because I'm not a computer expert, she thought. "*Cranston* needs to get gone soon," she said, gesturing towards the docking collar at the far end of the corridor where their tiny mother ship was attached.

"You got time."

"Barely," Rachel said. She yelled down the corridor at her crewmember, anchored at the docking collar leading to the *Cranston.* "Get them secured and get ready to leave!"

Chuckles ducked back down the ladderway wordlessly, followed by Eggman. Rachel descended last, and quickly arrived at the main crew deck of the *Price.*

Like most deep space ships, that part of the ship was a cylinder, spun to produce artificial gravity.

"Like a bug in a can," Rachel said under her breath, stepping on the floor of the main crew area.

"Huh?" Chuckles said, his breath fogging in the cold.

"Nothing," Rachel replied. She looked down the long main corridor, struggling to override the appearance that the corridor curved uphill. It wasn't—by the time you got somewhere, the spin put you at the bottom again—but Rachel found it disorienting, especially when the ship was dark, illuminated only by emergency lighting.

Something popped loudly, and everybody jumped a little bit.

"Thermal contraction," Eggman said.

He's probably right, Rachel thought. With no fans humming, all sorts of noises that would normally be masked weren't. *A dead ship, and if I don't get off soon, I'll die with it.*

They came to a door off of the main corridor and stepped into the "day bridge" of the *Price.* There was a separate "maneuvering bridge" for docking and close work, a zero-gee space with a real window looking out into space, but this room was used most of the time while underway.

The room wasn't ever that brightly-lit, but with the loss of ship's power it was even darker than usual. The number of amber and red warning lights from the various mostly-useless consoles gave the room a reddish tinge. The far end of the wall was dominated by a digital display. With main power off, most of the sensors were down, so the display was largely dark. However, the navigational computer was up, and a schematic showing their position in relationship to Mars was clearly visible. Also visible on the display was a flashing yellow warning, reading "collision imminent" in both English and Spanish.

"Any luck on the computer?" Chuckles asked.

"Not a computer problem," Bam Bam said, looking up from her console. She was clearly frustrated as she pushed a shock of black hair out of her face. "It's a reactor problem. I've got maneuvering control, but with no power, I can't move anywhere."

"What's wrong with the reactor?" Eggman asked.

"If I knew that, I'd fix it!" Bam Bam said.

"What about the special cargo?" Rachel asked.

"I have no idea." She waved at a desk off to the side. "Cargo manifest is on the Master's computer."

"So?" Chuckles asked.

"It's down," Bam Bam said. "Shut down automatically when we lost power to save juice for critical shit. Besides which I'll need the Old Lady's login."

"Can you bring it back up?" Rachel asked.

"Give me fifteen minutes, sure," she replied. "Fifteen minutes I haven't had."

Fifteen minutes they didn't have, Rachel thought, not counting the time they'd waste to crack the passwords and find the manifest.

"Charles," Rachel said. "We have to leave. Now."

"Why?" he asked.

"If we don't leave soon, we'll be too close to Mars for the *Cranston's* engines to pull us clear."

"Not a good idea to leave," he said. "The investors..."

"Fuck the investors," Eggman said. "What are they going to do..."

"If we don't pay them?" Chuckles said, his face drained of color. "If we're lucky, they'll just kill us quick. If not..."

Who exactly is bankrolling this operation? It was hard to scare stupid, and anybody capable of scaring a rock with lips like Chuckles had to be a serious Mike Foxtrot.

"We need a tow, Captain," Eggman said, looking at Rachel.

"Don't get stuck on stupid," Rachel said. "*Cranston's* barely got enough delta vee to get clear herself, let alone pull this out." The ship class was referred to as a Mosquito by its manufacturers, and not without reason.

"Then we just give them back their money," Eggman said. "Sell the *Cranston*."

Chuckles just glared at Eggman. Probably blew through most of the cash already, Rachel thought.

"Let's call for help," Bam Bam said.

"Call who?" Eggman asked.

Good question, Rachel thought. There were hundreds of settlements on Mars, technically under the control of dozens of countries on Earth. In practice, most of the settlements were on their own, and cared little for anything that happened outside their airlocks. Hell, Bensonville, the one-airlock town that was sponsoring this outing, was a good example of that.

"Space Rescue," Bam Bam suggested.

"Those Boy Scouts?" Eggman said.

"Why not?" Bam Bam said.

"Anybody got any better ideas?" Chuckles asked. Nobody said anything. "Okay, then, let's make the call."

"I got to get gone," Rachel said. "Or Space Rescue will be pulling two ships out of the shit."

"Go," Chuckles replied.

Rachel left, thinking that she'd never heard of a stupider idea in her life. But at least she'd get out.

Chapter 2

Thursday, 30 Virgo Year 15:45 local (March 1, 2074, 15:46 GMT) Docked at Stickney Base, Phobos, Mars Orbit

"PERMISSION TO ENTER THE BRIDGE," asked Chief Astronaut Bill Kelly.

"Granted," replied Lieutenant Peter Grant, perched on an equipment console. "Come and save me from death by boredom."

Kelly smiled. *I was like that once, chaffing at the bit for action.* He suppressed a frown. *Before I stuck my neck out for some General's brat. Got me bounced right out of the Air Force.*

Kelly grabbed the handrail and pulled himself hand-over-hand into the pilothouse. Phobos, Mars' inner moon, had barely enough gravity to get dust to settle, if you were a patient sort. Their ship, the Volunteer Space Rescue Service Vessel *Luidas Volodka*, was on alert, and was docked on the rim of Stickney crater. The planet itself filled the forward bridge window, the half-lit part glowing a surprisingly warm and friendly orange, the dark part dotted with small lights.

"I wanted to go over the training schedule with you, sir," Kelly said, in the neutral tone he'd long ago learned to use when dealing with 'superior officers' young enough to be his kids.

The bridge-to-bridge radio crackled. "Mayday, Mayday Mayday, vessel *Charles S. Price* calling, over."

"I hope that's not a Mayday Madeline," Peter grumbled, his hand reaching up to activate his headset.

They had been having a run of bogus mayday calls, Kelly thought. *As if the Service, badly overstretched and underfunded, didn't have enough to do.* Kelly pushed off towards the direction-finding console. Unlike the ship's original consoles, enclosed in beige aluminum, the add-on direction-finding console was an open rack with various components bolted in, and a barely-organized nest of wires visible in the back.

The mayday wasn't sending an automatic emergency beacon. *Strike one.*

"Grab the DF would ya, Bill?" Grant said.

"We're hot," Kelly said, activating the tracking program.

"This is Space Rescue to the vessel calling mayday, over," Grant called into the radio microphone.

"*Price* to Space Rescue. Request assistance, inbound Mars, over." It sounded like a female voice.

Kelly watched the display as it attempted to get a fix on the transmission. "Got three stations tracking, bearing correlates."

"Enough for a fix?"

"Negative," Kelly said.

"Copy," Grant said, and took a breath. "*Price*, this is Space Rescue. Please state your position, course, speed, and nature of emergency, over?" Kelly glanced over at Grant. A note of excitement was creeping into the kid's voice. Well, he was only twenty-something.

"Space Rescue, this is *Price*. Our position follows."

Kelly keyed in the position information while watching the DF run its calculations. The *Price's* reported position was almost exactly in the middle of the probability box calculated by the computer.

"Solid correlation," Kelly said, then turned to see Grant hovering at his shoulder.

"Let's scramble."

"Before we know the type of emergency?" Kelly asked. *Let's not go off half-cocked.*

"*Price*, what is the nature of your emergency?" Grant said, keying his headset.

The only reply was static. Grant reached past Kelly and pointed to the display. "Bill—looks like she'll have to make a change for orbital insertion soon."

"Looks that way, sir," Kelly replied. The ship was well out past Diemos, Mars' outer moon, but approaching quickly.

As they watched, Grant repeated his radio call. Still no reply.

"I guess we're scrambling," Grant said.

Kelly looked over his shoulder as Grant mashed the big red alert button, sounding alarms all over the ship. The grin on Grant's face wouldn't look out of place on a five-year-old riding a fire truck who'd been allowed to turn on the sirens.

The first person to arrive in the pilothouse was Captain Tony Chen, a short and wiry man with close-cropped gray hair. Since his cabin was the next compartment over, it wasn't a surprise.

"Bill, how'd you beat me here?" Chen asked.

"I was already here," Kelly replied.

"Syracuse loose again?" Chen asked, nodding in Grant's direction. "Come to collect from your boss?"

"I don't think they play until tonight, sir," Kelly said. "I was up to discuss the training schedule."

"Oh," Chen replied. He looked at Lieutenant Grant. "So, Peter, what do we have?"

"Mayday, ship inbound, lost contact."

Chen pulled himself over to his chair and somersaulted into it. "Have we started a track yet?"

"Yes," Kelly replied. He had told the system to put a track out. Nobody had bothered to set up a radar traffic control system for Mars, although even on Earth, the track would be out of radar range for most systems, so the track was the computer's best guess based on the DF data. "Track Five-Four-Zero-Four."

Kelly turned to see Midshipman Jack Williams pushing himself into the pilothouse, then sliding behind the navigation console. Lieutenant Lee, the ship's navigator, was on compassionate leave for his father's funeral, so Williams was filling in.

"Track 5404," Kelly said.

"Thanks, Chief," Williams replied, his dark face a mask of concentration. If they were going to fly an intercept, Williams would have to calculate it.

"*Price*, *Price*, this is Space Rescue," Grant said, "We are not receiving you. Please state the nature of your emergency, over."

"Power failure?" Williams asked, gesturing with his chin at the radio speaker.

"Possibly," Kelly replied, strapping himself in his chair as the tiny bridge filled up with people. He opened up a home-brewed database program the Service maintained, trying to get some information on their potential target.

Lieutenant Carla Ortega, the ship's second in command, pulled herself to her console, asking as she moved, "Did they say what the problem was?"

"No—just a position," Grant replied. "Then they went silent."

Ortega nodded her head, her short and dark hair bobbing, then started strapping herself in while her console booted up.

"Chief, any data on the *Price*?" the Captain asked.

"Sir," Kelly replied, not looking up from his screen, "the only *Price* in the records is registered to Tri-State Cargo out of Chicago, USA."

"Never heard of them," the Captain said.

Kelly shared Chen's lack of surprise. The ships from the big operators rarely had need of their services. It seemed like the majority of calls came from a collection of Mom-and-Pop outfits, underfunded and badly managed, pushing worn-out tin.

"Somehow I doubt they're registered with a tier-one nation," Williams said wryly, his teeth glistening white against his dark skin.

Complying with the spaceship regulations for so-called 'Tier One' nations was expensive, Kelly thought while pulling up a ship registry database. It also meant that the crew had to be in one of the higher-paying chapters of the Merchant Spacer's Union.

"Ethiopian," Kelly answered, reading from his screen. "And there's no indication Tri-State has a Martian office."

"Voyage plan?" Williams asked optimistically.

"Not on file," Kelly replied, adding "big surprise," under his breath.

"Mister Williams, time to intercept?" the Captain asked.

"Thirty-three minutes, assuming we launch in the next five. If not, we miss completely."

The *Price* had to be way out of position for her terminal maneuver, Kelly thought. The *Volodka*, formerly an orbital tug, was a high-performance ship and usually they had much broader windows.

"Looks like it's time to do some good," Williams said.

Kelly glared at Williams. 'Do some good?' The kid treated Space Rescue like they were on a mission from God or something. It was just a job. Kelly glanced at the Captain, who was nodding approvingly. When Chen had started the Service, the 'Volunteer' part of their name had meant no pay. Now the Service got some subsidies from insurance firms and was able to pay wages. Not big wages, but then he wasn't away from home for six months at a shot either.

"I truly hate these blind calls," the Captain said, nodding approvingly at William's remark. "But we get paid to keep the living alive. Ortega, query Earth. Chief Kelly, sound maneuvering. Mister Grant, departure calls please."

Kelly reached up from his console and pressed the button. An audible alarm sounded throughout the ship, letting people know they were going to accelerate. "All hands, stand by for gees," Kelly said over the ship's intercom, "repeat, all hands, stand by for gees." Then he sounded the alarm again while sweeping his eyes around the console looking for loose binders and other stuff.

Kelly turned his head to report to the Captain and saw Grant, floating parallel to the deck, brace his feet against a column behind him.

"Attention all ships, attention all ships," Grant said over the radio. "Space Rescue ship *Volodka* underway from Phobos on a priority call, standing by for traffic channel 16."

"Ready, Mister Grant?" the Captain asked, a smirk on his face.

"Yes sir," Grant replied, then repeated his radio call.

"Engage, Ortega," Chen said.

The ship's rocket engines fired. The sudden appearance of gravity mentally changed Kelly's orientation in an instant from sitting horizontally to lying on his back. He glanced over to his boss, now standing upright on the column. Grant's blond hair, usually kept short, was falling on the man's face.

"One of these days showboating like that will get you hurt, sir," Kelly said.

Grant's grin looked almost painful. "Only one gee, Bill," he said.

"Inertia's a bitch, Peter," Chen said.

Chapter 3

Thursday, 30 Virgo Year 52 16:00 local (March 1, 2074, 16:02 GMT) VSRS Ship *Volodka*, underway

"ONE OF THESE DAYS, Mr. Grant," Kelly said and the *Volodka's* rockets cut out, "you're going to sprain something doing that."

"I'm very careful not to," Grant replied, his voice strained.

He should be straining, Kelly thought. Inertia *was* a bitch, and as soon as the rocket quit, Peter went from 'standing' on the stanchion to doing a handstand on the radio. Captain Chen was smiling at Grant indulgently, as if Grant was his favorite grandkid.

"We're in the groove for rendezvous," Ortega reported. "Intercept time thirty-three minutes."

"Nice plotting, Jack," Kelly said. It was, after all, the kid's first solo intercept.

"Thanks, Chief," the midshipman replied.

"Very good," the Captain said, acknowledging Ortega's report.

"Chief, get the team ready," Grant said.

"Aye, sir," Kelly replied. Kelly picked up the intercom mike and said, "Now muster the Rapid Response Team in the Rescue Locker. Make manned and ready reports to the bridge."

"Permission to strike below?" Grant asked.

"Granted," the Captain said, gesturing at his console. "We'll see if we can extract any information from the *Price*."

"Aye, sir," Kelly said and fell in behind Grant, heading aft to the suit lockers. He pulled himself hand-over-hand down a padded tube that served as the ship's central corridor, passing at various points shorter lateral corridors and compartments.

They quickly arrived at the space suit locker. It shared a lateral corridor with the rescue locker where they stored their equipment, and at the end of the lateral corridor, attached to the exterior hull of the ship, was a small ship-to-ship shuttle or 'launch.'

"Any scoop on the Mayday?" Alan Nomura, one of the Able Astronauts on the rescue party, was in the space, suiting up.

"Nope," Grant replied, opening up his locker in the suit-room.

Kelly reached his locker an instant later, and opened it up. You could wear a suit over street clothes in a pinch and Kelly had, but that got uncomfortable real quick. Thankfully, they had time, so Kelly gratefully changed into a skintight suit liner.

"You still have the Disney picture?" Kelly asked, gesturing at his boss's locker door.

Grant chuckled ruefully at the gentle ribbing. "You know I do."

Kelly had seen it before—it was Grant, age seven or eight, posing with his helmet on his hip, just back from his first space walk, taken during a family vacation to the old orbital Disney.

Personally Kelly liked the other picture better. That was the one from when his boss was sixteen. The kid had gotten some kind of internship at the Disney Farside resort on Earth's moon, taking little kids out on moonwalks. The picture showed Grant and Katy Tunstall, the first person on Mars. The grand old lady had come out to Farside for some PR event, and Grant had been assigned to escort her around. She died a week later, just days before she was to address Kelly's class at the Air Force Space Command.

"You look kind of serious, sir," Alan Nomura said from his nearby locker.

"First time I've had somebody waiting for me to get back," Grant replied.

"Who's that?" Kelly said.

"Girl I've been seeing," Grant replied, pulling his suit liner over his face.

"She got a name, sir?" Nomura asked.

"Janet," Grant replied. "Got a kid too."

"Not yours?" Nomura said.

"No," Grant replied.

"Good to hear," Kelly said. Maybe the kid will settle down some. Kelly started to pull on his suit liner. Doing so always put you in a spin—the trick was to know how to stop spinning.

"There are times I wish I didn't have people to go back for," Alan said.

"Oh?" Kelly replied, still spinning.

"Stevie's teething."

Alan had two wives, which in Kelly's opinion was one more than anybody needed, and was working on a baseball team of kids.

"So you come here for peace and quiet, huh?"

"That and money," Alan said, clipping his helmet to his oversuit. "Two weeks on, two off. It's a good job."

"That it is," Kelly said.

"I'll meet you at the rescue launch, sir," Nomura said.

"Get the rest of the team organized and in the launch," Grant said. "I'm heading back to the bridge. Maybe *Price* decided to talk."

Kelly left a minute later, heading for the bridge. When he arrived there, Mars was looming in a corner of the bridge window, but noticeably smaller.

"Any updates?" Kelly asked.

"No," the Captain replied.

"How long until we get a visual?" Grant asked.

"We're rolling ship now," the Captain replied.

Kelly grabbed a handhold as the audible 'attitude' alarm sounded. A second later, he heard a faint jet of gas, the sound carried by the ship's hull, and the ship changed orientation. Stars swam past the bridge window and a light force tugged at him.

"We're steady on this orientation," Carla said. She put a bit of unnecessary body English into the ship's sometimes balky control for the telescope. "Got it—feed seven."

Kelly pulled himself over to a video console and punched up the feed, aware of Grant looking in over his shoulder.

"The ship looks okay," Jack said from his console. The *Price* was centered in the screen, and then jumped as Carla increased the magnification.

"Exterior views don't tell you much," Grant said.

No they don't, Kelly thought. An electrical fire, for example, could fill the ship with toxic smoke and render it uninhabitable. Still, you'd think somebody would get into a spacesuit and use a handheld radio.

Kelly looked at his suit's external wrist display. According to the time, any reply from Earth would be just coming in.

"What do you make her to be?" Williams asked.

"Well, Midshipman," Captain Chen said, "you're supposed to know common ship types. What do you hold her as?"

Kelly smiled. Captain Chen was having one of his "trainable moments" at the expense of Midshipman Williams.

"Daewoo Type-15?" Williams said.

"Are you asking or telling?" the Captain said.

"Daewoo Type-15," Williams replied, trying but failing to sound certain.

"I concur," the Captain said. "Pull up the standard schematics."

Williams routed the output to a second screen just below the first. Daewoo was a Korean company, and their Type 15 was an older model, designed for containerized cargo.

"She's a steamer," Williams said.

"Great," Grant replied sarcastically.

Most deep-space ships used high-efficiency ionic engines powered by fission reactors for propulsion.

"You'd think Daewoo would quit selling pressurized water reactors," Grant continued. "Damn things scram when you look at them sideways."

"More power output for the mass," Kelly said, feeling a bit defensive. "It's a good technology." Most companies nowadays cheaped out, and put pebble-bed reactors in, which, instead of using water and steam, passed nitrogen gas over sealed golf ball-sized chunks of uranium.

"Doesn't the US Air Force use pressured water reactors exclusively? Grant asked.

"Yes sir, they do," Kelly replied. "And they work fine."

"If you maintain them," Chen said. "But it's not much more power for the mass, and damn tricky to work with."

"Maybe their reactor scramed," Williams suggested.

"Maybe," Chief Kelly said, a note of irritation in his voice. "But a scram shouldn't take down the Cee-cubed systems."

"Depends on why the reactor scramed," Grant said, stating the obvious, "which for all we know it didn't."

Something was fishy. Cee-cubed stood for 'command, control and communications' and was always powered from multiple, independent, sources.

"Infrared?" Kelly asked.

Ortega grunted and switched feeds.

Williams tapped his monitor. "Crew quarters look kinda chilly."

He was referring to the saucer-shaped segment at the rear of the vessel, visibly spinning to produce artificial gravity.

"I'm more interested in the reactor," Chen said. That was housed in a boxlike and normally-zero-gee engineering space, just aft of the crew area, which formed the ship's stern. These areas showed pale pink in the display.

Warmer than ambient but not nearly as warm as they should be. She'd been without power for several hours. But even if she'd been without power for a day or so, there should still be enough air for people to live.

"Hypoxia?"

"Asking or telling, Mister Williams?" the Captain said.

"Neither, sir, merely suggesting."

"Why'd the reactor shut down?" Kelly asked.

"Simple. Computer did it automatically," Grant said. It was looking like this mystery was solved.

"Maybe," Kelly said, a note of doubt in his voice. *If so, who called it in*?"

"Remember the *Hanjin Conveyor*?" Grant asked.

"Yeah," Kelly drawled. It had been their first rescues together.

The *Hanjin* had been unresponsive to radio calls and way off course. Kelly shuddered from the remembered cold. The ship's life support system had slowly failed, depriving them of oxygen. Either the watchstander had ignored the alarm or silenced it. Not that it mattered - everybody died, most of them asleep in their bunks. Then they froze solid as the ship cooled down.

"Hanjin was a Daewoo Type 15," Grant said.

"Well, somebody called this in," Kelly replied. "Which means somebody is, or was, still alive."

"You may be right, Grant," Chen said, "but we won't know until we get aboard."

She's not under thrust, Captain," Williams interjected. "And given her current course, she either gets moving in two hours or she'll miss insertion." Orbital insertion was the maneuver to change course from flying at Mars to orbiting around it.

"Short or long?" Kelly asked. Short meant crashing into the planet, while long meant flying past it.

"Short," Jack said. "Six hours to impact."

"We better get moving," Grant said. "Unless Mars needs a new crater."

"Concur," the Captain said. "Range to target?"

"Passing 5,000 kilometers," Ortega replied.

"We'll match course and hold at five clicks," the Captain said. "Mr. Williams, lay in a plot."

"Intercept in ten minutes," Williams replied.

"Striking below," Grant said.

"Grant," the Captain said.

"Sir?"

"Let's take this one extra careful, please."

"Yes, sir."

"Checklist complete," Kelly said over the radio link. "Just need the boss."

"I'm going EVA," came Grant's voice over the radio.

Volodka's thrusters fired again as they were matching courses with the *Price.*

"Range to target three-zero clicks," Ortega said over the bridge-to-bridge radio, patched into Kelly's left earpiece. "Intercept in two minutes."

Kelly was sitting in the pilot's chair of the larger of the *Volodka's* two ship-to-ship cargo pods, and with his checklist complete he had nothing to do but wait. The boxy vehicle, which everybody referred to as a launch, bore more than a passing resemblance to a small cargo container with a rocket on the back end, and wasn't much bigger. Alan Nomura, the other exterior rider, was in position, "standing" on a platform jutting out from the starboard side of the launch.

The rest of the team was inside, where Grant should be, Kelly thought. But the kid wanted to "lead from the front" and since rules required two exterior riders, the better to gain entry into a dead ship, Grant rode from outside.

A minute later the hatch to a small, one-man airlock just forward of the launch opened, and a Grant emerged, looking bulky and clumsy in his spacesuit. There was a length of green nylon rope, knotted every meter or so, running from the airlock hatch to a point on the ship at the nose of the launch. Grant pulled himself out of the hatch, allowing his body to straighten out nearly perpendicular to the *Volodka*, and grabbed the rope.

He pulled himself hand over hand along the rope until he arrived at a plastic tube mounted vertically on the face of the launch. Grant grabbed the tube, using the tacky surface of his glove to stick to the plastic. *Have to give it to the kid—he's damn good at EVA work.*

Grant then hand-walked up the tube, his body pivoting at the waist, and used another tube to hand-walk around to the port side of the launch to a platform welded on the side of the launch, where the platform was, just out of view of Kelly's window.

A minute later, Grant's voice came through Kelly's right ear. "Comm check on the wire," Grant said, referring to a data cable running from Grant's suit to the launch.

"Five by five," Kelly replied. "You ready?"

"Yes, let's go," Grant said.

Kelly disengaged the hold-down clamps, which sent an audible clunk through the launch, then Kelly pulled away from the *Volodka* using the attitude jets. He walked it a few meters away then tripped the main rear-mounted rocket engine. The rocket wasn't very powerful, producing maybe a quarter of a gee at full thrust, but for guys outside it would still feel like they were falling off the side of the launch.

"There she is," Grant said as they rounded the *Volodka* and the *Price* came into view. The *Price* looked tiny against the black—like something you'd hang on your keychain.

"Engine cut in three," Kelly said.

Grant grunted audibly as the rocket cut off, his inertia trying to fling him into space.

"Be a more comfortable ride inside," Kelly said.

"Better view here," Grant replied. "Besides, somebody's got to be here."

Suit yourself, Cowboy.

"Let's run a sweep from bow to stern, target's starboard side," Grant said. *Volodka* hadn't been able to see the starboard side with the telescope.

"Copy, making run," Kelly said.

As they made the approach, Williams, on the *Volodka*, made another call to the *Price*.

"Merchant Vessel *Price*, this is Space Rescue ship *Volodka*, five kilometers on your bow. We are sending over a launch. If you are receiving us, please flash your running lights, over."

The darkened running lights didn't even flicker.

Kelly swung in a sharp ninety across the *Price's* bow, a flat slab of sheet steel, then made a square turn. Once they were turned, Kelly made a short burn on the rocket, which sent them drifting down the starboard side. That part was in shadow, so Kelly pointed the launch's nose at the hull and hit the floodlights.

"Full load," Nomura said over the wire-link.

"Looks that way," Grant agreed.

No shit, guys, Kelly thought. Empty slots meant wasted money, so every slot on the *Price* had a shipping container in it. Bulk material, like glass and steel for agricultural domes, brick for building and the like, was made on Mars. Manufactured goods, from computers to residential nuclear reactors, were containerized and imported from Earth or her moon. Mars sent back some raw materials, but it was mostly a food basket for asteroid mines and Earth's waterless moon.

As they drifted down the side of the ship, Kelly noted a few scuffs and dings from the cargo handling equipment, but nothing at all unusual. The ship was still dark and lifeless. Even the standard suit radio frequencies were silent, which Grant didn't like at all. Surely *somebody* had enough smarts to get a suit on?

"Must be a life support problem." Grant said.

"Maybe," Kelly replied. "Or maybe not."

"You getting cold feet, Chief?"

Kelly bit off his first and intemperate response. "There are old Rescuemen, and bold Rescuemen, but there's no such thing as an old, bold Rescuemen," he finally said. *Cocky. The kid has talent, but not enough experience.*

"Copy, Chief. Stand off the rescue airlock," Grant said. "And get in line of sight with *Volodka.* Nomura and I will go over on suitjets."

"Copy," Kelly said. He arrested the launch's motion with a quick, fuel-efficient burst from the main engine and pointed the launch's stubby bow at the *Price's* emergency airlock, ringed with yellow and black stripes. "Your range is six-five meters."

"Make the call," Grant said.

"Copy," Kelly said. Then, over the bridge-to-bridge frequency, Kelly said, "Merchant Vessel *Price*, this is Space Rescue. We are sending over assistance to your starboard airlock. If you read, please flash your running lights, over."

Nothing.

"Unplugging now," Grant said. "Comm check on digital radio, over."

Now that the exterior team wasn't connected via intercom, Kelly set up his right ear for a digital radio link to *Volodka* and the team members, which included video from a helmet-mounted camera.

"Five by five, good pictures, over." Kelly said. Nomura, on the same radio channel, completed his comm check.

"Grant away," Grant said. His spacesuited figure now appeared in the side window of the launch, slowly heading towards the *Price*. The kid gave a single burst from his suit jet.

"Nomura away," Nomura reported, following right behind Grant.

As Kelly watched, the two men approached, then rolled to orient feet first. Their shadows, caused by the floodlights from the launch, grew as they approached.

Suddenly all the *Price's* exterior lights came on, including a floodlight aimed right at the launch. This was followed by a loud squeal from the analog radio set.

"What the hell?" Grant yelled over the digital link.

Kelly could barely hear him over the squeal from the analog suit radio in his left ear. He mashed the squelch control on the console.

"Two flares, negative, two launches from the *Price*, outbound fast," Fencl said, pointing from her seat next to his.

"*Volodka* has two bogies inbound, ship's launches!" Chen said over the digital link. The analog channel was completely jammed by the squeal. "What's going on, over?"

"I have no idea," Grant replied.

"The emergency airlock is opening," Nomura said.

Kelly looked down and could see a spacesuited figure in the lock. He shivered for a second.

"Man in lock has a gun," Kelly said, desperately wishing it wasn't so. "We're coming in to get you!"

"Negative!" Grant said, landing feet first on the deck of the *Price*. "Break off, Kelly!"

"We can't leave the Lieutenant!" Novak said.

Kelly saw a second airlock opening. "Shit!"

"Kelly, break off now!" Grant said.

"God damn it!" Kelly said. He fired a reverse thruster. "We're gone!"

"*Volodka* copies," Chen said over the link as the thruster fired.

As they backed out, Kelly saw Grant's hands go up.

I just abandoned two shipmates, Kelly thought, his gut heaving.

Chapter 4

Thursday 30 Virgo Year 52 16:25 local (March 1, 2074, 16:27 GMT) VSRS Ship *Volodka*

JACK WILLIAMS HIT *VOLODKA'S* MANEUVERING ALARM as the helmsman fired a burst from the main rocket, pushing the ship forward. The two launches coming from the Price were directly inbound. *Pirates. Had to be pirates. Who the hell hijacks an ambulance?*

"Prepare to repel boarders!" Captain Chen shouted. "Helm, shake them off!"

Oh shit, Jack thought. He looked at his console. There was nothing he could do.

"Carla!" the Captain shouted. "Get to the weapons locker and take Jack with you! Everybody clear the bridge!"

"I'm gone," Carla said.

Jack unstrapped from his seat and pulled himself over it. As he did, he saw Captain Chen grab a radio handset.

"Port Lowell, this is *Volodka*," Chen said. "We are under attack by pirates, over."

The weapons locker. They shouldn't need a weapons locker at all. It had recently been added at the Captain's orders. *We're the good guys!*

Volodka could jinx, but unless they were prepared to abandon Lieutenant Grant, Chief Kelly and the rest of the Rapid Response team, they had to stay in the area. He didn't sign up to shoot people, but now it looked like he would have to.

Jack left the bridge and pulled himself aft along the central passageway on the heels of Lt. Ortega, trying to hold on and make time as the ship shimmied underneath him. A metallic clang rang throughout the ship, coming from the outer hull. It didn't matter much what maneuvers they did now. Now it was a question of how long it would take to force open an airlock. His stomach churned.

Two of the engineering ratings, Chief Astronaut Krauss and Able Astronaut Pacht, waited at the small arms locker when Jack arrived. "Nice of you to join us," Krauss said, trying to sound nonchalant. The sheen of sweat on her pale face gave her away.

"Fast as we could," Ortega said, pulling the key from her pocket. She unlocked the hardened steel padlock securing the weapons locker, and quickly got the lock off, then swung the sturdy door open. There were six pistols inside, sleek black semi-automatics, each with two loaded clips stored beside them.

"Grab them all," Ortega said, stuffing a pair of pistols into her belt.

"Spacesuits," Pacht muttered, fumbling with his pistol. "We should be in suits."

"They can't blow pressure." Krauss chambered a round. "The air would prevent them from getting in."

"They can blow it once they're in," Pacht said.

An audible alarm sounded. The airlock opening alarm.

"They're inside," Ortega said.

"Can they blow pressure from the bridge?" Jack asked.

"No—life support," Krauss said.

"Get there and hold it," Ortega pointed aft. "Jack and I can hold them at the junction." She sounded a lot more confident than Jack felt. "Chief, we got a boat of people out there. What can we do to get them inside?"

"Nothing until we get comms with them," Krauss said.

A burst of gunfire rang out, sounding like it was farther forward. *I guess we'll see how good our self-sealing hull really is.*

"Fuck," Jack said, "They've got the bridge."

"Maybe," Ortega replied. "We know the ship better than they do." She turned and looked over her shoulder. "Krauss, put them in the dark."

The woman grinned. "Gladly."

Ortega gestured forward, towards the bridge. "Let's move out."

"Aye aye, Ma'am," Jack said.

Jack and Lieutenant Ortega arrived at the junction, the centerpoint for anybody moving inside the ship, just as the lights went out and the ventilation fans stopped running. A trio of emergency lights was the only illumination in the area. A string of curses echoed down the passageway from the forward area.

"Doesn't sound like they're very happy, does it?" Ortega said, a wicked smile over her face, half in shadow.

"No Ma'am," Jack said.

Jack looked at the junction. It wasn't much, just a wide spot where three sets of tube-like interior passageways met. The long passageway they were in went forward to the bridge and the empty mess decks. Heading aft, behind them, were crew quarters, the rescue locker, and engineering. The pair of short cross-corridors went to access airlocks, one for each of the four sides of the tubular ship.

"With the breakers tripped, they have to come back here to manually reset," Ortega said.

She reached up and turned off the emergency light in the dorsal side of the passageway. The other two lights, on each side of the lateral passageway, lit up the junction. Jack and the Lieutenant could see their targets, but people coming from the bridge couldn't see them.

"We should move back a bit," Jack said. It's darker back there.

"Yep," Ortega replied, backing down the corridor.

As they started to move, Jack turned to look forward into the junction again and saw a space-suited figure, weapon in hand, pull himself into the corridor, facing away from Jack.

"Look out Carla!" Jack shouted, and pointed his gun at the figure. He pulled the trigger as the suited figure twisted on his axis. The gun went off with a deafening bang, and the recoil slammed Jack into the side of the corridor. Jack reflexively pulled the trigger again, realizing after he did so that his feet were suddenly in the way of the pistol's muzzle. The gun didn't go off, and in fact the trigger didn't seem to want to move. He started to shout "I'm jammed" when three or four more loud bangs tore through the space.

Jack managed to stop his spin and brace up against the wall. The slide of his gun was stuck halfway back. With shaky fingers, he pulled the slide back, clearing out a live round, and chambered another.

"You okay?" Lieutenant Ortega called from across the hall.

"Yes," Jack said, his voice cracking. He looked down the passageway, struggling to get oriented after his tumble. A space-suited figure was in the junction, the suit backpack caught on a fire extinguisher stanchion.

"He dead?" Jack asked.

"I certainly hope so," Ortega replied.

"Did I hit him?"

"Yes," she said. "Better to be lucky than good."

She gestured down the corridor with her pistol. "His buddy is back down the passageway. We traded a couple of shots. I don't know if I hit anything."

From ambulance driver to murderer in five minutes. Then he realized that Lieutenant Ortega was talking.

"Pardon?"

"You should have anchored first."

"Sorry."

"Don't get sorry, get good," Ortega said, no malice in her voice.

"My gun jammed," Jack said. "I need to get a working one."

"Nothing wrong with your gun, kid. You limp-wristed it."

"Oh." Jack thought for a second. "What's that mean?"

"The slide needs to move back to chamber a round, Mister. If you're moving back, it doesn't complete its travel," Ortega said. "Cover me. I'm going to add that guy's rifle to our arsenal."

"Aye aye, Ma'am." Jack felt sick, and struggled to keep his food down. "How long before they try again?"

"Five minutes, maybe less," Ortega said, calmly approaching the dead pirate. "And they'll send more people next time."

Chapter 5

Thursday 30 Virgo Year 52 15:45 local (March 1, 2074, 15:45 GMT)
Port Lowell, Mars

TWO HOURS OFF OF THE SHIP FROM EARTH, Sean Yeargan felt dizzy, just like he had for the first week or two he'd been on the *Lufthansa Berliner*. He looked around, taking in all that he could see of Port Lowell, Mars' biggest city.

Not that you could see much. Locals called the pressurized buildings on Mars domes, but to Sean's eyes they looked like enclosed shopping malls back home. He stopped at a corner and glanced at the map displayed on his PDA. The habitation areas of Port Lowell were a series of brick tubes covered with dirt, running along on the surface. Where they could, the architects burrowed through natural hills.

Yeargan shook his head, trying to clear the dizziness. It worked, sort of, so he resumed walking, smiling wanly.

How much of this dizziness is caused by Mars' lesser gravity?

Probably not much, he decided. He'd always suffered from spin sickness, caused by the inner ear trying to adjust to the centrifugal force used to simulate gravity. Once you got adjusted to the spin, re-adjusting to gravity could have the same effect. It was why he'd gotten a desk job with the insurance company in the first place.

His son hadn't suffered from that problem.

His dead son. The reason Sean volunteered to go to Mars.

Stop thinking about that. He patted the receipt for his air tax in his pocket.

Gotta make our own air, he thought. Plants do that nicely, and will grow just fine under glass in Martian sunlight. At convenient intervals, the locals had plopped glass-and-steel agricultural domes, which showed on his map as green blobs, to provide oxygen and some food. Despite the plants, air wasn't free.

Sean looked around and found a street sign, blue with white letters, mounted on the side of a wall. He turned right and walked down another 'street.' The ceiling, about three stories above his head, was an arched brick barrel, lined with lights and ventilation ducts. Stores and businesses occupied the first level, their doors opening onto the walkway or street. Above them were two levels of apartments, apparently accessed via open hallways let into the rows of businesses.

An open-sided electric trolley, its body made of brightly colored fiberglass, rolled down tracks in the middle of the open gallery, accompanied by the ringing of a bell. Sean noted that there was no driver in the trolley, but that it stopped to avoid pedestrians in the way. Labor on Mars wasn't cheap.

Sean's destination, 221 McKinley Street, Sector U, Port Lowell, proved to be a small bar-restaurant. A fiberglass sign hung from a pole over the door proclaimed the place as "Dutch's Watering Hole." The owner had fenced off a segment of the street, and placed a couple of small chrome tables out.

"Sean Yeargan?" a woman called out, sitting at the table farthest from the door. She was dressed casually, jeans and a tan tank top. Her blonde hair was long and straight, and had bubblegum pink highlights.

"Yes," Sean said. "You are?"

She stood up and offered her hand, pulling a strand of hair out of her face with the other. "Janet Pilgrim. I'm sorry about your son."

It had been almost four years since his son Alex had gone missing, and two since Janet, the sole surviving crewmember of that ship, had reported his death. It still hurt. "Thank you," Sean said, not knowing what else to say. He joined her at her table.

"Something to drink?" she asked, beckoning at a small e-menu attached to the table with a stout wire.

"Whatever you're having is fine, but I'm buying."

"Two house bourbons," she said, punching buttons on the device.

"I thought local time was early afternoon?"

"It is. My lunch time, in fact. So?"

I guess it's five o'clock somewhere on this planet. "You must have studied my picture, to pick me out like that."

"Actually no," she replied, a wry smile on her face. "I just looked for somebody fresh off of the boat. Between your bouncing up and down and that five-degree lean into a non-existent spin, it was easy."

Space legs, they called it, Sean thought, trying to avoid showing his embarrassment. A waiter arrived with the drinks, sparing Sean the need to reply. He took a sip of his bourbon, and barely avoided sputtering. *Bourbon my ass!* The damn stuff tasted like moonshine, and must have been concocted on-planet, probably in somebody's bathtub. He noticed that the vile stuff didn't seem to faze Janet, who took a long drag on hers.

Despite the bullshit he'd told his boss, there was only one reason for him to come to Mars. "Tell me how my son and Kate died," he asked.

Kate Yeargan had been his daughter-in-law, and captain of Janet's ship.

"Kate went quick," Janet replied, looking him straight in the eye. "We weren't expecting trouble, and she was off watch. The pirates tried to cut the high-gain antenna off with a laser. Being pirates and lazy, they hadn't practiced, and so sliced a hole in the growhouse."

Sean hated that slang term for greenhouse, and wondered if Janet knew the connotation. But that wasn't important.

"Kate was in the greenhouse?"

"Yep. Picking apples off one of our miniatures." Janet took another stiff sip of her drink. "The 'house vented out almost instantly."

"And my son?"

"I told you in my emails."

"You said he was shot. I want details."

"You might not like details."

"Try me," Sean finally said.

"Alex was in shock, I think," Janet said. "He knew his wife was dead. The pirates told us to assemble everybody not on watch on the quarterdeck. Alex and Ken did so."

"Alex was supposed to be on watch."

"Sir," Janet said, reaching for her drink and then apparently thinking better of it, "I said you might not like it."

Sean didn't, and could feel his face flush. "Tell me."

"The two men went to the quarterdeck, and a launch from the pirate ship docked there. I watched on the CCTV."

"Yes?"

"Ken attacked the pirates when they entered. Unarmed. Alex I think was just in the way."

Sean looked away, not wanting her to see the tears in his eyes. The street was deserted.

"Who buried them?" Sean asked.

"One of the pirates must have taken care of Alex."

Probably jettisoned with the trash, Sean thought. After they'd rifled through his pockets, of course.

"We couldn't get to Kate until I finished welding the patches on," Janet said. She fumbled in a pocket of her tight jeans and fished out a small gold band. "Her wedding ring."

Sean felt his eyes water again. According to the reports, both from the media and the private ones, they'd kept Janet, the pirates had, more or less as a slave. Yet she'd hung onto the wedding ring.

The waiter came back and put down another pair of drinks. Sean drained his first, the raw alcohol burning as it went down.

"Thank you," he said to Janet.

"For what?"

"For surviving." He held up the ring, his eyes watering. "For this."

Janet blushed and looked away. "Just lucky, I guess."

Survivor's guilt, Sean thought. Mixed with a little Post-traumatic Stress Disorder. She'd personally killed four of the sons of bitches to get her freedom.

Sean understood that. It was easy to see what you've fought in yourself. Every time it snowed in Chicago he remembered the fighting in Pyongyang during the Second Korean War. The look on that man's face when Sean gutted him was as clear as if it was yesterday, despite being over thirty years ago.

"You seeing somebody?" Sean asked.

"Like a boyfriend?"

"Therapist," Sean said. He pointed at her drink. "Self-medicating is not a good idea. Been there, done that and got the T-shirt."

"I'm fine."

So you say, Sean thought. "Do you know where the other pirates went?" Especially that red-headed bitch Storey, Sean added mentally. She's the one that got away.

"No. Why?"

"Professional interest."

She snorted. "What does Zurich North American Insurance want with pirates?"

A short walk out an airlock minus suit would be nice. "Mars' piracy problem is getting out of hand."

Janet smiled. "Getting in your pocket, are they?"

"Quite a bit, actually. Between the losses of ships and crews, it's expensive."

"Death benefits that high?"

"The people who took your ship weren't very smart," Sean said. "Now we're getting hit with ransom demands."

"You pay?"

"We have to," Sean said. "Union rules—'must fund rescues.'"

"I'm surprised you guys don't cut deals with them. Buy them off."

"That assumes we can find somebody to buy."

"Mike Gerulitas not returning your calls?"

"It's complicated." Mike was a fence and fixer who had provided papers to his son's murderers so they could resell the ship on Earth.

"Mitsui Marine Insurance tried to buy off Gerulitias. SOB didn't stay bought." Sean took a sip from his second drink. It didn't burn as much—the alcohol must have numbed his sense of taste. "The other problem we've got is a lack of intelligence."

She smiled. "You're stupid?"

"No, the military type of intelligence, which I know is an oxymoron. We don't know who these pirates are."

"What do the returned crews have to say?"

"Not much," Sean said. "Seems like most outfits are smart enough to keep their identities hidden."

"Sounds like a real problem," Janet said. She knocked back a healthy gulp. "Wish I could help."

"Well, you could," Sean said. "Like I said, we need intel on these guys."

"Got a job, thanks. Besides, what are you going to do with the intel—make sure the 'Pay To' on the checks is spelled right?"

"More like stop writing checks."

"I would ask whose army you're going to use, but I suspect that you've got that worked out."

Would that we did, he thought. Blackwater's quote had been ridiculous, and Triple Canopy's CEO had laughed them out of the room. "We weren't born yesterday," he punted.

"Hope that works out for you." Janet drained her glass and pushed back from the table. "My lunch break is over."

Sean noted that it was a liquid lunch.

"About our piracy problem?" Sean said.

"I've got a kid and a job, so I don't see how I can help you."

"We'll pay," Sean said to her back.

"Trying to make a quick buck is how I got to Mars in the first place," she said over her shoulder as she walked away.

Chapter 6

Thursday, 30 Virgo Year 52 16:30 local (March 1, 2074, 16:32 GMT)
VSRS Rescue Launch One, near VSRS Ship Volodka

"*Volodka* is bucking like a bronco," Kelly said, trying not to think about the men he'd just left behind. "The second launch can't dock while she's jinxing like that."

Not that he'd ever seen a bronco. The closest he'd gotten to any animal before moving to Mars was the Bronx Zoo. Now his wife brought live chickens home for dinner. *Ex-wife, actually. Had to remember that.*

"We gotta go back for the Lieutenant!" Fencl, their medic, said. She was sitting in the co-pilot's seat to his right.

"We will, as soon as we got something to go back with," Kelly said. "Where's that second launch?"

Fencl, now that she had something to do, seemed to calm down. "There, on *Volodka's* stern. Ventral—seven o'clock."

"Got it," Kelly said. "Everybody, go on suit pressure now." Kelly pointed the snub-nosed launch at the apparent hostile, painted an incongruous shade of day-glow yellow.

"You're not going to do what I think you are?" Fencl asked.

"Check your seat straps," Kelly replied, closing his faceplate with his other hand. God I hope this works, he thought. Kelly fired the main engine for a long burn while pressurizing his suit.

Whoever was piloting the second launch was clearly not a rescueman, Kelly thought. His situational awareness sucked. The pirate was so focused on the bucking *Volodka* that he completely forgot about her launch. Kelly closed on the pirate launch rapidly.

"Son of a bitch!" Fencl yelled as the pirate launch grew in the front window.

"Brace!" Kelly said, jerking the controls to skew his craft sideways. His side window was suddenly filled by the pirate's ship.

The impact slammed him against his seat straps, and the crunch of metal was clearly audible though his helmet. The launch started to spin rapidly, and Kelly heard a string of curses over the intercom. The alarm indicating loss of air pressure started to squeal, but faded rapidly as the air rushed out.

He gave the main rocket a brief burst at full throttle, which took some of the spin off, then cut thrust and let the auto-stabilizer handle the rest.

"Everybody okay?" Kelly asked.

The crew's training kicked in and they sounded off by the numbers. As they did, a squeezebottle of water drifted by, the water inside trying to boil and freeze at the same time in the cold vacuum.

"Get all your shit secured!" Kelly barked.

"When did you learn how to do that?" Fencl asked over the intercom.

"Just now," Kelly said. "See if you can raise *Volodka*."

As Fencl worked, Kelly pivoted the launch on its center of gravity, looking for the pirate ship. Parts of his main window had frosted over, complicating his search.

"Got you, you sons of bitches," he said. The pirate launch was spinning like a top, off-gassing and steering jets firing furiously. Several pieces of exterior fuselage had come off, and were spinning around as well.

"*Volodka*, this is Scout, come in please," Fencl said.

Kelly realized that the jamming signal on the analog frequency had stopped, and that there was communication coming over it. He dialed the squelch up.

"Rescue launch, we have your ship," came over the analog. "Bring in our second crew or we'll kill some hostages, over."

"Bullshit," Kelly said, making sure he wasn't transmitting over the external circuit. A spacesuited hand reached over him and grabbed a portable drill, spinning silently.

"One of the tool kits busted open," somebody said apologetically over the intercom.

"Get it in one sock," Kelly growled. He scanned the sky, finally locating the *Price*, silhouetted against Mars, then glanced down at his radar display. "The lights are on but nobody's home," he said.

"What?" Fencl asked.

"The *Price*," Kelly said, pointing to the radar display. He noticed that his hand was shaking. "She's not moving."

"She can't, her crew's on our ship," Fencl said.

"But she's not closing in on us, either," Kelly said. "We're both pulling away."

Kelly felt a tap on his shoulder. "Getting something on digital two," Lewis, their second Able Astronaut, said.

Kelly dialed up the channel, ignoring a repeat of the bullshit from the pirates over the analog channel.

"Ortega to any station, come in please, over."

"Ortega, this is Kelly. What's your status, over?"

"Pirates have the bridge, we have the engineering spaces."

"The captain?"

"Last seen on the bridge, over."

Kelly looked over his shoulder, confirming that the other members of the crew had heard that. "Ms. Ortega, you're senior, Ma'am."

"Copy. We have four spare weapons. What is your status, over?"

"Hull ruptured, but we're all okay. Do you control lock seven five delta, over?"

"Affirmative, but we've killed power to the ship. Can you open manually, over?"

"Affirmative," Kelly said. They were Rescuemen, after all. "Request you have suited man and weapons in the lock, over."

"Wilco. Williams is bringing the weapons."

"Copy, we're in route, alongside in five, out." Kelly turned and looked over his shoulder at the rest of the crew, not that it was needed, since they were in vacuum and communicating over an interior hard-wired circuit. "Lewis, you're senior. Take Otarski and Diep with Mr. Williams."

Kelly pointed at the *Volodka*, filling their forward screen. "Fencl, see that pirate launch?" he asked, pointing at a craft sitting on the exterior of their ship." You're going to take that for a spin. I'll make sure that other fucking boat of theirs stays away. Got it?"

"We got it, Chief," Lewis said.

"Aye aye," Fencl said. "Glad I got cross-trained."

"Let's do it, then," Kelly said, ignoring Fencl's snide remark. *Christ Jesus, there's got to be an easier way to make a living. Mars was supposed to be a place to start over, not die on.*

Jack shut the inner door to the airlock, putting himself in total darkness except for the lights in his heads-up display. From a dark hallway to a dark airlock, he thought. At least we held the boarders at the junction.

He pounded on the airlock hatch with a hammer. Whoever was out there would 'hear' it through their feet or whatever else was in contact with the hull.

The pressure started to drop in the tiny space. His skintight spacesuit felt even tighter as the pressure bled off. When the outer door silently opened, he was blinded for an instant by the glare of sunlight from outside, until the helmet viewplate caught up.

"Kelly?" Jack said.

"Able Lewis, sir," the radio crackled back on the digital link. "Kelly wants us to go hard."

Jack waited a second to let his eyes adjust to the glare, then handed the spare weapons to Lewis, and finally pulled himself outside the ship. Lewis passed him a wirejack, which he plugged into his suit's comm port.

"What the hell's that!" Jack said, reacting to a flare from a rocket.

"Fencl's taking the pirate launch for a spin," Lewis said. "Chief's on our boat. Your orders, sir?"

My orders, Jack thought. How the hell am I supposed to know what to do? Jack glanced around at the trio of Rescuers. I'm senior, he thought. That's why I'm supposed to know what to do. He looked at the time in his helmet's heads-up display. An hour ago I was rescuing people. Now I'm going to kill people.

"They entered at Lock 2," Jack said. "We'll go in through there."

"They'll know we're back-dooring them once we try to cycle the lock," Diep said, her voice flat.

Jack thought for a second. "I got an idea."

Jack led the others alongside the exterior of the ship. It was slow going, but the group eventually arrived at Airlock #2. The airlock was designed for equipment and cargo access, not personnel. Jack figured the pirates had used it because it was the most obvious airlock close to the pilothouse. Besides, #1 airlock, right behind the radio room, was barely big enough for one person. #2 was cavernous by comparison, two meters on a side, and several people could fit into it at one time. Any idiot could look at the size of the respective hatches and tell.

The *Volodka*, still spinning slowly from their earlier maneuvers, took that instant to put the exterior of the ship in shadow.

Then the area was suddenly flooded with light from above. Jack glanced toward the light instinctively, even as he realized Kelly had used the launch's floodlights to help them. To Jack's surprise, the floodlights revealed that the door was completely open. Jack carefully pulled himself along the hull, and poked his head into the airlock.

It was empty. Jack waved behind him for the rest of the Rescuers to follow, then clambered in. Unlike a lot of ships, the hatches were of two-piece construction and slid open and closed sideways, much like the doors of an elevator.

Jack looked at the doors from inside. It was a bitch to maintain the airtight seal that way, since the doors had to be closed so tightly, and there was a safety issue in that you could open the doors with pressure on the other side, but the locks were faster to get in and out of. *That's going to work to our advantage.*

Once all three Rescuers were in, Jack waved at the Chief's launch and gestured at Diep to close the airlock door. She made an OK sign and started to close the hatch. Although there was a manual crank, designed to override the motors, Diep simply pulled first one then the other door closed.

It wasn't an airtight seal, but this plunged the space into darkness until Lewis activated a chemlight. In the sickly green glow, Diep used the crank to tighten the seal. Once she did, she manually dogged the hatches together with a special wrench mounted in the space.

Lewis touched his helmet to Jack's.

"No power," Lewis said.

"No shit," Jack replied. The recommended way to re-pressurize the space would be by opening either of two valves that would allow air to flow in from the interior. But that was slow, and the inrushing air was noisy. Jack had a better idea.

"We'll manually slide the doors open," Jack said.

"It will get gusty," Lewis said.

"Who cares?" Jack tapped Lewis on the chest. "Pass it on."

Lewis did so, and with Otarski took up a position on either side of the interior doors, which were identical in design to the outer doors. Jack took a spare wrench and manually undogged the inner hatch, then braced up on the outer door. Diep did the same next to him.

Jack held out his free hand with three fingers up. Once the two Rescuers signaled they were ready, he counted down, three, two, one, closed fist.

On the closed fist, Otarski and Lewis pulled the doors open. A wave of air rushed inside, slamming against Jack. Without waiting for the wave to subside, Jack pushed off with his legs from the door and leaped into the passageway beyond. The pop of gunfire, muted by his helmet and the roar of air, proved that the pirates weren't stupid.

Whoever they left behind was, however, a lousy shot. Jack hit the far side of the passageway and rolled into a ball while trying to get oriented. Besides creating a strong but brief wind, the rapid opening of the airlock had dropped the temperature enough to create a fog in the space. It made finding a target impossible. Jack pointed his gun in what he thought was a good direction and fired. The gun barked once, the flash illuminating the fog. The recoil shoved him back down the passageway, his gun jammed.

I wonder whose bright idea it was to bring an automatic into space, because it was fucking stupid.

Fortunately, Otarski and Lewis were able to brace up, and poked their guns out of the airlock, each firing several rounds. Even more fortunately, they seemed to agree with Jack as to the general direction of the threat.

Jack managed to brace up and clear his weapon. He popped open his helmet faceplate.

"Lewis," Jack yelled, "Did you hit anything?"

Several cracks of a rifle from down the hallway suggested that he had not.

"You okay, sir?" Lewis yelled.

"Fine. Call Kelly and tell him to send in the second crew at Airlock 5," Jack yelled back.

"Roger," Lewis said.

"You're bluffing!" A man yelled from down the passageway. Lewis and Otarski both fired in that direction.

"You wanna die here?" Jack yelled. "This fog's lifting and we're between you and your ship."

Several shots rang out from somewhere deep inside the ship. Jack could distinguish between the sharp cracks of the pirate's rifles and the quieter, deeper sound of the pistols.

"Coming in," Lewis said over the echoes from the firing.

"Stay put, damn it!" Jack said. "Wait until the fog clears!"

Lewis didn't respond, and in the dark Jack had no idea where he was. A shadow loomed in front of the airlock. Jack decided to slide to port.

"Sir, what's your location?" Lewis yelled. It might be from the airlock.

"Pirate's moving!" Jack yelled.

The barely-seen figure twisted and fired, the recoil from his gun pushing him back. Jack fired, and now that he was braced up, he got a pair of shots off. The group in the airlock fired, the sound deafening in the tiny space.

"I'm hit!" Lewis yelled.

Jack stayed quiet, trying to sort out who was who, when something soft and warm bumped into him. He pushed back, then clicked on his suit light.

The light illuminated a dead body, drifting randomly in an unfamiliar spacesuit. The body of a kid, Jack noted. Maybe sixteen Standard years old. Jack floated over and checked for a pulse. Who in the hell took a kid like that out to be a killer?

"The pirate's dead," Jack said.

Several gunshots echoed through the ship.

"Ortega, this is Williams," Jack said after toggling his radio to voice-activated. "One pirate down, one crew wounded, over."

Chief Krauss' voice replied. "Two pirates dead, but the lieutenant's hit."

"Krauss, get me power and maneuvering," Jack said. "Diep, recall the Chief and Fencl." With two people hit, they were going to need her.

"Captain Chen?" Jack said, pulling himself onto the bridge. The lights came on, revealing a soccer-balled-sized globule of blood just inches from Jack's face. He squirmed franticly to avoid the blood, which changed course as the fans started up. *Maybe he's just wounded.*

The radio crackled, causing Jack to jump. "*Volodka, Volodka,* Phobos Rescue on one-six, reply please, over."

Jack pushed off a console with his foot, drifting towards the radio handset. He stopped his forward motion with a hand on a seatback and grabbed the mike, twisting to look back towards the rear of the compartment.

"Phobos Rescue this is *Volodka*, over," he said while twisting.

Then he found the Captain.

He was dead, his lifeless eyes open, and his body wedged between a circuit breaker box and the inner hull. The blood, or some of it, was coming out of a large area in his chest. On the opposite side of the hatch was a man's body, red hair and beard, face frozen in surprise, duct-taped to a stanchion. The ax-end of a Hallagan tool was buried in the man's chest.

"*Volodka*, this is Phobos Rescue, what is your status, over?"

They must be rattled back at base—they didn't ask him to change off of the distress and hailing channel. Good question—what is our status?

"Phobos Rescue, this is *Volodka*," Jack said over the radio. He gave a brief report, leaving names and ranks off. The local news monitored their transmissions, and Jack didn't want Chen's family hearing about his death from a reporter.

"We hold the ship, over," he concluded. For now, he added mentally. *Price* and whatever mother ship the pirates were using were still out there. Jack pivoted and pulled himself over to the captain's console. The short-range radar was still warming up, indicating ten seconds until it went active.

"Copy, Captain. Interrogative your intentions, over."

"Stand by, *Volodka* out," Jack said, using the captain's mike. He looked at it. For the moment, it was his mike, and he *was* the captain. A wave of sheer panic washed over him. Then the radar beeped, and Jack forced himself to look at it.

One thing at a time. The nav computer was still booting. Apparently it had gone down hard, so until he got it fixed, navigation was manual. He carefully checked the range setting on the display, and waited for three sweeps of the scope. Short range was clear. *Where's our launch?*

They docked, you idiot. Christ, get a grip. He opened up the display to a medium setting, immediately picking up a single contact at about 100 kilometers out. Jack punched the button for engineering on the captain's bitch box. Only Chen called it an 'intercom.'

"Engineering, bridge, what's my status on maneuvering?"

Pacht's voice came back. "The Chief's spinning up pumps now. You'll be at India Five in a minute."

India Five was five seconds to rocket ignition. They could hold at that level for hours, or light rockets and be gone. He centered the tracking bug on their lone radar contact and let the computer determine its course and speed. "Copy," Jack said, then pushed the button for sickbay. "What's the status on our wounded?"

"Lewis got it in the ass," Kelly said, "but he's just nicked. Fencl's still working on Ortega."

"Copy. Chief, get up here and see if you can find me a helmsman."

"On my way."

The computer beeped and provided an estimated course and speed for the contact. It was pulling away from them at a fairly good clip. Jack started to figure out where they were in relation to Mars. Running into a planet was bad. He'd just calculated their position and was preparing to feed it into the course computer when Kelly arrived.

"Is there some reason that you didn't move the captain?" Kelly asked, pulling himself into the space.

Jack, hovering over the captain's chair, looked back at Kelly. "Yes. I wanted to keep the living alive." *Keep the living alive. Chen's motto for any rescue.*

"Understood, sir," Kelly said, his voice softer. "I've got a guy ready to go back with me."

"Go back?"

"To the *Price*. We left two men there."

"Manuevering reports at India Five," the bitch box squawked.

"Copy," Jack said in reply.

"*Volodka*, this is Rescue Phobos, request update on your status and intentions, over."

Kelly nodded at the radio. "What are your intentions, sir?"

Jack patted the pistol he'd stuffed between straps on his spacesuit. "Don't you think enough people have died?"

"We don't leave people behind!"

"If we can rescue them, no." Jack turned and gestured at the radar scope. "The contact I *think* is the *Price* is 150 clicks away." He turned back and looked at Kelly. "Look me in the eyes and tell me you can pull off a rescue."

Kelly looked away silently.

"I'm sorry," Jack said. "They're my friends too." Jack picked up the radio handset. "Rescue Phobos this is *Volodka.* We are RTB best speed, will need medical standing by, over."

"Copy *Volodka* return to base. Medical alerted. Rescue Phobos standing by for all traffic channel one-six, out."

"*Volodka* out," Jack said. He turned and looked at Kelly. "Chief, sound maneuvering."

Chapter 7

**Friday, 31 Virgo Year 52 02:20 local (March 2, 2074, 03:00 GMT)
Bensonville, Republic of the White Race, Olympus Mons, Mars**

IT'S A MIRACLE THAT IDIOT CHUCKLES didn't get them all killed, Rachel thought, settling into a threadbare chair in the lounge. The idiot in question, Charles Benson Junior, scratched his balls expressively with one hand as he poured a drink with the other. Notably, nobody else was being offered anything.

She'd gotten to the *Cranston* and pulled away just as the *Price* sent out her Mayday call. By the time Space Rescue showed up, *Price* was just a blip at the end of the radar screen.

Although apparently the idiot had been persuasive enough. Somebody had fixed the Price's engine problems.

"Hostages all tucked in, son?" Charles Benson Senior, Senator of the White Race and Mayor of Bensonville asked, his voice gravelly and soft. He was sitting on an arm chair at one end of the lounge area, his gray face a stark contrast to the pastel sheet hung like a tapestry against the dark stone wall of the lounge.

"Yes, sir," Chuckles answered, plopping down in a faded low-backed arm chair almost at the opposite end from his father. "We've got them locked up in town."

"Good. I'd hate for them to get loose."

That's why I moved them. The hostages on her last ship, the *Witchcraft*, *had* gotten loose and retaken the ship. It had cost her a lot of money and nearly her life.

"Are all of the Class A shareholders present?" Senior asked.

"Except for Brenda, yes," Chuckles replied. The room was full, but everybody had a seat. When they'd had the last meeting, just before leaving, it had been standing room only.

"And the four dead shareholders," Senior added. "Who speaks for them?"

"I do, sir," Tony Lords said, fussing with his gray pony tail while sitting on a couch. "And Brenda's on the way."

Senior nodded, and went into one of his famous coughing fits. The rumor was that Charles Senior was dying of lung cancer. The hospital in Turner Springs, capital of the Republic of the White Race, might be able to help. McQue, Benson Senior's personal physician, apparently had other thoughts. Rachel sometimes wondered if McQue wasn't really working for Junior.

Brenda "Bam Bam" Lords walked into the room as Senior's coughing stopped, her sneakers squeaking on the floor of polished volcanic rock. Rachel noted with mixed emotions that Bam Bam had dressed for the occasion, her ample breasts rather skimpily contained by a bikini top worn over faded jeans. It was clear how she'd earned her nickname.

"Sorry I'm late, sir," she said, taking a seat next to her dad on the couch. "The B team had some questions."

"The meeting of the Bensonville Space Marines will come to order," Chuckles said. "All voting members present in person or by proxy."

It would be funny if it weren't so serious, Rachel thought. The 'Bensonville Space Marines' were what this group was calling itself, modeling their structure and payouts after the Somali Marines, the most successful sea pirates of the century. The fact that a bunch of white supremacists were literally lifting pages from a book written by a black man from Africa was beyond ironic.

"Would somebody like to tell me exactly who had the brilliant idea to invite Space Rescue to the party?" Senior asked.

"Calling for help was my idea," Bam Bam said. "But I didn't want to attack their ship."

"Like your idea woulda worked!" Chuckles said.

"It would have been a damn sight better then what we did!" Tony Lords said. "We lost four good men!"

"What exactly was the idea?" Senior said.

"Tell Space Rescue that we were the rightful crew," Bam Bam said. "How would they know otherwise?"

"But they'd still want to get paid!" Chuckles said.

"Tri-State has a billing arrangement," Bam Bam shot back testily. "It's not like we'd have to hand over cash. By the time Tri-State figured it out, we'd be gone."

"So should I take it that the second attack was your idea, son?" Senior said to Chuckles.

"Yes, sir, it was."

The two men glared at each other for a minute or two. Chuckles finally looked down.

"It's not something I would have done," Senior said, "had I been consulted."

"This damn mountain was on the wrong damn side of the planet," Chuckles said with ill grace. "We couldn't contact you!"

The Republic claimed all of Olympus Mons, a single mountain the size of the state of New Mexico. Bensonville was on the eastern rim.

"Mere common sense would suggest that it was unnecessary," Senior said. "Nevertheless, now we have to deal with the consequences." Senior looked at the rest of the group.

"The only consequence I see is that we picked up two additional people to ransom," Bam Bam said. "The Jap and the officer."

"I thought Chop Suey Man was a Chink?" Tony Lords said.

"Very adamant that he doesn't like chop suey," Bam Bam said. "Also very handy with reactor controls."

"What was the problem with the reactor?" Rachel asked.

"The main control panel was locked out," Bam Bam said. "The Rescue dude was able to physically jumper around it."

"So the *Price* is fully operational?" Senior asked.

"We'll need to reload the reactor control software for full functionality," Bam Bam said, "but the current jury-rig will work for now."

"Miss Storey, any word on our hostages yet?" Chuckles asked.

"I won't be able to get started on that until later," Rachel said. *Since when did I become 'Miss Storey?' You don't call me that when you're trying to get into my pants.*

"Any advance thoughts?" Senior asked.

"The *Price's* crew is worth some money," Rachel said. "Not as much as the Master and Engineer would have been. Of course, now that the crew knows Brenda was in on it we can't ransom her. I don't know how much we can get for the Rescuemen."

"Not much, I suspect," Senior said. "That organization is almost as poor as we are. Miss Lords, where do we stand on locating the special cargo?"

"Locklin was supposed to be the computer guru," Bam Bam said.

Locklin Richards had been in the first shuttle, the one that had actually gotten people inside the Rescue ship. Since the news reports weren't talking about prisoners, he was assumed to be dead. Rachel felt a catch in her throat. They'd been more than friends, even though Locklin refused to leave his wife.

"Yes, and we mourn for him," Senior said. "So what is Plan B?"

"A copy of the ship's manifest was kept on the Master's computer," Bam Bam said. "I brought the box down with me. We'll have to find somebody else to crack the encryption."

"Any other good news?" Senior asked sarcastically. He didn't wait long for an answer, continuing, "Well, we all have work to do. Any questions?"

There were none, so Chuckles adjourned the meeting.

It could be worse, Rachel thought, walking out of the Benson residence after the meeting. She had seen worse—after the *Witchcraft* fiasco which had gotten her stuck here in the first damn place. She shuddered, remembering the rage in one of the ex-hostage's eyes as he came at her with his homemade knife. Still, Rachel couldn't shake the fear that getting Space Rescue so directly involved in this was a mistake.

The dark and drab streets of Bensonville didn't help her mood as Rachel walked home. Rachel had grown up on Mars' Utopia region, where habs were built out of light-colored sandstone. Her home hab had gone an extra step, and painted the ceilings light blue. The effect was light and airy.

Here on Olympus, they built hab spaces out of cut volcanic rock. The floor, the walls, and the roof, three levels above them were all of dark volcanic rock, cut by lasers. Even if all the overhead lights had been on, and they weren't (every other one was off as an economy measure) the hab just sucked light.

You'd think two A shares would be worth something. Or maybe not.

Under 'Somali Rules,' Charles Senior, as mayor of Bensonville, got 10% of the ransom off the top for 'anchoring rights.' The investors usually got 30%. But since the investors seemed more interested in "the special cargo" then the ship, the investor cut was only 15%.

People taking less risk, like those guarding the ship in orbit, were 'B' shareholders, and got $100,000 each, but no vote. There were also some people, like those guarding the prisoners in the town, who got paid on a straight daily rate.

Each pirate part of the actual attack got an 'A' share, which was an equal cut of the money left over after everybody else got paid. Skilled pirates, like Rachel who was qualified to command their mother ship, got an additional 'A' share.

Let's hope that there's something left for the 'A' people, Rachel thought as she arrived at her house. Not surprisingly, the front door to her store / house was unlocked. Typical Minty, Rachel thought, feeling a flash of irritation at her younger sister. Although an unlocked door would only be a problem if anybody actually *wanted* anything from her store.

Rachel entered and closed the door behind her, locking it by feel. The lights were off, and the switch was on the far wall, but enough light was spilling through the open door to the family room in back for her to see.

She could feel the unevenness of the floor through her soft-soled deck shoes as she walked across the room. This part of the town was below grade, and the floor was cut lava bedrock. The front half of the room was partitioned into several smaller spaces, the better to showcase the prints and decorative wall sculptures. Rachel had used some of her inventory of tapestries and curtains for that purpose. *They won't buy it if they can't see it.*

Not that anybody was buying much.

A long set of curtains, these not for sale and half-open, hung from the ceiling, dividing the room in half. A few boxes with her remaining inventory was behind the main curtain.

Minty was sitting in her usual place, sprawled in front of the video unit, her long and straight black hair the only thing visible from behind. A wine glass, half-empty, sat on the coffee table. She'd picked up drinking from their uncle. Unlike their uncle, she seemed to be able to drink socially.

"I don't suppose you found time to get dinner," Minty said, not looking up from the ballgame playing on the video.

"You suppose correctly," Rachel replied. "We got anything to eat?"

"Spaghetti in the fridge, and a bottle of so-so Chianti on the counter."

Rachel walked to the kitchen, pausing to kick off her shoes.

"Don't leave those shoes out," Minty said, glancing at her from the corner of his eye.

"I thought I was the older sister," Rachel said.

"Yeah, but I have to clean up after you."

You're nothing if not predictable, Minty, Rachel thought as she warmed up a plate of spaghetti. The girl turned eight and a half Martian years, or Mears, old next month. It was sixteen standard years, but the girl acted as if she was twice her real age.

"Any messages?" Rachel asked from the kitchen, shouting over the noise from the microwave.

"No customer calls, if that's what you mean."

Rachel stifled a curse. The hicks in this jerkwater town wouldn't know good art if it bit them on the ass.

The microwave beeped, and Rachel took out her plate. She walked into the living room.

"Tell me you weren't running around out dressed like that," Rachel said. Her sister was lounging on the couch, wearing a much-too-small cropped T-shirt and her dark hair, flowing loose, was more accent then concealment for the pink leather collar she was wearing. A half-empty glass of wine sat in front of her.

"Just school," Minty said.

"My God," Rachel said. "And where in the hell did you get that pink collar?"

"Ordered it from Bradbury. I think it's cute. A little big for me, but cute."

Rachel shook her head and resisted the urge to point out that she could see a slight pants malfunction It wasn't like the other girls in this town dressed like sluts. *Well, except for Bam Bam.* But Bam Bam's look was more white trash, while Minty's seemed to be stripper chic.

Rachel put her stuff on the coffee table and plopped down on the floor in front of it.

"When you're an adult, you can wear whatever you want, Arminta Ann Storey. In the meantime, put some clothes on when you go to school."

"Yes, Ma'am," Minty replied.

"I'm serious," Rachel said, irritation creeping into her voice. "Your alligator mouth is going to get your hummingbird ass in trouble."

A look of rebellion flashed across Minty's face, followed by her blank 'whatever' look.

It's like talking to a stone wall. Rachel took a sip of the wine. "What's wrong with this wine?"

"It's too complicated to explain." Minty slid a coaster at her, even though the table was stone-topped and wouldn't stain. "Did you see the news?"

"No."

Minty sat up on the couch. "Space Rescue ship got jumped by pirates. Four pirates dead, plus the Rescue captain." She turned off the video. "You?"

"Me what?"

"You, Ms. Dread Pirate Storey."

Rachel ate a forkful of spaghetti, debating if that was some movie line she was supposed to appreciate. *I wonder how much she knows?*

"Not sure I know what you're talking about," Rachel said after she swallowed.

"Jennifer Rachel Storey," Minty said, using Rachel's despised first name, "this is entirely too small a town to hide shit like that."

"I was on a business trip up to Phobos to buy art."

Minty smirked. "Nice try. You launched when Phobos was on the wrong side of the planet."

"Since when did you take up the study of orbital mechanics?"

"The name *Randal Cranston* mean anything to you?"

Christ Jesus. What doesn't she know?

"It's none of your business."

"You're my sister, Rachel," Minty said. "Of course it's my business."

You're not tough enough to handle it, kid. "Fine. Why don't you tell me what you think you know?"

"Chuckles and his merry band just 'jacked a cargo ship. Conveniently one that Bam Bam was crewing. Y'all wanted to take the ship before they posted double watches, so you had to buy or steal something with range. The only person I know in this one-airlock town who's qualified to operate a deep spacer is you. How am I doing?"

Dead on the money. "Go on."

"Except something went wrong when the merry band got on board. Probably one of them got excited and accidentally shot somebody important."

Actually, if Tony Lords shot somebody, they needed to be shot.

"What I don't know is whose idea it was to call for a tow," Minty said.

"Charles thought of that," Rachel said. "He figured to get two ships."

"That's the first honest thing you've said to me in a week." Minty took a sip of her wine. "So what's your involvement in this?"

"Hired ship driver, nothing more."

Minty frowned mockingly. "Please don't lie to me. I know about *Windy City* and *Odyssey*."

Those were two other ships Rachel had had a hand in stealing, the first one almost two mears or four standard years ago. "I don't know what you think you know, young miss..."

"I read the Interpol report," Minty said. "And that interview Janet what's-her-face gave."

"Pilgrim. And don't believe everything you read."

"So you're telling me that Charles Benson Junior, the guy you call the dumbest man in town, came up with an idea to steal a ship for ransom all on his own? And that a woman who just happened to be involved in three piracies, and is losing her shirt trying to sell frou-frou art to a bunch of bigots, didn't put him up to it?"

"Actually it was his dad's idea." Which had the advantage of being true. "Then I got asked to help," which was also true. Rachel took a sip of her wine. "Your point?"

"My point is this—I want in."

"Why in the world would you want 'in'?"

"Because if this thing goes sideways, which it's already starting to, I'll be in just as much trouble as you are."

"It won't go sideways," Rachel said.

"Did you say that before or after the crew revolt on *Witchcraft*?"

Rachel sputtered for an instant. *Witchcraft* wasn't in any Interpol report, at least not under Rachel's name, and deliberately so.

"Don't know what you're talking about."

"Space ship *Witchcraft*," Minty said. "Attacked about a mear ago by you and some African mercs. What happened—somebody fall asleep?"

No, Rachel thought, the guy guarding the hostages was awake when he got shanked, right at the start of the riot. Good thing—his screams gave me time to escape.

But since the crew took the ship back, Rachel didn't get paid for that gig. Her cuts from the other two ships had been small—and what hadn't been spent was tied up in inventory nobody in this shit town wanted to buy.

"I don't know what you *think* you know..."

"Jean-Paul Thierry ring a bell?"

Second Mate on the *Witchcraft*. "Should it?"

"He visited our cousin Eunice last month. Said he was an old friend of yours."

Jean-Paul and the dead captain of the *Witchcraft* had been lovers. He'd blamed Rachel for the captain's death. Jean-Paul had also led the crew riot which recaptured his ship.

"Yes, I was involved in the attack on the *Witchcraft*."

Minty smiled triumphantly. "Thank you for telling me the truth. Now, what exactly is your role with the *Price*?"

"You familiar with Somali Rules?"

"Yes. How many 'A' shares do you have?"

"Two for skippering the *Cranston*. I'm also supposed to handle the ransom negotiations."

"I hear you have a computer problem?"

"Just exactly how do you know that?"

Minty smiled. "Let's just say some of your friends are talkative."

So much for secrecy. "We do."

"I can fix it. For a 'B' share."

"Senior said he's paying cash."

"I'm sure I can find other ways to earn my share."

"Not my call."

"Don't you get to bring a friend under Somali Rules?"

Actually, you did. And a hundred grand extra would be helpful. Rachel looked at her sister. *It's not like she'd be at risk trying to hack a computer. Besides, I can keep an eye on her.*

"I'll put your name up," Rachel said. Something wicked came over her. "But you will need to do more than crack a computer. We need proof of life."

"What?"

Rachel smiled evilly. "Nobody pays for dead bodies, dear. I thought you knew that. We need proof that the crew is still alive."

"Video?"

"Yes." Rachel took a bite of her spaghetti. "All of them. Tonight."

"Tonight? But it's late!"

"And Port Lowell is eight hours ahead of us. We need something on their screens ASAP." Rachel smiled. "You said you wanted in."

"I guess so," Minty said.

"Go get some paper."

"What am I, your maid?"

"It's not for me," Rachel said with a grin. "It's for you. You need to take notes."

Minty got up from the couch. "Aye aye, Miss Captain Ma'am," she said, walking away.

There were guards at the prison, Rachel thought, so Minty wouldn't be in any real danger, but maybe getting barked at by a pissed-off Mexican would take some of the wind out of her sails.

"That's more like it," Rachel said to her sister's back.

Minty returned a minute later, notepad in hand.

"We're keeping them at Joe's on Second, yes?"

"Correct."

"Okay," Minty said, pen in hand. "Proceed, oh font of wisdom."

Chapter 8

Friday, 31 Virgo Year 52 09:45 local (March 2, 2074, 10:45 GMT) Volunteer Space Rescue Service Headquarters, Port Lowell, Mars

JACK WALKED DOWN THE HALLWAY at Rescue Base Port Lowell, headquarters for the Service. He'd docked the *Volodka* at Stickney Base, and they'd offloaded the wounded. Lieutenant Ortega was still at Phobos General Hospital, too bad off to move, while they'd sent Lewis down to the planet. Now, Captain Edwin Newindale, commander and senior officer of the Volunteer Space Rescue Service, his office at the end of the hallway, wanted to see Jack "post haste."

The hallway ended at a real wood door, one of the few he'd seen since leaving Earth as a kid. It was expensive, shipping wood out to Mars. Jack walked in, his first visit to the office, and found himself facing a wooden desk, manned by a pale young man.

"Midshipman Williams of the *Volodka* reporting," Jack said.

"I'll tell the Flag Officer that you're here," the orderly said, his face an impassive mask. "Please have a seat, sir." The man's dark blue dress uniform was impeccable. Jack was glad he'd at least had time to shave. His khaki work uniform was wrinkled, and looked like he'd slept in it.

Not that he'd gotten any sleep. He sat down in an overstuffed armchair as the orderly slipped into Captain Newindale's office. An antique mechanical clock sitting on a wooden cabinet ticked, the only sound in the room. Jack looked around, trying to stay awake. Wood came from Earth, and if half the furnishings here were real wood, the place must have cost a fortune.

Captain Chen should be making this report, Jack thought, an image of the Captain's dead body flashing unbidden into his mind. Or Lieutenant Ortega. Fencl had just barely been able to prevent her from bleeding out, and Carla was still in critical condition at

Phobos hospital, too weak to move down to the planet. With Peter Grant a captive on the *Price*, that left Jack in command.

"Midshipman?" The orderly said, holding the door to the inner office open. "He will see you know."

Jack stood up and followed the orderly into Captain Newindale's office. The orderly stopped in front of Newindale's desk, a massive wooden monstrosity which the cost of shipping from Earth alone must have been more then Jack's salary, came to attention and said, "Senior officer, *VRSS Volodka,* Sir."

"Midshipman Jack Williams, reporting as ordered, Sir," Jack said, standing at attention to the orderly's right.

"Thank you, Petty Officer," Newindale said, not looking up from his paperwork. "That will be all."

The orderly turned smartly and marched out of the office, closing the door behind him.

"How is Lieutenant Ortega," Newindale said, looking up from his paperwork.

"Weak, sir. The docs think she'll make it."

"Your after-action report is, shall we say, spare," Newindale said, gesturing at the printout on his desk. It was one of the few things on the massive dark wood surface, looking almost forlorn. "For instance, who exactly gave the order to commence firing?"

"Sir?" It wasn't the question he was expecting.

Newindale grimaced. "Who gave the order to open fire?"

"Nobody, sir."

"Nobody?"

"Sir, there was no order to commence firing. The pirates shot their way onboard and we shot back."

Newindale frowned. "Was there any attempt to negotiate?"

"Negotiate, sir? With whom?"

"With the so-called pirates."

Jack blinked, and struggled to clear his eyes. "So-called, sir?"

"I grant you, Midshipman," Newindale said, "that these individuals acted very aggressively. However, I'm not aware of any decision to militarize Martian space. Especially not by the Space *Rescue* service."

Jack's ears started to buzz, and he felt suddenly hot. "Who the hell said anything about 'militarize'? We went out on a rescue call, and got jumped. I lost three good people, and two more are in the hospital. We were fighting for our lives, and you want to know who told us to 'open fire'?"

"Three? How do you count that?"

"The captain, Lieutenant Grant and Able Nomura." Jack deliberately left off the 'sir.'

"Why would they kill Grant and Nomura?"

"They're pirates?"

Newindale scowled at Jack. "Son, they needed us for something, don't you think?"

Huh? "Not sure I'm following."

Newindale looked like he'd bitten something sour, then his face softened. "When was the last time you got some sleep?"

"I got a bit in the waiting room at Stickney General," Jack said.

"Sit down, son, before you drop." As Jack did so, Newindale said, "Want some coffee?"

"No thanks," Jack said, adding, "sir."

"The Mayday call had to be a trick," Newindale said. "If the ship was operational, they wouldn't have called attention to themselves."

True, Jack thought. "What does that have to do with Grant?"

"My guess is that they made him fix whatever the problem was in exchange for his life. And Nomura's."

"So he's a hostage."

"Probably."

"Have they asked for a ransom?"

"Not yet," Newindale said. "Not that I intend to pay one. It would encourage further acts like this."

"Sir, it's not like these pirates are just going to hand them over."

"I intend to resolve this matter peacefully. There's been gunplay enough in this matter." Newindale reached for a printout. "Now let's flesh out this after-action report."

At the end of their conversation, the fact that Jack had ordered the *Volodka* RTB without Grant aboard came up.

"It's my fault," Jack said. "Chief Kelly wanted to go back for them."

"Would Tony, I mean Captain Chen, have let Kelly do that?" Newindale asked.

Jack was surprised by the question. "I don't know," he finally said.

"Trust me, he wouldn't."

"If you say so, sir."

Newindale sighed again. "Tony and I go back a ways. He is, or rather, was, an idealist. But not stupid. You did the best you could."

"Thank you, sir," Jack said. His mouth felt like ashes. "Anything else?"

"No, that will be all."

Jack stood up and walked out. He still didn't feel better about his decision. Peter Grant and Alan Nomura were in some hellhole, and Jack had had a chance to prevent that. In Captain Newindale's outer office, he stopped the orderly and pointed at the inner office. "If he asks, I'm on a notification call."

"Notifying whom, sir?"

"Grant's girlfriend." Jack pulled out his PDA and fumbled for an address. "Any idea where 1749 N. Harding would be?"

"No, but let me pull up a map," the orderly replied.

I hear they've got something called Gee Pee Ess on Earth, and you don't need maps.

"Thanks," Jack said, after the orderly handed him a printout. "I'll be back later, and spend the day in the ship's office." There was a shitload of paperwork awaiting him.

"Very good, sir," the orderly said. "If I may, you did well out there."

"Thanks," Jack said, feeling his face blush. *If I did better I wouldn't be helping to plan a funeral.*

1749 N. Harding proved to be a blank brick wall with a large vehicle door, open. A sign above the door proclaimed the place 'Methods and Materials.' Jack walked in, and found a small gray-haired man pushing a pallet-jack.

"Know where Janet Pilgrim is?" Jack asked.

"Weld shop—in back," the man said, gesturing vaguely.

Jack walked off in the direction indicated, and found Janet standing next to a workbench looking at a plumber's nightmare of pipes and valves with a young man, short and wiry, about Jack's age. As Jack approached, the man spit into a paper cup in his hand.

"I told Mfume he'd have his manifold on Friday," the man said, "and that's tomorrow."

"Actually, I need to talk to Janet," Jack said.

She turned and looked at him, a welding rod in her hand. "What brings you out here?" She asked. Her voice sounded tight.

"You see the news last night?" Jack asked.

"No." She gestured at the manifold. "It's a rush job."

"We got jumped by pirates," Jack said.

"And?"

"They got Peter."

"You mean they killed Peter," she said. There wasn't a trace of emotion in her voice.

"We don't think he's dead," Jack said. "The pirates needed him to fix something, we think."

"You think," she said.

Jack was expecting her to show some emotion. This was like talking to a robot. "We got called out on a Mayday. When we got there the ship was cold iron and late for insertion."

"So you think he got them running?"

"Last track showed them under power."

"Take the day off," the man said. "I'll finish this."

"Thanks Marty," Janet said, "but I got it." She looked at Jack, her eyes steely. "Anything else?"

"Not that I can think of," Jack said. "I'll call when we know more."

"If you want to," Janet said. She dropped her welding hood down over her face. "Watch your eyes."

"Let me buy you a cup of coffee," the man said to Jack.

"Sure," Jack said. "You are?"

"Marty Mackovic. I own the shop. Watch your eyes."

Jack turned his back as the welder fired up. The stink of burning metal filled the air, and even with his back turned, the flashes of light from the arc bounced around the shop.

The man put his hand on Jack's shoulder and pointed him towards a metal open staircase. They walked up and into a sparsely-furnished office. The man walked over to a small coffeemaker, which had been white once.

"What do you take?"

"Just black, Mr. Mackovic."

"Call me Marty," he said. "Have a seat."

Jack looked around. Practically every surface in the office was covered with piles of various paper and manuals, mostly grease-stained. Jack found a guest chair with a ripped cushion and sat down.

Marty handed Jack a black mug, steam rolling off of the top. He took a sip of his coffee and winced. It had been on the burner too long and tasted like ass.

"So Space Rescue is going to buy their people back?" Marty said, talking around what had to be a wad of tobacco in his mouth.

"I guess so," Jack replied. "We haven't been contacted yet."

"They carry insurance? Space Rescue, I mean."

"I have no idea."

"I ask," Marty said, pushing some papers aside to perch on a countertop, "because they're usually broke." He pointed with his chin out the door. "They owe me for material on that manifold. Most places won't do work for them unless it's cash in advance."

"So why do work for them?" Jack felt his face flush, and immediately regretted asking.

"Mfume saved my life," Marty said, emotion flashing over his face. "I owe him."

"Janet going to be okay?"

Earl shook his head. "Woman's a genius welder, even when she's hung over. Which is good 'cause that's a regular occurrence with her."

Jack took another sip of his coffee. He'd heard that comment about Janet before. Not that Peter Grant was unfamiliar with bars. "I should be going," he said.

"I hear that the insurance companies sent somebody up to fix this piracy shit."

"Oh?"

"Yeah. Head guy's named Yeargan."

"Sounds vaguely familiar," Jack said.

Marty sat down his spit cup. "You should go talk to him."

"You think he can help?"

"He'll be better than that idiot Newindink."

"You mean Newindale."

"I mean Newindink." Marty stood up and walked to his desk. "Let me get you Yeargan's contact information."

Chapter 9
Friday, 31 Virgo Year 52 11:15 local (March 3, 2074, 11:55 GMT)
Port Lowell, Mars

AFTER HIS MEETING WITH JANET AND MARTY, Jack returned to Space Rescue. The paperwork he'd been dreading proved less impressive, or at least less urgent, than he'd been dreading.

Jack found himself looking at the contact information Marty had given him about the insurance weenie. It listed him as 'contact via Roger McNally at McNally and Associates.' Jack called up that business in the local directory to discover that McNally handled shipping insurance claims. Not only that, but Space Rescue's database showed McNally as the owner's rep for the *Price*.

"Maybe I ought to see what this dude has to say," Jack said to himself. The paperwork would wait.

He left, and caught a street car to the address on Schiaparelli Street. It wasn't exactly the ritziest part of town, but rather an area where respectable if cost-conscious businesses set up operations. Jack walked in, the jingle of bells over the door announcing his arrival.

"In back," a man shouted from the other side of a head-high cloth partition. Jack walked around it to find a frumpy looking older black man sitting at a gray metal desk.

"I'm looking for Sean Yeargan," Jack said.

"He's in the back," the man said, standing up and revealing more than a little paunch. The sound of a toilet flushing came from the back. "My name's NcNally, the man said, offering his hand. You are?"

"Jack Williams, Space Rescue."

A white man, fairly trim with graying hair and beard, walked out of the back area, wiping his hands with a paper towel.

"Sean, meet the other Jack Williams," McNally said.

"They usually refer to me as 'Black Jack,'" Jack said.

"I met the other guy," McNally said. "Guy's so white he's practically pink."

Sean offered his hand, still damp, and Jack shook it. "Pleased to meet you, Mr. Yeargan."

"Call me Sean, Jack," Yeargan replied. "Drink?"

"Coffee would be nice—black."

Yeargan grabbed a plastic thermos from a faded Formica-topped side table and poured Jack a mug. "What can we do for you, Lieutenant?"

"Midshipman," Jack replied. Yeargan handed over a mug emblazoned with some insurance company logo. Jack took a sip, thinking he was practically living on coffee. At least this stuff was fairly fresh.

"You heard about the *Price*?" Jack said.

Yeargan grimaced. "You could say that."

"Captain Newindale thinks that our guys are still alive—held for ransom."

"Oh, The Dink does, does he?" McNally said. He walked out from behind his desk and settled into a metal low-backed arm chair close to a folding table.

Apparently that's the conference room. Jack pulled up a similar but not matching chair and sat down.

Yeargan, standing by the coffee area, sent a sharp look McNally's way, the overhead fluorescent lights casting a weird shadow on his face. "They might be, but to answer your next question, nobody's called us yet."

"How does this work, anyway?" Jack asked. "Ransoming a crew, I mean."

"You Space Rescue's point man on this?" Yeargan asked, a dubious look on his face.

Jack felt his face warm. "No, this is an unofficial visit."

"Well, assuming they want to play the ransom game," NcNally said, "it goes one of two ways. One, they have the ship's captain call his ownership via radio. Or two, some lawyer or similar greaseball calls us. Then we talk until we agree on a number."

"Either way, we're screwed," Yeargan said, joining them at the makeshift conference area.

"How so?"

"We don't know where the ship's at," Yeargan said, gesturing dangerously with his coffee cup. "Other than 'Martian orbit' which is too vague to be of use."

"I'm missing something," Jack said. "Why do you care where the ship is?"

"Yeargan's been sent to put the kibosh on this piracy shit," McNally said. "But it's hard to kibosh somebody if you can't find them."

"Oh," Jack said. "Why you?"

"You heard of the *Windy City*?" Yeargan said.

"It's before the kid's time," McNally offered.

"I know all about *Windy City*," Jack said. *Now I know where I heard Yeargan's name.* "I just had to tell Janet Pilgrim that her boyfriend's been captured."

"Oh Christ," Yeargan moaned. "How'd she take it?"

"Cool as a cucumber."

"Fucking wonderful," Yeargan said. His tone seemed to imply that it was anything but wonderful. Jack decided to parse his reaction to Janet some other time.

"What kind of 'kibosh' are you talking about?" Jack asked.

"The nine-millimeter kind," Yeargan replied. "Send a few of these fucks back in bags and maybe they'll stop."

"We sent four back already," Jack replied. *At least one of them was killed by me personally.*

"Yeah, but if they get a big payday, and they will," Yeargan said, "They'll keep at it."

"They're not going to get a payday out of Space Rescue," McNally said.

"Why not?" Yeargan asked.

"They're chronically broke, for one thing," McNally said.

"Captain Newindale was very reluctant to pay a ransom," Jack added.

"Newindink," McNally spat. "Man's a classic example of the Iron Law of Bureaucracy."

"What's that?" Jack asked.

"Dreamed up by a writer named Pournelle," McNally said, setting his coffee on the battered conference table and leaning back. "Pournelle's Iron Law of Bureaucracy states that in any bureaucratic organization there will be two kinds of people: those who work to further the actual goals of the organization, and those who work for the organization itself. Your boss Newindink is an example of the latter."

"Still doesn't explain why he's not paying," Yeargan said, leaning into the group.

"Not paying benefits him, because he can look tough to the other captains. He also keeps his costs down."

"But why not launch a commando raid?" Yeargan asked.

"Commando raid?" Jack said. "We're not a police force or a military."

"Well, somebody on this fucking planet needs to be," Yeargan shot back.

"Ain't gonna be Space Rescue," McNally said. "Too risky, for one. If some Rescueman gets himself shot, the blame falls to Newindink."

"The reward..." Yeargan said.

"Is a pat on the back from some shippers, and a metric shitload of grief from every station in the boondocks." McNally drained his coffee cup, obviously satisfied with his observation.

"Huh?" Yeargan said.

"How do you think a place like Viking Chryse keeps the lights on?" McNally asked.

Jack didn't know exactly where the station 'Viking Chryse' was, but Mars' Chryse Planitia was sparsely populated, even by Martian standards. God knows what kind of crooked shit they were up to that far out in the boondocks.

"You're the local expert—enlighten me," Yeargan said. There was more than a touch of sarcasm in his voice.

"All these little one-airlock stations are either pirate bases or buying stolen goods at pirate auctions," McNally said. "Nuclear reactors ain't cheap, even the little-bitsy two-fifty kay-double-you ones, but everybody needs one."

"So, Mr. Williams," Yeargan said, favoring Jack with a quizzical look, "if you're not The Dink's point man, what exactly is your role in this?"

Good question. What is my role? "Right now, I'm acting commander for the *VSRS Volodka*."

"I've heard of rapid promotions," McNally said, "but isn't that a bit quick?"

"Captain Chen's dead. Our First Officer was off on bereavement leave. Lieutenant Ortega's in the hospital and Lieutenant Grant was captured."

"Thin command structure," Yeargan observed.

"We're not the US Air Force Space Command," Jack replied. That organization was notoriously rank-heavy—supposedly they had more generals than ships.

"Which is too busy glaring at the Chinese and the Indians in low Earth orbit to bestir themselves here," Yeargan said. "So, mister Acting Captain, any idea where our missing ship is?"

"Last I saw her, the *Price* was on course for insertion to low northern orbit latitude," Jack said.

"Huh?" both men asked at once.

"Once we got the ship back, our ship I mean, I had *Price* on radar for maybe twenty minutes. She was on a course for a low northern latitude orbit."

"How low?" Yeargan asked.

Jack thought for a minute. "Between sixteen and twenty north."

"Cuts out Viking," Yeargan said.

"Sixteen north is also sixteen south on the flip side," McNally offered.

"Which is too far north for Boxtown," Yeargan said. "They're at twenty-four south." Yeargan looked at Jack like a man dying of thirst looking at a pitcher of water. "You got more details?"

"It's a pretty broad window," Jack said.

"Which already cut out two known pirate hotspots," McNally said. "You opened your mouth, kid, might as well go all in."

"I'm a Rescuer, not a soldier," Jack said.

"There's two of your own being held," Yeargan said.

I know. I left them.

"We're just looking for data," Yeargan said. He didn't say 'right now,' but Jack knew that's what Yeargan meant.

"I'll provide data, but that's it."

"You do that, kid," McNally said. "We'll do the rest."

Chapter 10

Friday, 31 Virgo Year 52 17:15 local (March 2, 2074, 17:55 GMT)

JANET WALKED INTO HER HOUSE AFTER WORK, casually pushing the door closed behind her. It was quiet as well—her son Mikey was at Penny's house. Janet tossed her keys down on the table next to the door. She flicked on the overhead light, but didn't bother locking the door.

Everybody I love dies.

She walked back towards the kitchen, dimly illuminated by a light over the sink she used as a night light, her shoes squeaking on the hard tile floor. When she got to the sink, she washed her hands again, trying to scrub off the grit she'd missed while washing up at work.

And the blood. People die because of me.

Raj didn't die because of me, another voice inside her said.

She smiled, remembering her first real boyfriend's face. *What brought him up*? Her smile faded. *So many people died because of me that I* forgot *about one*!

The sting of the hot water caused her to jerk her hands back. She turned the faucet off and reached for a hand towel to dry herself.

The towel she usually left hanging on the oven handle wasn't there. Mikey had spilled something at breakfast, and she'd used it to clean up after him. Her hands still wet, she opened up the high cabinet above the refrigerator, the only one that (so far) Mikey couldn't get into.

The gun was there, sitting next to the last two clean hand towels. She dried her hands absently with a clean towel while looking at the gun.

It wasn't very impressive, that gun—a cheap snub-nosed .38 revolver, older than her dad, with a well-worn rubber grip. It did work, though—she'd used it.

On people.

Did the Grissom twins really have to die? Did I really have to kill them?

Janet dropped the towel on the floor and took the gun down. She flipped the cylinder open with a practiced motion. Five copper-colored bullets filled the chambers. She closed the cylinder, and bent down to pick up the towel while still holding the gun in her left hand.

She went to the kitchen table, the only piece of furniture in that part of the house. Just like the rest of her stuff, it was battered and second-hand. A previous owner had left a too-hot pot on the table, creating a circular scorch mark near the middle. She spread out the towel and laid the gun on it.

I can't go on. I just can't.

A glint of something caught her eye in the dim light. She looked closer and saw one of Mikey's fire trucks. Even that had been second-hand—she'd bought it at an auction and had to remove a tag with some other kid's name on it before giving it to Mikey.

I can't even give my kid a fucking new toy! How can I be a real mother for him?

She laid her head on the table like a kid taking a nap at school, feeling very tired.

I'm not his mother. Not really.

Mikey did call Janet 'mommy,' but he also used the word for Penny. In fact, just that morning, Mikey had asked her if they were going to "mommy down the street."

He'll never miss me. Penny can raise him, and when he gets older, show him my picture.

The phone rang.

Janet looked at it, startled. She could see from her seat the caller ID—Sharpe, Penny.

The phone rang again, insistent.

"Go to voicemail," Janet said.

The phone, too cheap to come with voice response, ignored her, and rang again.

Janet didn't move. "It will eventually go to voicemail."

Then she looked at the gun. *I better answer it.* She jumped up and got it in the middle of the last ring.

"Yes?" Janet said.

"You coming over to get Mikey?"

"Yes," Janet lied. "I'll be there in a few. I just want to shower first."

She hung up the phone before Penny could reply. *If Penny thinks I slipped in the shower, she'll come over alone. Mikey doesn't need to see me.*

Janet sat back down at the table, and looked at the gun.

Headshots are messy. Sure, but messy. Also closed casket.

She wondered what kind of bullets the gun was loaded with, so she opened the cylinder and dumped the rounds out into her hand. They were all hollow-points, with a soft lead ring.

A shot into the chest should be good. Cleaner. She looked around, wondering if she still had that plastic tarp from when she'd re-painted her bedroom.

No, that would look too deliberate. An accident would be better. Her Mom had paid for some insurance on her, and the money would go to Mikey. *Maybe he could use it to go to college, when he gets older?*

She re-loaded the gun, noticing a slight tremor in her hands. When she was done, she set the gun down on the towel.

"Okay, Mister Coroner," she said, her voice echoing in the empty room, "I'm sitting here cleaning my gun, and the damn thing went off. Who knew it was loaded?"

She looked around. *Yeah, but cleaning it with what? A damp towel?*

Her hands were sweaty, and she wiped them off on her T-shirt.

"Christ," she said. "How many shitty t-shirts do I have?" Most of which are probably only fit for rags anyway. And the WD-40 is under the sink.

Should I leave a note? "Not where Mister Coroner would find it, no, dumb shit!"

But maybe someplace Penny would find it? Like in Mikey's dresser. She'd have to pack up his stuff sooner or later.

Janet heard the front door open.

"Janet, you okay?" Penny called out.

"I'm fine," Janet said, looking at her gun with a feeling of desperation. "In back."

Just get her the fuck gone and do this!

"It's dark," Penny said, her shoes clicking on the tiles as she walked towards the kitchen area.

"Leave it off," Janet said.

Penny walked into the room and stopped at the hallway leading into the space.

"What's with the gun, dear?" Penny asked.

"I was going to clean it," Janet said, struggling to keep her voice level.

"Cleaning a loaded gun?"

"It's not loaded."

"You sure?" Penny walked up to the other edge of the table. "What are those copper things I see on the cylinder ends?"

Janet shrugged, but didn't say anything. *Go away*!

"You really should unload the gun first," Penny said.

"I will." Janet gestured at the gun on the table. "How do you know about guns?"

"The first thing they taught me in boot was to unload my weapon before cleaning it."

"I thought medics didn't carry guns."

"Doctors don't, or don't have to. Medics do."

Janet looked at the gun, then picked it up, her finger on the trigger. It felt right, somehow.

"Do you know how I got this gun?"

"No," Penny said. "How?"

"Mikey's dad."

The pirate who raped me. A bastard just like the bastard who killed Peter Grant.

"I thought he was a shotgun type of guy?" Penny said.

"No, I killed him with a shotgun. Not his."

The 'family heirloom' I'd taken from the Grissom twins. After I emptied this into them.

"Could I see it?"

"It's nothing special. Just a cheap-ass pocket piece."

"I'd like to look at it," Penny said, slowly sitting down across the table from Janet. "If you don't mind."

"Why would I mind?" Janet said with a shrug.

"I don't know," Penny said, reaching out for the gun.

Janet looked at Penny's outstretched hand.

"Please?"

Janet sat and watched as her hands, operating as if they had a will of their own, put the gun in Penny's hand.

Penny slowly wrapped her fingers around the gun and brought it to her. She unloaded it, and put the bullets in her pants pocket.

"Mikey loves you," Penny said.

"I know," Janet wailed, a flood of tears in her eyes.

Penny tossed the gun away, the gun clattering as it skidded across the tiled floor. Janet could barely see as she felt Penny's arms around her.

"Tell me what's wrong," Penny said.

"I just can't deal with another dead man," Janet said, finishing her story about Peter Grant's capture and probable death. They were still at the kitchen table, but Janet had somehow ended up sitting on the other side, with her back to the hallway.

"It's hard," Penny said.

Janet looked up. "My God, where's Mikey?"

"Alanya took him out for a burger."

"Who?"

"A friend of mine," Penny said. "You want more coffee?"

Janet looked down and realized there was a mug of coffee in front of her. She had no idea how it got there, and when she took a sip, it was cold. "No, thanks."

"I need a refill," Penny replied, getting up stiffly.

"You don't know," Janet said, looking over her coffee cup. "About losing people."

"I do," Penny replied over her shoulder from the counter. "Two weeks before we were to rotate out of Haiti, my platoon sergeant caught a bullet in the groin. He bled out on me in the dirt. I had to tell his wife and kids."

"I'm sorry. What was his name?"

"Felix Lightfoot. Man—hell, a kid, younger then I am now—from Toledo, Ohio."

Janet looked at the clock. "Oh, shit! You're supposed to be at work!"

"I got somebody to cover for me."

"I really do owe you," Janet said. She looked at her hands. *My God, I was going to kill myself!*

There was some commotion at the front door, and Janet turned around to see Mikey coming in with a woman about Janet's age. The woman had some takeout bags of food, which she waved at Janet.

"Dinner's here," The woman said.

"You must be Alanya," Janet said, talking around Mikey's head as he wrapped her in a big hug.

"Let's eat," Penny said from the corner of the family room.

Janet looked over and noticed that Penny's front pocket was bulging. A bulge about the size and shape of a small pistol.

I guess you better keep that for now.

Chapter 11

Friday, 31 Virgo Year 52 9:00 local time (March 3, 2074, 17:40 GMT)
Bensonville, Republic of the White Race, Olympus Mons, Mars

RACHEL WALKED OUT OF HER BEDROOM, rubbing sleep out of her eyes. She'd been up late telling Minty how to get the proof of life she wanted. *Hopefully it won't be too screwed up.*

When she got to the kitchen, she saw, right on the middle of the counter, a datastick sitting on a note.

"Here's your videos," the note said, in Minty's florid hand. "Gone to Bam Bam's to look at the computer."

Rachel took the datastick, coffee and toast up to her office and plopped down in front of her computer.

My God, she actually paid attention. Each member of the crew was sat in front of a plain cloth tarp as a backdrop, and allowed to talk for one minute. They each said the date, time and gave their Merchant Space Union ID number. There were no other voices on the recording and the date and time stamp had been erased. The camera was a low-res job designed for home use, so there was enough information to prove the people (six men, four women) were alive, but not much else.

She put a call into her contact in Port Lowell. They were eight hours ahead, so he should still be in the office, unless of course one of his girlfriends was feeling frisky.

There was a moment's delay after the call went out, during which Rachel stared at the very generic Bryce Associates greeting screen. As far as she knew, the only "associate" Steve had was whichever bimbo he was keeping on the payroll and calling a secretary.

"Hi Steve," she said when Bryce's face came up on the screen.

"Rachel, nice to see you," Steve replied. His tie was undone, and his jowly pale skin hung loosely.

"I'm calling you about that business in orbit," she said. The link was not only scrambled but buried, hidden in a seemingly normal video-call ostensibly between Steve and his aunt in Bradbury. But since she didn't know who was in his office or otherwise out of the pickup's range, a little discretion was good.

"Nasty, that." He waited for her lead.

"I've come in possession of some people and merchandise," Rachel said.

"Oh. This merchandise related to the incident in orbit?"

"Yes."

Bryce nodded, his jowls quivering. The man had a bit of a five o'clock shadow. "I'm not in the business of moving merchandise."

"Actually, I was hoping you'd help me return it. For a finders' fee, of course."

The slimebag produced a reptilian smile. "Of course. And a broker's fee?"

"A few percentage points."

The smile faded. "My usual fee is 15%. Take it or leave it."

"5% - you're not the only shark in the ocean."

"We seem to have agreed on 10%. What do you have for me?"

There's another 10% down the toilet. Still, although there were other sharks in the ocean, none were as cheap as Bryce. "The ship, seven crew plus two Space Rescue guys."

"Ship undamaged?"

"Yes. And the hostages are healthy."

"Good. Proof of life?"

"Check your usual spot."

The usual spot was an anonymous file share on a third-rate data service. Even if somebody knew to look there, everything pointed to people who didn't exist. She waited as Steve downloaded the data.

"Got it," he finally said. "It clean?"

"I think so, but give it another wash."

"Aren't we the paranoid type?"

"No, just not a data wizard. It's the stuff you don't know to look for that kills ya."

"I'll take it home and look at it tonight."

"How fast—what kind of turnaround are we looking at?"

Bryce shook his head. "I have no idea. I hear that the Consortium sent a fixer—I'll see if I can get on his calendar."

He meant the North American Insurance Consortium, a collection of US, Canadian and Mexican insurance companies, a group of 'concerned entities' who were going to be paying the ransom.

"This fixer any good?"

Steve shrugged. "I guess I'll find out. Do you need me to set up a dummy account?"

"No, we've got that already."

Bryce nodded. "Been planning, huh?"

"For a while. What about valuation—on the ship I mean?"

"I'll get somebody on it tonight, but to a certain extent it's driven by their insurance."

"Okay," Rachel said. "Call me when you get something. Oh, one more thing."

"Yes?"

"The second ship..."

"The Space Patrol boat?" Bryce said, smiling at Space Rescue's derogatory nickname. "What about it?"

"There were some people who got onboard."

Bryce's smile faded. "Dead. One caught an ax with his chest, the rest got shot. Don't tell me you want the bodies back."

She did, but that would be stupid. "No. Just want to confirm their status. Thanks."

"I'll call you when I get some news," Bryce said.

She hung up. *A fixer, on Mars. Great! Things should move faster now.*

That evening, Rachel stepped into Hill's, the town's only funeral home. It didn't feel right to leave the bodies at Port Lowell, but anonymity was more important than feelings. It also didn't feel right to just ignore the deaths, so they'd set up a group visitation. Should have had dinner first, she thought, looking at the crowd.

There were four guest books in a row outside the main parlor, and a line at each. Rachel decided to skip that, and walked into the parlor. It was a somber place, gray wallpaper and dark drapes. There had been three men and one woman killed in the attack, and large, portrait-sized pictures of them were grouped at the far end of the long room.

The families of the dead were sitting in a row next to the pictures, and a long line had formed, snaking past the families, then the pictures, and then dispersing into the rows of folding chairs set up facing the pictures.

Minty was already there, talking to one of her friends. *Do you own anything that's not slut-wear?* Although, for Minty, the black mini-dress wasn't that over the top.

Minty apparently excused herself and walked over to Rachel.

"Before you get in line," Minty said, "let's talk."

"Sure, sis," Rachel said. They walked over to a quiet corner and settled into a pair of ancient plastic folding chairs.

"I was just leaving," Minty said, "so I'm glad I caught you."

"I'm caught," Rachel said.

"We cracked the code."

"That was quick. How?"

"It wasn't easy," Minty said with a smile.

Apparently I'm going to have to hear the whole story before you get to the point. "Go on."

"The PC had biometrics, so we had to pull the DASD out and put it in another PC. Then we still had to do some social engineering."

"Social engineering?"

"We had to guess the Old Lady's password. Took us dozens of attempts."

"All this is fascinating," Rachel said, squirming in the uncomfortable chair, "but could we cut to the chase?"

"Row 8, slot 4, position 3."

"Which is where, exactly?"

"Almost exactly in the middle of the cargo area," Minty said. "Position 1 is on top," she continued, gesturing at what would be the top of her imaginary spaceship. "Position 3 is two boxes in, sitting on the load-bearing frame. Four through six are underneath the frame," gesturing towards the bottom.

"'Top' and 'bottom' don't mean shit in space, dear," Rachel said, "but I got the picture."

"There are six slots left to right," she continued, making a chopping gesture, "and slot 4 is two from the right side."

"So no matter what we do, we have to move at least two containers just to get to the special cargo," Rachel said, mentally substituting port and starboard for left and right.

"Pretty much," Minty replied.

That was going to be a problem, Rachel thought. The containers didn't 'weigh' anything, but they had a lot of inertia. Phobos Port and the handful of orbital stations had specialized manipulators that could easily load and unload containers, but they couldn't very well just show up at one of those places with a stolen ship.

"We'll have to get a cargo tug," Rachel said.

"A what?"

"A cargo tug. It's a small orbital space ship with grabbers that can shift the containers." The things looked like flying beach balls, although man-sized, with exterior manipulator arms.

"I don't suppose we get those at Tugs-R-Us," Minty said.

"Not really."

"That does beg the question of how our investors were going to get the container down?"

"There are things you shouldn't ask, young lady," Rachel said, glancing at Minty. Besides, there was any number of ground-to-orbit birds that could handle at least one container. None of them could fly off of Bensonville's shitty 'spaceport,' which wasn't much more than a flat piece of dirt, but getting the container to the ground was the investors' problem.

"You tell anybody about this yet?" Rachel asked.

"No."

"What about Bam Bam?"

"She and her dad left for dinner just after we cracked into the main drive."

"Well," Rachel said, standing up, "let's pay our respects and then go tell Junior."

Chuckles proved to be holding court in one of the back rooms of The Eagle's Lair, the town's more popular bar. The bar's owners had installed fiberglass fake-wood paneling—paneling so fake-looking it practically hurt Rachel's eyes.

Bam Bam and her dad were at the bar too, all sitting at Chuckles's table. Rachel couldn't help but notice that Bam Bam was wearing the same black dress as Minty, but filling it out much better.

Wonder how bad Bam Bam would freak if I hit on her, Rachel thought, unbidden. *Maybe that's why I've been so weird around her.*

"Got a minute, boss?" Rachel asked.

Chuckles gestured at the only free chair while taking a big gulp of his beer.

Rachel sat down and, with Minty standing behind her, told him about the location of the special cargo. She also mentioned the problem they would have in moving it.

"You sure you couldn't use one of the orbital launches we have to shift those boxes?" Chuckles asked.

"No way to grab on to them," Rachel said. "Besides, the containers are linked together with special connectors."

"Couldn't we unlink them by hand?"

"Maybe," Bam Bam said. "But it would be a bitch. Besides, trying to move those containers with our dinky orbital rockets would be tough."

"You could do it, right?" Tony Lords asked.

"Maybe," Bam Bam said. "It would be really slow going."

"Why don't we kick this problem to the investors," Tony said. "Let them either come and get it or pay extra for us."

"That's a really bad idea," Chuckles said. "I don't want them to know where the *Price* is."

"Just how were we going to get them their box?" Tony asked.

"*Cranston* was going to fly it to a set of coordinates," Chuckles said, gesturing at Rachel.

Leave me hanging out to dry, huh.

"Can we rent a tug?" Minty asked.

"What?" Chuckles said, glaring at Minty. Clearly he didn't want to hear from her.

"Rent a tug," Minty said, ignoring the glare. "I assume one of you girls can fly it."

"I can fly anything," Rachel said. "But who's going to pay and where are we going to rent one from?"

"I worked in one weekends while going to school," Bam Bam said, winking at Junior, "and there's at least one rental place on Phobos."

"How much?" Chuckles said.

"About what we're paying for dirtside guards," Bam Bam said. "Plus fuel."

"If the *Cranston* could carry a container, I assume it could carry a tug," Minty said.

"Mosquitoes have two exterior hardpoints," Rachel said. "We'll need both—one for the container and one for the tug."

Chuckles looked confused.

"We'll need the tug to put the container into whatever ship the investors meet us with," Rachel said.

"Sounds like we've got a plan," Tony said. "When can you leave?"

"Isn't there something we're forgetting?" Minty said.

"Not now," Rachel growled.

"I suppose the kid wants in," Junior said with ill grace.

"Well," Minty started.

"Fine," Chuckles said. "One Class B share, but she pulls a shift on guard duty topside."

"Deal," Minty said.

Rachel gulped. Guard duty on orbit was a bit more dangerous.

"Maybe she could pull a shift down here?" Rachel said.

"No," Tony replied. "Those guys are hourly and besides don't need relieving." He looked at Minty. "Get your shit, then. Zeb's coming down for the memorial tomorrow, on account of Locklin being his kin, which means you're going up

Rachel noted Minty's smile slip for an instant. *Maybe getting in a bit over her head would cool her jets a bit?*

"Can I borrow your pistol, sis?" Minty asked.

"Class B brings their own gun," Chuckles said.

"Take your AR-15," Rachel said, keeping her voice calm. "Bam Bam and I will call tomorrow and set up a rental, then we'll come and pick you up."

Tony drained his beer. "You launch in two hours, Minty," he said. "I'll go radio them that you're coming up."

Chapter 12

Monday, 33 Virgo Year 52 11:06 AM local (March 5, 2074, 13:06 GMT)
Port Lowell, Mars

SEAN YEARGAN STOOD UP FROM HIS DESK and stretched. He wondered how Janet was taking the news of her boyfriend's kidnapping. *I guess it depends on how serious they were.*

Roger McNally, his office mate, looked up from his computer screen.

"My butt gets tired from sitting," Sean said by way of explanation.

"I know the feeling," Roger replied, leaning back in his chair.

"How are you doing on the cargo claims?" Sean asked. Roger was the Mars-based claims rep for most of the shipping insurance companies, so the *Price's* cargo claims had landed on his desk.

"Just finished booking the last one," Roger replied.

Each shipper had the option to purchase insurance on their containers. Most shippers did, because the ship's insurance only paid a flat rate per kilogram.

"That was quick," Sean said.

"Not many shippers," Roger said, taking off his glasses and gesturing at a printout. "Half the containers were for Stormy."

Stormy was the nickname for Sturm and Associates, a large consumer wholesaler on Mars.

"Still, almost five hundred containers."

"Five hundred seventy-six. All but three insured."

"Our per-kilo payout is pretty stingy, and insurance is cheap," Sean said. "Who would go without?"

"Two of the containers were humanitarian medical equipment, shipped by somebody called Mission Outreach."

That made sense—the church people probably could just afford the shipping. Either that or they just put their trust in God. "And the third?"

"A container of 'machine parts' consigned to Aguilera and Spears, LLC."

"Who are they?"

Roger shrugged. "Damned if I know. Why?"

"I guess I just don't like mysteries," Sean said.

"They don't bother me," Roger replied. He rummaged around his stacks of paper on the desk and produced a single sheet. "Here. Everything I got on that container."

As Sean took the sheet, his cell phone rang. He picked up the phone and put his earpiece in, then pressed the answer button. Video popped up on the tiny screen.

"Sean Yeargan?" asked the face of a white man, mid-thirties and jowly. The name strap below the man's face said "Bryce and Associates."

"Yes. This is?"

"Steve Bryce."

"Hi, Mister Bryce. What can I do for you?"

"I understand you speak for the ownership of the merchant ship *Charles S. Price.*"

"I do."

"I represent the people who currently control the ship."

Sean felt his face redden. "You mean the cut-throat pirates."

"Please, sir, let's try to stay professional."

"Okay, the professional cut-throat pirates." *I have to deal with the SOB, but that doesn't mean I need to like him.*

Bryce grimaced. "If you wish."

"I do."

"Perhaps we should meet. I hate having these discussions over the phone."

"Sure," Sean said. "Come on over to my place."

"I suspect that my reception there would be rather too warm," Bryce said. "Perhaps someplace neutral?"

Sean glanced at Roger, who'd been catching Sean's half of the conversation. Sean muted his phone. "The pirates want to talk. Some guy wants to meet locally."

"Who?"

"Steve Bryce. Ring a bell?"

Roger grimaced. "Favorite lawyer for the local sleazeballs. We could meet at the Captain's Club. It's close."

Sean took his phone off mute. "Captain's Club?"

"Yes. When?"

"Half an hour?" Sean asked, glancing up to see Roger nodding yes.

"I'll be there," Bryce said.

The Captain's Club was a hotel—restaurant which also rented small offices on an hourly basis. Its clientele consisted largely of ship's officers who needed someplace dirtside to conduct business on a temporary basis.

Sean and Roger arrived at the Club first, entering through a very generic-looking stone and glass lobby, decorated with standard-issue ferns and a cheap fountain. Other than the gravity, the place could have been anywhere in the solar system.

The two men booked a small conference room on the second floor, decorated with a large geometric print. Sean had just set down his briefcase in the room when Bryce called Sean's cell. Sean gave him the room number and they took their seats.

In person, Bryce was short, coming just under Sean's nose, and was working on a swivel-chair spread. The three men shook hands coldly, then sat down around a round laminate-topped conference table, which was the main piece of furniture in the tiny and windowless room.

"We're all ears," Sean said.

Bryce produced a datastick from his pocket. "We have the ship and ten individuals..."

"There were ten on the *Price*," Sean asked. "What about the two Space Rescuemen?"

Bryce held out his hand as if to calm Sean down. "I have eight from the *Price* and a pair of Space Rescuemen."

"We'll want to know about the two missing *Price* crewmembers," Roger said.

"I'll have to ask my principals," Bryce replied. He pointed at the datastick. "Proof of life."

Sean picked it up and plugged it into a spare tablet pad. Bryce would be stupid to try and pass him a virus, but better safe than sorry.

The datastick proved to contain one file, a video of the ten hostages, which Roger and Sean watched.

"Captain and Chief Engineer are missing," Sean said. "What happened to them?"

"Again, sir, I don't know," Bryce replied. "I will have to find out."

"We'll want the bodies back, Roger said. Sean glared at him. *He's only saying what happened.*

"I'll pass that along."

"How much do you want?" Sean said.

Bryce smiled, a reptilian grimace that Sean dearly wanted to smash down the man's throat. "I was hoping you had some idea of the value of the ship and crew."

"We'll get back to you," Roger said, looking at Sean. "Perhaps you should copy that file to the local drive."

Sean nodded yes and did so. When it was done copying he handed the datastick back.

"We have your contact information," Roger said. "We'll be in touch."

"Soon, I hope," Bryce said, standing up and offering his hand.

Roger shook the man's hand, but Sean didn't.

"That guy gives me the creeps," Roger said.

"The sons of bitches killed two men," Sean said. "And now they have the balls to ask for money."

"You're taking this a bit personal, aren't you?"

"Fuck yes," Sean said. He stood up and started to pile stuff into his briefcase. "Know anybody who could plant a bug?"

"Pardon?"

"Bug. Office. His." Sean pointed at the door Bryce had left through. "Also car, bike, hell, the man's underwear, if he wears any."

"You need to cool down."

"No, God damn it," Sean said, pounding his hand on the table. *Well, maybe I do.*

"Yes, you do," Roger said. "And I get your frustration. But for all we know all he's got is a generic email account. Burn him and those people are fucked."

"This whole God damned planet is fucked."

"Maybe. Let's hope it's not beyond repair." Roger patted Sean on the back. "Let me buy you lunch. They do a great buffet here."

Roger was still praising the buffet after they left, although Sean was hard-pressed to remember what he'd eaten. As they walked down the street, a storefront caught his eye.

"You remember what address that 'Spears and Aguilera' container was going to?"

"No," Roger said, "Although I think you mean Aguilera and Spears."

Sean pointed to the storefront. "Spears and Aguilera—Family Hair Care" read the sign over the window. He crossed the street, noting the address—18 North Tinsdale—on the front door.

He walked in, and the receptionist said, "Can I help you?"

"Maybe," Sean replied, looking at the older woman. "Is this all there is? I mean, is there an office upstairs or in back?"

"This is it," the lady replied. "Mister Spears—the owner—has the two upper floors as his apartment."

Apparently hearing his name, a balding man with a bad comb-over got up from a chair and walked over.

"I'm Spears," he said. "Help you?"

"Just curious," Sean said. "Who's Aguilera?"

Spears gestured at a rather large black lady, washing somebody's hair farther in back. "My partner. She does mostly women's hair. Why?"

"Either of you expecting a shipment of machine parts from Earth?" Sean said.

Spears gave them a weird look. "Does it look like we would be?"

"Thanks," Sean said. "I'll let you get back to work."

"Sure, friend," Spears said. "Hey, when you need a haircut, come back. Half off for first time customers."

"Thanks," Sean said, waving at him.

Out in the street Roger said, "What the hell was that all about?"

"Maybe nothing."

When they got back to the office, Sean pulled the sheet of paper on the "Aguilera and Spears" container of machine parts. It was a bill of lading, with the 'deliver to' address listed as 18 North Tinsdale, Port Lowell.

Sean showed it to Roger. "Wanna bet that the 'contact on arrival' number rings to that shop?"

The number proved to be out of service, and never issued. They also checked the loading docks generated before the *Price* had left Earth. That container had had almost the maximum allowable mass, it was pre-paid and a last-minute addition.

"Somebody just paid a bunch of money to ship a container to Mars," Roger said, "but nobody was around to pick it up."

"It's almost like somebody was expecting that ship to get hijacked," Sean said. "Any guesses as to why?"

"The ship was due to hit Phobos Port," Roger said, "and clear European Union customs."

"Whatever was in that box wouldn't clear the inspection," Sean said. "We better see what Earth knows about this container."

"I'll do that," Roger said. "You should get that video to Space Rescue. They'll want to see that their guys are alive."

Chapter 13

Friday, 31 Virgo Year 52 19:30 local (March 3, 2074, 05:50 GMT)
Spaceport, Bensonville

"MR. LORDS SAYS I'M GOING UP," Minty said, trying to keep the excitement out of her voice. Finally, she thought. I'm eight and a half and I'm finally taking a rocket flight! About time to get into the action. Although having to pack in two hours was rushing it.

"Got all your stuff?" McIlhaney asked.

"Yes," Minty said, holding up her duffle bag.

"That gun real?" he asked, pointing at her AR-15.

"Of course," she said, trying not to turn as pink as the fore-grip of her gun. She'd been five Mears old when it was given to her, and back then she wanted *everything* to be pink.

"It loaded?"

"Of course."

McIlhaney scowled. "Well unload it. Last thing we need is an accidental shooting." He walked away, shaking his head. She heard him say, "So green you can hear her photosynthesize" under his breath.

I've been wearing spacesuits since before I was potty-trained, and shooting a gun for Mears. How hard can this be? Minty dropped the mag and cleared the chamber, then put the loose bullet into her ready mag and stuffed it into her duffle bag.

"You my passenger?"

"I guess so," Minty said, looking up to see a tall, horse-faced woman staring back at her.

"Hi, Ms. Tharp," Minty said.

"You can call me Twyla," she said, offering a hand. "Arminta, right?"

"Everybody calls me Minty," she replied, shaking hands.

"Well, Minty, grab your stuff."

They clomped thru the sparsely-furnished 'departure lounge' and into a large airlock. There was an electric pickup truck parked there, its bed full of bundles in cargo nets. As the pressure went down, Twyla took Minty's duffle bag and gun and stuck it into one of the netted bundles.

When pressure equalized, the outer door opened and they stepped out to the Martian surface. Dirt had been piled up to make a ramp, and McIlhaney, driving the pickup, drove down it, followed by Twyla and Minty on foot. It was dark out, but the immediate area was reasonably well lit by some floodlights mounted on the wall of the rocket port.

Twyla's ship, a small cigar-shaped thing with four retractable landing feet, was sitting on the dirt about 100 meters away. They covered the distance quickly, but not as quickly as the pickup truck. When they got there, McIhaney was halfway through loading the cargo containers into the basket of a cherry-picker mounted on the back of another pickup truck.

"You ladies want a lift?" he said, his voice booming over the radio.

"Beats climbing," Twyla said. The three of them tossed the rest of the cargo into the cab of the cherry-picker, then Minty and Twyla rode up, standing on the outside of the cab. As they did, Minty saw recessed handholds on the hull of the vehicle. They obviously were somebody's idea of a ladder.

"That doesn't look like fun," Minty observed.

"It ain't," Twyla replied. "Unless you like getting down in a hurry."

The cherry-picker reached the top of the rocket. The crew compartment, such as it was, looked like you could seat five people, counting the co-pilot, as long as everybody was friendly.

"You sit in the right front seat," Twyla said. "Get strapped in and don't touch nothing."

"Copy," Minty said, clambering in awkwardly.

Getting strapped in proved interesting, especially with the rather rude strap that came up between her legs. She couldn't look behind her in a suit helmet, and the cheap mirror mounted on the instrument panel as an after-thought didn't show much. But it didn't take a rocket scientist to figure out that Twyla was trying to get all the cargo secured.

Minty jumped as somebody touched her left arm.

"Ready?" Twyla said.

"Yes," Minty replied.

The door, which also proved to be the roof of the vehicle, descended and latched into place. Twyla did some manipulations to the controls, and then popped open her suit helmet.

"Save your air," she said.

Minty came off of suit pressure and opened her helmet. She coughed at the strong gunpowder smell, caused by the Martian dust reacting with moisture and oxygen.

"Now what?" Minty asked.

"We wait," Twyla said.

"For what?"

Twyla gestured at a display in the middle console, equidistant to them. "For the *Price* to get into position."

"That doesn't mean a damn thing to me."

"See that blue line?" Twyla pointed to the display. "That's where *Price* is. The dotted line is where she's projected to be. When the ship gets to the green square, we launch, and meet up at the green circle. Got it?"

"Sure," Minty said. That didn't explain the half-dozen other lines and dots on the screen, or the numbers, but okay.

"Set your suit radio to 227," Twyla said. "It's our working channel."

Minty did so, noticing that the dot representing the *Price* was rapidly approaching the green square. It didn't look like a long wait.

As soon as it entered the square, and without saying a word, Twyla pressed a button causing the rocket to roar to life underneath them.

Minty quickly felt heavy, as if her limbs were made of lead, then even heavier, as if somebody was piling bags of lead on top of her.

"Heavy," Minty grunted, surprised at how much effort that took.

"Only three Gees," Twyla said.

Which is only nine fucking times more than I've ever pulled! Minty struggled for breath, and wondered for an instant if she was going to pass out. But apparently the laps she'd ran in PE paid off, because she was able to keep breathing and conscious.

As suddenly as the rocket had started it stopped, and Minty jerked against her straps. The crotch-strap proved especially sensitive, bringing a tear to her eyes.

"Welcome to orbit," Twyla said. "First time?"

"Yes," Minty said, swallowing hard. Her stomach felt like it was trying to climb out of her throat. "Does it show?"

Twyla chuckled. "If your eyes were any bigger they'd explode."

As she said that, they rolled onto the day side of the planet, and Mars, her home, sprawled before her, orange and welcoming.

"My God," Minty said.

"Seeing a planet from orbit for the first time is impressive," Twyla allowed.

You've seen at least two, Minty thought. "What's Earth like?"

"Blue. White clouds, shitloads of them. But mostly blue."

We've got white clouds too, Minty thought, noticing a few wisps off to her right.

"Jupiter, now that's impressive," Twyla said. "Red, yellow, white. Giant bands the size of planets. On the night side, lightening like you'd never believe."

Earthlings always talk about lightening, Minty thought, like it was something special. From what she'd seen on videos, it was overrated.

"There's our ship," Twyla said.

"Where?"

Twyla pointed at what looked like a star, rising on the edge of Mars. "You sure?"

"Yes, I'm sure."

"If you say so."

"Heh, kid," Twyla said. "If anybody talks about an 'initiation' for first-timers, call bullshit on it."

"Why?"

"Well, 'cause the 'initiation' is to get you to believe that there is an initiation. There isn't."

"Thanks." *I wonder why she's telling me this.* Minty swallowed hard, trying to keep her stomach down.

"Shake your head, like you got water in your ears."

Minty did as advised, and her stomach suddenly felt better. "Wow."

"Your inner ear's all fucked up," Twyla said. "You do remember how to clear a puked helmet?"

"Yes," Minty said. Not that she wanted to. She'd done it for practice on a school outing and been hoarse for a week.

"Good."

Minty noticed that the ship was now apparently bigger than a grain of rice, and growing larger by the minute.

"Go on suit pressure," Twyla said.

"Why?" Minty asked, even as she closed her helmet.

"You see a docking collar on this thing?"

Well, no, Minty thought, not that I'd know what a docking collar was if you hit me with it.

The *Price* was growing by the instant, and now was clearly a spaceship, dominated by rows of multi-colored cargo containers. It looked like something that a toddler would put together with Legos. Minty thought about asking how big the *Price* was, but decided that Twyla was too busy for small talk.

She was glad she hadn't asked. The *Price* was huge—at least two hundred meters long, maybe more. They were—at least in Minty's conception—underneath the *Price* (they were between Mars and the ship)—and about ten meters away. Twyla opened the hatch / roof, and Minty found herself sitting in full vacuum for the first time ever.

An airlock 'above' them opened, and a pair of spacesuited figures were inside. One of them tossed a white nylon rope at them, and Minty grabbed it. She handed the rope to Twyla, who secured it to a metal ring in the console between their seats.

"Okay," Twyla said. "You go up the rope, hand over hand. Don't get in a hurry, and don't let go of the rope. Got it?"

"Yes," Minty said, wondering why her mouth was so dry. She unbuckled her straps, and carefully pulled herself along the rope. When she got to the other end, the inside of the *Price's* airlock, one of the suited figures helped her secure her feet in a pair of straps and connected her to a safety line.

"I'm going down," one of the suited figures, a male voice, said over the radio. Whoever was speaking pulled himself down, trailing a second rope.

No fair, Minty thought. He gets a safety line and I didn't!

The figure disconnected the safety line and handed it to Twyla, then he connected another line to Twyla's rocket. Twyla took the line she'd been handed, and connected it to one of the cargo nets. The other suited figure in the airlock pulled the cargo in, then pushed it at Minty.

"Secure this stuff to that hook," the voice said, gesturing vaguely.

"Copy," Minty said, recognizing the speaker as Russ Nelson, who was in charge of the topside crew. She awkwardly maneuvered the bundle over to one side, discovering as she did the difference between weight and inertia. By the time she'd gotten that bundle moved, Russ had pulled in and secured a second bundle, and a third was on the way.

Working in this fashion, all six bundles, including Minty's luggage, were hauled aboard. After the last bundle was in, the main line to Twyla's rocket was disconnected and Russ pulled it in.

"Closing lock," he said, and the outer doors silently slid shut. A rotating yellow light went on, and when Minty could hear the audible alarm, she depressurized her suit.

"Where do you want this stuff?" Minty asked.

"I'll handle it. Which bundle has your stuff?"

"The pink rifle," Minty said, gesturing.

"You take that to the *Cranston*," Russ said. "You might as well bunk there."

"Okay," Minty said. She looked around for a second at the cylindrical hallway on the other side of the inner airlock door. "How do I get there?"

"*Cranston's* dorsal to us," Russ said. "Starboard airlock."

Minty looked around for another instant. "Sorry, sir, that's not helpful."

Russ shook his head. "Can they find me somebody any greener?" He took her hand. "See those red hash marks on the wall?"

"Yes."

"The hash marks point to port, and 'cause they're red we know we're port of centerline. Green would be for starboard of centerline. Hashes are on the forward bulkheads, dots on the aft bulkhead. See the blue stripe?"

"Yes."

"That's dorsal."

Minty thought 'port' was what space-geeks called 'left,' and she made a mental note to figure out what the hell 'dorsal' was later.

"Got it?"

"I think so," Minty said. She grabbed her stuff and started to pull herself along the hallway, trying not to bang too many times into the wall.

The transition into the *Cranston* had proved to be a tube about a meter wide. Ian, a kid just a Mear ahead of her in school, had met her at the airlock.

If he's old enough to be up here, so am I!

Getting down into *Cranston's* crew area proved interesting, as it involved stepping from a stationary to a rotating segment of the ship. Once you were on the rotating platform, gravity, small but noticeable, took hold.

"It feels funny down here," she said, stepping onto what had to be the lowest level of the *Cranston's* centrifuge.

"One sixth-gee," Ian said. "Like Titan or Luna."

"Oh," Minty said. "Where am I bunking?"

"Doesn't matter," Ian replied, starting to climb back up the ladder. "We're all over on the *Price*."

"Food is over there too?"

"Yeah. It's help yourself. I gotta run—I'm on watch."

"Okay," Minty said to his back. She looked around, noticing that only every third light was on. She wondered why, then wondered how to turn them on, as there was no obvious light switch.

I may be in a little over my head.

"If I were a cabin, where would I be?" *Or a bathroom.* From her point of view, either way was 'uphill' from where she was standing.

Be careful what you wish for, Minty thought, because you just might get it.

Chapter 14

Monday, 34 Virgo Year 52 18:00 local (March 5, 2074, 20:00 GMT)
Port Lowell, Mars

"SPACE RESCUE ISN'T A MILITARY ORGANIZATION," Jack said, looking at the concerned faces of his parents on the videophone. "We're just civilians trying to help people."

"Then why are they out fighting pirates?" his mom asked.

"We're not," Jack said. "We got jumped." *Something that probably wasn't a problem for ground-side accountants.*

"I want you out of Space Rescue, Jackson Robert Williams, and back home where you belong."

His mom was bobbing her head with emphasis. Her hands were twitching, and Jack was glad that she couldn't reach through the videophone to grab his ears.

"Mom, I'll be OK." Jack's mind flashed back to his meeting with Yeargan and McNally. *Although I could be an insurance guy.*

"Son," Jack's dad, Robert Williams, interjected, sitting on the couch next to his mom, "you said that before. Right before the *Wan Hai* fire."

"But that was different," Jack said. *I don't need this shit after Captain Chen's funeral.*

"How?" his dad asked. "And before that, it was the *Action Alpha* collision."

"Nobody got hurt on *Action Alpha*," Jack reminded him. Although the bow of the *Alpha* looked like an accordion and the ship she'd T-boned, the *Leda Maersk*, was a total loss. Both ships had been maneuvering around Phobos port and had collided with only a couple of meters per second relative velocity.

"The point, son," his dad said, using the controlled tone of voice that suggested trouble lay ahead, "is that when everybody else is getting the hell out of the way you're running *into* the problem."

"That's what Space Rescue does, dad," Jack said, feeling his face heat up. "You knew that going in."

"We assumed you'd get out by now, son," his dad said. "Or take a desk job. Use your accounting degree."

"We don't need accountants," Jack said. How many people does it take to count to zero, he added mentally. Although Newindink's office must have cost a pretty penny. Shipping wood to Mars wasn't cheap.

"Son," his dad said, "I do not want to have to come to your funeral."

"I don't want to go to mine either," Jack said, trying to force a smile. A vision of Chen's younger daughter clutching her doll as the flag-draped coffin of her father passed down the church flooded his mind. "But I have a job to do here."

His mom opened her mouth to say something but a touch from dad stopped her. "When are you coming to St. Mary's for a visit?"

"I don't know," Jack said. "My schedule's a bit up in the air at the moment."

"When you figure it out," his dad said, "give us a call. We miss you."

"I will," Jack said.

Everybody said their goodbyes and hung up. Jack glanced at the phone. *Maybe I should get out. I left two men behind.* He took a deep breath. That call had been only the second-hardest call he'd made today. Just before going to Chen's funeral, he'd gotten a video-mail from Peter Grant's parents.

How do you tell a man that you abandoned his son? The time delay makes it even harder. You send a message, spent twenty minutes thinking about how you could have said it better, then get a reply.

Jack got up and walked barefoot to the bathroom. He had just unzipped his fly when the phone rang.

"That's why God invented voicemail," Jack said to the print of a fish his mother had hung over the toilet on her last visit.

After finishing his business, Jack padded into the bedroom of his tiny apartment, taking off his dress uniform tie as he walked. The call proved to be from his old college buddy Ted. In typical fashion, Ted took a minute to leave a message completely devoid of all information except "call me."

"Call Ted," Jack said to the phone as he unbuttoned his shirt, "privacy mode."

The call went through and Ted's pasty face with its receding hairline popped on the screen just as Jack pulled his sweaty T-shirt over his face. The church had been warm, and the place they held the funeral luncheon at was overflowing. Jack had made the mistake of going back to headquarters. The ship maintained a groundside office there, and he'd spent the rest of the afternoon talking about Chen and re-watching the video the pirates had sent of Grant and Nomura.

"Got a hot chick there or what?" Ted asked, his face bobbing on the screen like he was trying to look around the privacy image.

"Or what," Jack said. "Just got back from a funeral."

"Who died?"

"Captain Tony Chen. I take it you didn't watch the news?"

"I'd heard y'all had a rough time," Ted said. "Didn't realize anybody'd bought the farm."

That would be Ted, Jack thought. If it didn't involve sports or sex Ted didn't give it much mind. "So what's up?"

"Having a little party at my place and wondered if you wanted to come."

Jack flopped on the edge of his bed and started to untie his shoes. "Last thing I'm in the mood for is a party."

"Beer's cold."

"Not really in the mood."

"Suit yourself, but Lois is bringing grilled tilapia."

On the other hand, I do have to eat. "Not interested. I'd be lousy company."

"Dohmeny's going to be there too."

Dohmeny was the HR rep for the accounting firm where Ted worked. Ted was perpetually trying to get him to apply.

"I don't want to get dressed up."

"It's beer at my place, dude. Dress code is 'no nudity.' Unless you're a hot chick of course."

"Thanks, Ted, but I'll take a raincheck."

"Suit yourself," Ted said before breaking the connection.

Jack tossed his T-shirt in the general direction of the hamper. It missed, and landed on the floor. "Can't even hit the fucking hamper," Jack said, walking over to retrieve the shirt, the floor cold on his stocking feet.

Maybe Dad's right. Get out before somebody has to leave me behind. I can at least take a look, see what's out there. And I'll keep contact with McNally. Just in case Mom's right.

"Phone," Jack said. "Call Ted—privacy mode."

The next morning Jack overslept, and scrambled into work late. The duty astronaut greeted him as he arrived.

"Good morning, sir."

"Good morning, Petty Officer," Jack said, walking into *Volodka's* groundside office. "The trolley broke down," Jack said, lying to cover his lateness. "Any word on Lieutenant Ortega?"

"They moved her groundside last night," the petty officer replied. "She called and asked for you to stop by. Also a Mr. McNally called."

"Thanks." Jack walked into the office and sat down in his cramped cubicle. He checked his email, then called McNally. The man's face quickly popped up on Jack's phone screen.

"McNally."

"You were looking for me?"

"Yeah. I got the personnel files for the *Price* crew members. Want to drop by?"

"You still think there was an inside guy on this hijacking?"

McNally shrugged his shoulders. "I've got nothing else to do until Earth gets back to me."

Jack looked at his inbox. Most of it would have to wait for somebody more senior anyway. "Sure. Put a fresh pot of coffee on."

McNally grimaced. "Fresh will cost you."

Jack sat his cup of coffee down on a round dinette table that McNally was using as a conference table. "Not bad."

"You are the pickiest person I know," McNally said.

"My dad grows coffee."

"I thought you said he lives on Mars?" Sean Yeargan said.

"He does. If you grow it here, you don't have to ship it in from Earth."

Yeargan nodded. "Good point. But getting it to grow on Mars must be a bitch."

"Just a matter of tweaking settings in your greenhouse," Jack said. "For example..."

"I'm sure it's fascinating," McNally interjected, "but how about let's talk crew profiles."

"Let's," Jack said. *I do tend to lecture when it comes to coffee.*

McNally started handing out hardcopies. "*Price* was operated by Gropo Espacial General de Mexico, which added a translation delay."

Jack picked up the first sheet, the personnel record for the ship's captain. "Twenty years experience."

"Which is probably why he's dead," Yeargan said.

"Shit," Jack replied. *I'd been so busy worrying about Grant and Nomura I forgot about the other ship.* "How much are they asking?"

"Nothing so far. This was just the 'get to know you' discussion."

"You know Space Rescue's not going to pay," Jack said.

"I didn't expect them to," Yeargan said. "Besides, they have no money."

"So what are we going to do about Grant and Nomura?"

"If I have my druthers," Yeargan replied, "we're not paying nobody nothing."

"How are you going to pull that off?" Jack asked.

"He hasn't gotten that far, kid," McNally replied. "Primarily because we have no idea where these people are."

"If you knew?" Jack asked.

"Then it's a different story," Yeargan said.

Then maybe we should figure out where these SOBs are.

"So, why are we looking at the *Price* crew's employment records?" Jack said.

"Easiest way to 'jack a ship is if you've got somebody on the inside," Yeargan said.

"Not that an inside person is always needed," McNally added.

"Got any other leads?"

"No," McNally said.

"Then we look here."

This is kind of like a drunk looking for his car keys under a streetlight instead of by where his car is because the light's better. But since we don't even know if the keys are missing...

McNally grabbed a stack of printouts. "Well, if this was an inside job, it has to be one of the watchstanding officers."

"Second or third mates," Yeargan said. "And we can't exclude a double-cross, so the Captain and Engineer are in."

Jack looked at one of the printouts. There was a picture included. "Are we sure this is right?" he said, pointing at the printout.

"I assume so," McNally said. "Why?"

"According to this, this woman was born on Earth and never went to Mars."

"Yes?"

"I could have sworn I met her here, on Mars."

"What's her name?" Yeargan asked, rummaging through his handouts.

"On this handout, she's listed as Lisa Maddow," Jack said. "But the woman I knew was called Bam Bam."

"Oh?" Yeargan asked. "What kind of name is 'Bam Bam'?"

Jack smiled and made a cupping gesture with his hands in front of his chest. "Bam Bam," he said, moving first one hand then the other.

Both men smiled at that remark.

"Maybe she's got a cousin back on Earth?" McNally said.

"Maybe," Jack said.

"The report said the mayday call was from a female voice," Yeargan said. "Did you listen to the recording?"

"I did," Jack said. "Didn't sound familiar."

"Audio quality on the recording was shit," McNally added.

"Where'd you meet her?" Yeargan asked.

"Well, that's it," Jack said. "Not sure I met her so much as saw her passing in the hallways. At intermediate flight, I think."

"So you probably wouldn't recognize the voice," Yeargan said.

"Not that it would make a difference," McNally said. He looked at Jack. "Can you check on her?"

"I'll make some calls."

Chapter 15

Tuesday 35 Virgo Year 52 13:15 local (March 6, 2074, 15:56 GMT)
Port Lowell, Mars

JACK SETTLED INTO HIS CHAIR at the *Volodka's* groundside office. The visit with Lieutenant Ortega had taken a while, and then he'd had other ship's work to attend to.

Should I really be helping Yeargan and McNally? He thought. It wasn't like he had any official authorization to even be talking to them, much less snooping around Mars checking up on their crewmembers.

He glanced up, and saw a picture on his desk. It was Peter Grant, Janet and him, taken at a local restaurant. Jack had just passed his Lieutenant's certification board, and they were helping him celebrate his impending promotion. A promotion that was supposed to come through later this month.

If I don't get fired screwing around with these weenies. He looked at the picture again. *Then don't get caught.*

"Where have I seen you?" Jack asked, looking at the hardcopy service record. He thought about what he was doing when he heard the name 'Bam Bam.'

Intermediate flight.

Jack had moved to Mars as a small child, leaving Earth halfway through kindergarten. Like most Martians, just living on Mars had taught him a lot about living in space, but some skills, such as flying a rocket, required more formal training.

He'd been taught how to fly a ground-to-orbit rocket and make a rendezvous at McBride Flight Training. *Me and about half of all rocket jockeys on Mars.*

McBride had all kinds of certification programs, and Jack was sure that Bam Bam wasn't in his program. She wasn't in any of his classes—he'd only actually seen her twice, both times in public areas.

"She's got great *assets*," Quinn had told him. *Alan Quinn—he of the perpetual hard-on.* Jack smiled at the memory. *Quinn would at least be able to tell me what program she was in. Without that I'm trying to find a needle in a haystack.*

The last time Jack had spoken to Quinn, which had been months ago, Jack realized with embarrassment, Quinn had been flying cargo lifts out of Port Lowell north. Most of those were flown during the local night—passengers wanted to fly during daylight. Jack dialed Quinn's home number.

Quinn's greeting screen, a cheesecake shot of some bikini model with Quinn's name on the side, popped up on Jack's videophone. The call was just starting to roll into voicemail when Quinn's face popped up.

"Yeah?" Quinn said. The man's hair was matted and his face sleepy.

"Sorry, I was just going to leave a voicemail," Jack lied.

"Jackson Robert," Quinn said, recognition dawning, "to what do I owe this call?"

"Well, I was just thinking we should keep in touch, you know," Jack said.

"We should," Quinn replied. "Of course, with me working third, it's tough." Quinn's eyes focused. "You're with Space Rescue now?"

"Yeah," Jack said. *That had always been my plan, like I told you.* Might as well cut the small talk. "Look, Alan,"

"Andy," Quinn corrected.

"I said that,"

"No, you said Alan."

"Oh, sorry." Crap. Jack had even filed Quinn in his contacts as 'Alan.' "Look, you remember a chick while we were going through training?"

"I remember a lot of chicks during training. Why?"

"I'm trying to find one of them. Girl they called Bam Bam."

Quinn smiled. "She's way out of my league, sport, let alone yours." Quinn's smile faded. "And I seem to remember she had real old-fashioned ideas about things."

"Such as?"

"She kept talking about 'Negros' and 'Orientals.' Weird."

That *was* weird. Jack hadn't heard the word 'negro' until high school biology. "You remember what program she was in?"

"Dude, what program she was in wasn't high on the list of priorities, if you know what I mean."

Yeah, I do. "Well, did you have any classes with her?"

Quinn scratched his head. "No, but she was in Advanced Celestial Navigation. They met just before my Flight Safety class in the same room."

"Great, Andy, thanks. We should get together for a beer sometime."

"Yeah, call me." Quinn broke the connection.

Jack pulled up the website for McBride Flight Training. He recalled that not many people took Advanced Celestial Navigation. A few minutes dinking around told him why—it was only required for one certification—Third Mate, Interplanetary.

Thirty minutes later, Jack realized that he'd exhausted the information available on the public web site. There was no directory of graduates or other online information about students. There was, however, a placement office phone number. Jack called it.

"McBride Flight, Placements," said a gray haired woman, who looked like somebody's Chinese grandmother.

"Midshipman Williams, Space Rescue," Jack said. "I'm trying to verify a reference and career history for a Ms. Brenda Lords. Can you help me?"

"If she's a graduate of McBride, of course."

Jack arrived at McNally's office on Schiaparelli Street just as the later man was changing the sign on his door to closed.

"Going home?" Jack asked as he opened the door.

"I wish," McNally replied. "Just trying to prevent people from walking in to sell me stuff."

"I got some information for you. Where's Yeargan?"

"Off signing a lease on an apartment. Come on in."

Jack went in ahead of McNally, who lingered behind to lock up. Jack took a seat in the guest chair in front of McNally's desk, noting as he did that Yeargan's desk was growing a pile of paperwork.

"Drink?" McNally asked, returning to the office area from the front door.

"Whatever you're having."

McNally grunted, and produced a bottle of whiskey and a pair of juice glasses. He poured a liberal amount into the glasses and handed one to Jack. The two of them settled into seats around his rickety conference table.

"Got the information back on 'Lisa Maddow,'" McNally said. "She's a Franklin job."

"Pardon?" Jack asked, struggling not to choke on the burning whiskey.

"Fake ID," McNally said. He took a gulp of his drink. "Guy back on Earth, some local bureaucrat, used to sell fake IDs. If you were in the know, you'd show up and ask to see 'Mister Franklin.'"

"So the guy's name was Franklin?"

"No, Ben Franklin's the picture on the US one hundred dollar bill." McNally leaned back in his chair. "The beauty of the scheme was that the IDs weren't actually fake. They were genuine Government paper."

"So how do you tell?"

"Lisa's got no history," McNally said. "A birth certificate, a passport, and a Third Mate's license, which she got by passing a test in Monterrey, Mexico."

"Makes sense." Jack looked at his barely sipped whiskey. He was much more of a beer drinker. Jack sat his drink down and opened up his briefcase. "Here's what I got."

Just then, somebody knocked at the door. "That's probably Sean," McNally said, standing up. "I'll be back."

McNally returned a moment later followed by Sean Yeargan. The Earthman sat down in the guest chair next to Jack while McNally poured another drink. Jack brought Yeargan up to speed on 'Lisa Maddow.'

"She's looking good for an inside person," Yeargan said. He sat down at the conference table. "Ya know, something about her 'proof of life' speech didn't seem right."

"Oh?" Jack asked.

"Play it for him," Yeargan said.

McNally shot Yeargan a look as if to ask if he was Yeargan's secretary, but the man got up and handed Jack a tablet PC with the video queued up. Jack watched it without comment.

"I don't see anything," McNally said.

"I do," Jack replied. "She's not nervous. She's also a lot cleaner than the others. Like she was allowed to take a shower."

"Why would she be nervous, if she was in on it?" Yeargan said. "So the SOBs will try to sell this Laura person back to us, huh?"

"Lisa," Jack said, handing over a printout, "but I think her real name is Brenda Lords."

The printout had a picture taken from the McBride Flight graduate directory. It sure looked like 'Lisa.'

"Sure looks like her," McNally said.

"Same mass, height and age," Jack replied. "And she took the Third Mate's course at McBride."

"So we know she's Martian," Yeargan said. "Still, this is a big planet."

"She went to high school in Bradbury," Jack said. "If that helps?"

"Oh?" McNally said.

"It's amazing what people will tell you over the phone," Jack replied, feeling proud of his detective work. He explained about using a job offer as a pretext.

"Especially when they think they're doing somebody a favor," Yeargan replied when Jack finished.

"Bradbury's too big to be a pirate base," McNally said. "Second largest city on Mars, pretty tightly run Still, I suppose we could start looking there. What high school?"

"Christ the Crusader," Jack said.

"Don't need to look," Yeargan said. He pointed at McNally with his drink glass, alarmingly less full than a minute ago. "Spit that name into a google and see what you get."

McNally went to his computer and did so, and said, "It's a correspondence school."

"Catering to white supremacists," Yeargan replied. "We put out an alert to all insured parties to treat that on a resume as a security risk."

"You thinking she's Republic of the White Race?" McNally asked.

"They do control all of Olympus Mons," Yeargan said, "which is dead in the middle of our best guess for *Price's* orbit."

"My source tells me that she had 'funny' racial ideas," Jack said.

"The pieces are coming together," Yeargan said. He drained his glass and slammed it on the desk. "Hit me again."

"I wouldn't go partying just yet, Sean," McNally said, reaching for the bottle. "Olympus is as big as Spain, so we've got a ways to go before we can send in a team. Not that you have a team to send in."

"Details, details," Sean said, apparently only half-sarcastically. "We're better off than we were this morning, yes?"

"I suppose so," McNally replied, refilling Yeargan's glass.

"We'll get a team together," Yeargan said, looking at Jack.

"Who's this we? I said I'd help gather information, and that's it," Jack said.

"For now," Yeargan said.

"Speaking of pieces," Jack said, ignoring the suggestion, "one piece we're missing is how the pirates got aboard."

"Shuttle," Yeargan said.

"Don't think so," Jack replied. "*Price* had been cold iron for at least six hours when we got there, and she was quite a ways out."

"What kind of ship would you need to make a rendezvous?" McNally asked.

"Either a high-performance orbital job or a deep-space capable boat."

"Not many of the former on Mars," McNally said, leaning back. "And we know who owns those." McNally looked at Jack. "What kind of deep-space ship?"

"Cheap," Yeargan replied.

"Stolen can be pretty cheap," McNally said.

"If you can steal a ship, why pirate another one?" Yeargan said. "Besides, everything we've got suggests this job was planned out at least a year ago, when Lisa—Barbie,"

"You mean Brenda," Jack said.

"What's-her-face went to Earth," Yeargan concluded. "No, the ship had to be in hand."

Something Jack had seen when he'd reviewed the data logs from the rescue clicked in his mind. "I think I got a lead on that," he said.

"Oh?" both men asked.

"Yeah—but I need to check it out at the office."

Yeargan looked at his watch. "I'm hungry, and still on the expense account."

"There's a very nice Italian place close by Space Rescue," McNally said. He looked at Jack. "You want to come?"

Vito's was good, Jack thought, if a bit overrated. But Vito's beat the leftover round steak in Jack's refrigerator. "If you don't mind a detour, Vito's it is."

Chapter 16

Thursday, 37 Virgo Year 52 13:45 local (March 8, 2074, 17:45 GMT)
West Gustav crater, Mars

ROGER MCNALLY STARED OUT THE WINDOW of the public rollalong at the rocky surface of Gustav Crater. The crater lip, starkly illuminated in the mid-day sun, was visible ahead, looming like a line of hills. He seriously hoped the man he was meeting had useful information about the pirate base ship. Especially since the man had asked for cash up front.

Next time, Roger, just write a memo. Or cut out the sauce.

It was the second whiskey that did it, Roger thought. They'd all had another snort at his office, then caught a streetcar to Space Rescue.

That was two days ago. The kid, Williams, thought he'd seen a contact on his scope just before they got jumped. When the three of them had reviewed the data logs, Williams was right.

"Has to be something small," Yeargan had said.

"But deep-space capable," Willams had said.

They'd discussed it more over dinner at Vito's. Roger made a face. Dinner at Vito's had involved at least two bottles of Chianti. At the end of it, they'd decided on a plan to figure out who owned the mystery contact. A plan which he was now implementing.

"West Gustav Station, end of the line," a conductor yelled, walking through the cab of the rollalong.

Roger started to toss his belongings into his briefcase, as did the handful of other passengers. The rollalong, a multi-wheeled bus-sized vehicle designed for roadless Mars, maneuvered to dock with an airlock on the West Gustav bus station. *At least I won't have to put on a space suit and look like the fuckin' whole-wheat Pillsbury Doughboy.*

There was a soft bump as the rollalong made contact with the dock, then a brief delay as they made a hard seal. When the forward cabin door opened, Roger got to his feet and made his way forward carrying his soft-sided briefcase.

Just inside the dimly-lit brick-walled terminal there was a half wall separating the main terminal from the disembarkation area. The only exit was via a counter, manned by two bored looking police officers. One line, marked "residents" by an overhead sign, was manned by a young cop, barely in his twenties, who apparently knew just about everybody by face and was waving people through. Roger got in the "non-resident" line, which was manned by an elderly woman with olive skin.

"Passport," the police woman sked speaking in a broad American accent.

He handed over his passport, which she ran under a scanner mounted on the counter. He put his hand on the fingerprint reader.

"Canadian, huh?" She said.

"Yes. Originally from Orillia, Ontario."

"Oh," the woman said. "What brings you to West Gustav?"

"Business."

The town was an old settlement, one of the first private ones on Mars. When he was a kid, the town's founding had been controversial. In part, the controversy had been expected—Gustav was the oldest private settlement on Mars. The other part of the controversy had been the fact that it was settled by Americans, mostly, but not governed by America.

"Welcome to the Vietnamese People's Deep Space Dependency of West Gustav," she said. The fingerprint machine beeped and flashed a green light, so the woman handed him back his passport. "Enjoy your stay."

Roger walked away, thankful she hadn't asked if he was carrying a gun. Sean Yeargan had given it to him, just before Roger left. The gun was sitting in a small pocket on the top of his briefcase. "You probably won't need it," he had said. "But just in case."

Not that carrying a gun was unusual on Mars, he thought, walking through the tiny and dingy terminal. Everybody packed, or so it seemed.

He stepped out of the terminal onto Main Street. A sign, so new he could almost smell the paint, proclaimed it the "oldest commercial district on Mars."

It wasn't very impressive. The street was barely four meters wide. The buildings that lined the street had started life as metal shipping containers. The containers had been dropped on the undulating surface and pushed into two more-or-less straight lines. Holes had been cut to form doors and windows, and various pieces of scrap metal had been used to construct a roof covering the walkway, with the whole mess covered in dirt and rock. The dirt both kept radiation out and prevented the interior air pressure from blowing the roof off.

Lighting consisted of various exterior fixtures mounted to the sides of the containers, giving it a dim, late-evening vibe. The 'pavement' had come later, and judging from the various types and styles, each storefront had done it itself.

He walked down the covered street, populated by a mix of stragglers from the lunch hour and his fellow passengers. Main Street quickly emptied out into the equally unimaginatively-named First Dome. He'd been a kid when Gustav West, back then just "Gustav City" had been founded, and had been fascinated by the whole thing.

In reality, First Dome wasn't that impressive, Roger thought, pausing at the gravel pathway / road leading to his meeting place.

Unless you were planning a mugging, he added, patting the wad of money nervously. The only people in sight were behind him, walking into a hotel. People had been killed in nicer places for less. Roger resumed walking.

Covering just over three hectares or seven acres, the steel-and-glass dome, which had been briefly the biggest structure on Mars, looked small. Roger continued straight, now on a gravel road that was flanked by small fields of tomatoes. The dome seemed empty, in part because the buildings in it were all underground.

Skywalker ranches. They were called skywalker ranches.

Roger vaguely remembered that whoever had come up with the concept had tried to call them something else, but the skywalker name stuck. The buildings were buried under a couple of meters of dirt, allowing the surface above to be used for agriculture, while providing radiation protection in the event of solar flares. Each building had a square or rectangular interior courtyard, opened to the sky above, and a small top-house on ground level, just big enough to provide access below.

The gravel road came to a T, passing around a small wooded area in the center of the dome. A sign indentified it as "First Tree Park." As the name suggested, these were the first trees planted on Mars, apple and cherry, and were now starting to touch the top of the low-ish dome. Roger crossed the nearly deserted street, and followed a narrow stone path into the woods. He was meeting his contact at the Crash Victims' Memorial in the center of the park.

The Memorial proved to be a circular area, sunk maybe half a meter deep, with a gravel surface and lined with pink stones forming a low wall and seating area. A large metal statue sat on a pedestal in the center of the circle, commemorating settlers who had died in a crash on arrival.

Roger felt a shiver run down his spine. *Well, technically it is public.* He'd wanted a public meeting place for his own safety. But between the deserted park, the trees, the lack of traffic and the buried architecture, he was completely out of human sight. He unzipped the pouch on his computer bag and retrieved the small automatic, which he slipped into the pocket of his sports coat. *One in the tube, six in the clip. If I need more then that I'm really screwed.* He thumbed the gun in his pocket, trying to remember how the safety worked.

He stepped down into the memorial and made a quick circuit, trying to find a good spot to wait. The best visibility was at the opposite end of the memorial from where he came in. It put his back to a small open field, and allowed him to observe the other entrances, except one. He settled in for a wait.

During the dinner at Vito's, Roger had agreed to call various ship brokers. Several of these brokers, like the man Roger was to meet, ran to the shady side.

Actually, Roger thought with a shiver, Yeltsin was more than just shady. Of course, he was the one who wanted to meet in person.

A couple of minutes later he heard the crunch of gravel underfoot. Roger stood and walked around the memorial to his right, where he came up to a man walking into the memorial.

"Boris Yeltsin, I presume," Roger said, struggling to prevent his voice from cracking. The man's blonde, short-cropped hair and broken nose screamed "Russian mob." Since he *was* Russian mob, that fit.

"Yes," the man replied. "Roger McNally?"

"I am." Boris held out his hand, and the two exchanged a limp handshake. Boris sat down on the statue pedestal, while Roger sat across from him on the stone bench. Boris was wearing a light windbreaker, zipped up. It wouldn't have been out of place in the chilly old town, but it was a bit warm in the dome for a jacket. Roger slid his hand to his sport coat pocket.

"What can I do for you?" Boris asked, looking over Roger's shoulder.

Roger took a brief glance back before answering. "We're looking for the purchaser of a ship."

"So you said over the phone."

Roger wetted his lips. "I believe I did. Do you have the information?"

"I might. At a cost."

"Of course."

Boris leaned back against the stone wall of the memorial. "It seems you know much already."

"We know that a ship, a Mosquito, left Phobos Port," Roger said. Yeargan's contacts had found that out. "The closest track to the *Price* was small. Too small to be anything but a Mosquito. And the *Price* was boarded too far out into space for a shuttle to reach."

"So this, 'Mosquito,' was the pirate's mother ship?"

"We think so."

A Mosquito was a tiny ship, made by Bombardier, intended as a rich man's 'space yacht.' It had not proven popular. People rich enough to buy what they wanted bought bigger ships, and the merely wealthy bought a cargo ship and upgraded the crew space.

"Surely there are many such mosquitos in Mars space," Boris said, again looking over Roger's shoulder.

"Only three. Two of which are cluttering up Phobos docks."

"And you wish to know who owns the third?"

Roger grimaced. "Yes, like I said over the phone." For some reason Yeltsin wanted to do this face to face.

Boris unzipped his jacket a bit. "Look, I am a businessman. People come to see me when they want a certain, discretion, in their business dealings." Boris looked over Roger's shoulder again.

Roger resisted the urge to follow Boris' eyes and faked a smile. "Please. They come to you because you're cheap."

"That as well," Boris said. If he felt ashamed, Roger couldn't detect it. "Look, perhaps you should just go back to your paperwork."

I'd love to, Roger thought. "Or you could just answer a question."

Boris started to reach into his jacket, and Roger pulled the gun out of his pocket. Or tried to—it hung up, but Roger jerked harder, heard something rip, and got the gun out.

"Whoa! Whoa! Whoa!" Boris said, putting his free hand up as if to stop the bullet.

"Whatever you're reaching for, bring it out real slow," Roger said. "I may be a fat old man, but I'm not dying here today."

"Take it easy, man," Boris said. He slowly took his hand out, producing a pack of cigarettes. "Smoke?" he said, waving it carefully in Roger's direction.

"No," Roger said, realizing that he was pointing the gun at Boris with both hands. He relaxed and sat the gun on his lap. "Cigarettes are bad for you."

"Fatal, or so I hear," Boris said, a wry smile on his face. "But not usually so quickly."

"Sorry."

Boris lit his cigarette and took a big drag before answering, the words coming out in a cloud of smoke. "All is well. Besides, I think your gun is still on safety."

Roger looked down. *Son of a bitch, it is.* He left it that way.

"It will cost you," Boris said. "5,000 Euros cash."

"Should I bother haggling?"

"Is it your money?"

Actually, no. Roger reached into his sports coat pocket. "I think this is five grand," he said, handing over a wad.

Boris casually fanned it. "Close enough."

Roger realized that his face was covered in sweat, sweat that had nothing to do with heat.

"I'm waiting."

"You are not a patient man," Boris chided. "It's not good for the heart."

"I don't want to miss the return bus."

"Fair enough," Boris said with a shrug. He gestured at his jacket. "May I?"

"Of course," Roger said, putting his gun in his pocket.

Boris produced a folded piece of paper. "The woman said her name was 'Denise Richards.' I doubt that is true, but here is a picture."

Roger took the paper and unfolded it. A third of the page was taken up by a full face picture of a red-headed woman, clearly a screencap from a video. The rest of it was a photo-fax of her ID paperwork.

"You took a copy of her ID?" Roger asked.

"She offered it," Boris said with a shrug. "Besides, I needed something to fill out the flag registration. Bolivia, before you ask."

Registering space ships had become a source of revenue for landlocked countries like Bolivia, Roger thought with a flash.

"This is all you've got?" Roger asked. *Hell, I have to provide more paperwork to rent a car. But it was another piece of the puzzle.*

"When they took possession, the rocket flew up from Bensonville," Boris said.

"Bensonville? You're sure?"

Boris shrugged. "I didn't watch the launch. But they said 'Bensonville' and the launch window fit."

That was actually more useful then the piece-of-shit paper he gave me. "Thanks."

Boris put out the butt of his cigarette. "I should leave first," he said. "Wait five minutes. My sniper is easily excited."

Roger sat wordlessly as Boris departed, wondering just how close he'd come to being shot in the head by Boris' sniper.

Chapter 17

Thursday, 38 Virgo Year 52, 21:45 local (March 9, 2074, 09:25 GMT) Yacht Randall Cranston, near CCS Charles S. Price, Mars Orbit

RACHEL GLANCED AT THE RADAR SCOPE in the tiny bridge of the *Cranston.* They were finally going to get the damn 'special cargo' put where it belonged.

It had been easy to rent a cargo tug on Phobos, although Rachel had had to be the one to go down and collect it. It wouldn't do, after all, for the 'hostage' Bam Bam to be seen in public.

"Range one-zero-zero," Rachel said over the radio, talking to Bam Bam on the cargo tug.

"Copy," Bam Bam said, her voice tinny over the radio.

"Minty," Rachel said, keying her mike, "are we ready to receive?"

"I am, over," came back the reply. Rachel felt a flush of pride. Minty had been absorbing knowledge like a sponge. Pity she had to get that knowledge by being a crook. *At least I'm up here to keep an eye on her.*

Bam Bam's small cargo tug approached. The tug was a boxy collection of tanks, manipulator arms and rockets, with a spherical one-person crew compartment more or less visible in front. The whole thing was only about half as big as the twelve-meter-long cargo container it was moving.

As Rachel watched out the bridge windows, the tug and its cargo slid silently past the *Cranston's* slowly-spinning crew area.

"I'm heading to the aft lounge," Rachel said over the radio. From there she could visually supervise the actual mate-up of the cargo container.

Bam Bam and Minty both acknowledged as Rachel pushed herself out of the zero-gee space, holding a hand-held radio. She left the radar in the bridge, since she wouldn't be needing it.

Rachel quickly pulled herself down a series of tubular passageways. She passed through the central hub region, where the crew quarters were accessed, and into a small utility area aft of the saucer-shaped crew quarters. She arrived at her destination, the 'aft viewing lounge' a large zero-gee space with a window, just as Bam Bam called "clear," on the radio.

"Clear," Minty replied.

The *Cranston*, like all Mosquito-class ships, had a twenty-meter-long and three meter-wide stalk running from the crew area back to the tanks and reactor for the ship's ionic engines. Rachel looked out and verified that Minty was indeed clear, perched on a hold about three meters from where the stalk met the crew areas.

"Coming down," Bam Bam said over the radio.

"Copy," Minty said. "You're in line."

Bam Bam slowly guided the tug down, pushing the cargo container up against the flat hard-point on the *Cranston* that they'd secure it to.

"Five meters," Minty said. Rachel, as safety observer, could wave Bam Bam off if needed, but there was no need.

Minty kept calling off the distance until the container clicked into place, a click that Rachel felt through the ship.

"Down, check four," Bam Bam said.

"Checking," Minty replied. Minty used a small hand-held thruster to scoot out and visually check all that all four corner connections of the container had locked in place.

"One-three latch didn't engage," Minty said after a minute or two, referring to one of the locks. As it happened, that lock was the one farthest aft, and the last one she'd checked.

"Copy," Bam Bam said. "Rachel, do you want to try and re-dock?"

Actually, I'm kind of hungry, and Chuckles would probably like us to dock with *Price* sometime tonight.

"Girls," Minty said, "I think I can manually get this to lock."

"You sure?" Rachel said.

"No, I'm not sure, but I'd like to give it a try."

Considering that the *Cranston's* best acceleration was point zero three gee, three hold-downs was probably enough. "What's your air?" Rachel asked.

"Four point seven," Minty replied.

"Try until your air is at four-zero, then come on in," Rachel replied. "Bam Bam, you're clear to dock."

"Bam copies and I'm gone."

The tug disengaged from the container and silently headed around the stem of the *Cranston.* Rachel pushed out of the space and went to the airlock opposite of the observation lounge to watch Bam Bam dock.

Thursday, 38 Virgo Year 52, 13:45 local (March 8, 2074, 17:45 GMT)
Port Lowell, Mars

Sean let himself into Roger's office. Roger was out on West Gustav meeting with a contact of his. Sean had signed a lease on his own space, but the landlord hadn't finished painting it yet. He burped, deciding that he should skip the onions next time he ordered the brat special at lunch.

Sean signed back into his computer, and pulled up his email. There was a message marked urgent from a .mil domain, so he opened it.

From: Slevnik, Mike, COL USAF, OIC, Criminal Investigative Division
Sent: March 5, 2074, 21:30 CST
To: Yeargan, Sean
Subject: Container number 245113-1

Sir:

1. Regarding subject container, shipped by "Drake-Mann Shipping," I believe this container actually contains property stolen from the USAF.
2. "Drake-Mann Shipping" is alias for BGEN Lewis Mandrake, USAF (retired), former commander Project Rhode Island Red.
3. Property may be conventional (high-explosive) ordinance. Request you handle accordingly.
4. Reward of $5 million USD for return of material

5. Discretion is important—DO NOT contact news media.

Mike
COL Michael C. Slevnik
CID Group West
Call: 01-445/245-5591

"Fucking wonderful," Sean said. "The Zoomies can't keep track of their bombs."

It would explain why whoever was receiving the container would be not happy to see it go through customs.

Thursday, 38 Virgo Year 52, 22:00 local (March 9, 2074, 09:40 GMT)
Yacht *Randall Cranston*, Mars Orbit

Minty hooked a suit tether into a hold-fast on the *Cranston* and glanced around for a second. Mars was off her left shoulder, half-lit, and Rachel's voice was in her ear as Bam Bam docked the tug.

Three days ago, if you'd asked me if I wanted to go on a space walk, I've have told you it was the coolest thing ever. She stretched, trying to use the suit to scratch part of her back. *Now I just want to take a shower.*

She unhooked and turned on her suit light, so she could see the one-three latch, which was mostly in the shadow of the ship. She pulled her face close, hovering a few centimeters from the latch.

Damn thing was busted, she thought. The metal do-hickey that actually latched in was busted off. Probably never latched, even at Earth. She backed off, using a short burst of her handheld thruster. *This is a funny container.*

To get to this container they'd had to shift several others, and it wasn't like she'd never seen a shipping container before. Most containers were painted a color, and had some company's logo on it. Some of them even had advertising. This one was flat gray, and other then a container number, painted in black, it was featureless.

It also wasn't sealed. She looked at her timer. Thirty minutes left. *What the hell?* Minty wasn't an expert on cargo containers, but she'd been told that they were sealed 'after inspection.' An unsealed container must not have been inspected.

Maybe that's why whoever's paying the bills wants this box. I mean, if they just wanted it to get here, why 'jack the ship?

The question now was what to do. She looked at her air. *Plenty left. They say knowledge is power.*

Opening the latch to the door was a little more difficult than she'd thought it would be, but after a few days in zero gee she was getting the hang of things. She swung the right-hand-door open.

Boxes. The container was loaded with grey plastic boxes. Although...

"Whoa," she said, then checked to see if her suit radio was on voice-activated. It wasn't.

Good, because all the boxes said "HIGH EXPLOSIVES" and "ORDINANCE" on them in big stenciled letters. She noticed some smaller letters to the side on each box.

Maybe that's a model number. She used her suit camera, for the first time ever, to take a few pictures.

Thursday, 38 Virgo Year 52, 23:01 local (March 9, 2074, 10:41 GMT)
Yacht *Randall Cranston* Mars Orbit

Bam Bam hadn't freaked at all when Rachel put a move on her.

They were docked with the *Price*, where the orbital watch was being kept, after having finished with all the cargo work. Minty was off taking a shower or whatever. The time was right, in other words.

"I was wondering when you were going to hit on me," Bam Bam had said.

"What makes you think I'm hitting on you?"

"Your hand on my ass, for one thing." Bam Bam put her hand on top of Rachel's, preventing her from removing it. "But I would like to keep this a little bit more on the down-low than you and Locklin."

"Did you have to bring his name up?"

"I could have mentioned Sara French, but that would be going back a bit."

"Damn, building up a file on me?"

"No, but you're about as subtle as a bull in heat, and as oblivious as well."

Rachel felt her ardor cooling. "You're not exactly putting out the warm vibes, Miss."

"Look, Red, let's not get all girly-girly about relationships and shit, okay? I've just spent three months in a tin can with a bunch of assholes and a busted vibrator. You wanna hit on this or not?"

"Well, if you put it that way."

Rachel was using the 'ship's master' stateroom, a narrow space, which was more like a hallway with delusions of grandeur than a room. It was in the crew cylinder, which was spun to produce gravity, in this case a comfortable 1/6 Gee.

The gravity was about all the cabin had going for it. Furnishings consisted of a long built-in couch which converted to a bed on the wall opposite to the desk. The couch made a handy if narrow landing strip. But unlike the owners stateroom, there was a built-in workstation, allowing Rachel to monitor the ship.

Bam Bam had been a little grabby, ripping Rachel's shirt in the process, so Rachel had fixed that problem with some rope formerly used to secure her luggage. Bam Bam's hands were secured to an armrest, safely out of the way, and her naked body was sprawled along the couch.

"Got a minute, sis?" Minty asked.

Rachel looked over her shoulder to find Minty standing at the door to the stateroom, a piece of paper in her hand, obviously trying to keep from giggling.

"Does it look like it?" Rachel said.

Minty made a show of trying to look around Rachel. "Look's like she's not going anywhere."

"I don't suppose we could cut to the chase," Bam Bam said.

Rachel, naked except for her panties, rolled off of Bam Bam and pulled over her desk chair, which she sat down in.

"You have my full attention," Rachel said.

"Hi, Bam Bam," Minty said, smirking. "I thought you were bunking over on the *Price*."

"I was, Arminta, but I changed my mind," Bam Bam said. "Forgive me for not getting up."

"Now that we've got the social graces covered," Rachel said, struggling to keep her voice down, "could you please tell me what the fuck is so important?"

"Do you know what's in our container?"

"Which container?" Rachel asked.

"The one we just fucking moved over here," Minty said.

"No, I don't, nor do I care."

"You should."

"Why?"

"It might fucking explode," Minty said. "We're carrying missiles."

"Huh?"

"Missiles," Minty said, a look of triumph on her face. "Here." She handed Rachel a print-out, which Bam Bam tried to look at from the couch.

"Son of a bitch," Rachel said.

"Somebody want to clue me in?" Bam Bam said.

"Air to air missiles, from the US Air Force," Rachel said.

"Cool," Bam Bam replied.

"Not just any missiles," Minty said.

"Look, dear, I'm sure you think this is important," Rachel said.

"Missiles modified to work as ship-to-ship missiles in space," Minty said. "I did some research."

"That is important," Rachel said.

"Which would explain why our paymasters want us to cut these out special," Bam Bam said.

Rachel felt a chill, which was not caused by her lack of clothing. "We need to tell Chuckles."

"Why?" Minty said.

"Because whoever's paying us might not want to keep us around," Bam Bam said. "Dead men tell no tales and all that shit."

Rachel looked at Bam Bam. *I've seriously underestimated you.* "Exactly."

"I'll get on the radio," Minty said.

"You'll do no such thing," Rachel said. "We'll tell him in person, tomorrow. No need to broadcast this shit to the world." Rachel waved a finger at Minty. "And that means you aren't going to tell anybody up here either."

"But..."

"But nothing," Rachel said. "This is need-to-know, and the three of us are the only ones who need to know. Got it?"

"Yes, Dread Pirate Rachel," Minty said.

"Good. Now get some sleep."

"I'll try," Minty said, looking at Bam Bam. "As long as you two don't keep me up."

"We won't," Rachel said as Minty backed out.

Rachel grabbed a sock from the floor, hers or Bam Bam's, she didn't know or care. "You'll keep it down, right?"

"Seems like I got the short end of this relationship," Bam Bam said.

"Somebody had to."

"Bitch," Bam Bam replied, sticking out her tongue.

Chapter 18

Thursday, 37 Virgo Year 52 19:45 local (March 8, 2074 23:45 GMT)
Port Lowell, Mars

JANET PUSHED HER PLATE OF HALF-EATEN LASAGNA aside. She glanced at Mikey, sitting in a booster chair at Penny's table. He had gotten almost as much lasagna on him as in him.

"How's work?" Penny asked, topping off Janet's glass of iced tea.

"Okay, I guess," Janet said, wishing that Penny had offered her something stronger to drink.

"Any news about Peter?"

Janet shrugged. "No. Why would I care?"

"I thought you two..."

"He was a good fuck," Janet lied. "That's all."

"Little pitchers."

"Nothing he hasn't heard before," Janet said. She looked at Mikey. *Kid needs a father. Grant might have been it. If he wasn't off trying to save the fucking universe.* Janet smiled wryly. *I'd been like that, once. Then reality hit.*

"I'm sure they'll get him back," Penny said. "I mean, we know he's alive."

"Like I said, who cares?"

Penny glared at her, clearly wanting to say something. Whatever it was, she thought better of it. "What about Hap?"

"Hap?"

"That guy—you had him over last month."

Janet was puzzled for a second, then she remembered. "He's harmless."

"Maybe harmless is good," Penny said.

"What's that supposed to mean?"

"Just that somebody with a nice safe job can be, a point of stability."

Janet smirked. "What is this, the twentieth century? 'You should find a good man and settle down, dear.'" The last part of her sentence was said in a fake-girly tone of voice. *Although, Penny did have a point.*

"Well, you do have a kid..."

Janet held up her hand. "Okay, got it, you're right. You're always right. But just where am I supposed to meet Mister Perfect?"

"Where'd you meet Hap?"

Janet laughed. "He was a set-up. Somebody's friend at work."

"You done?" Penny said, pointing at Janet's plate.

"Yep," Janet said, pushing the plate away. "Need help?"

"Why don't you clean up Mikey and I'll do dishes?"

"Deal," Janet said, picking up her son. They retired to the half-bath downstairs, where Janet plopped her son on the vanity to clean him off.

"You just like playing with food, don't you!" Janet said to Mikey.

The kid grinned like a little pig in shit.

Janet wetted a rag and started to work on her son. She did owe Penny a lot. There'd been a brief flurry of local fame when Janet, the sole survivor of the *Windy City*, brought the ship in, but that had faded quickly, and Janet had been on her own. She'd been five months pregnant—really too late...

She looked at her son, giggling as she wiped his face. *It's not your fault.* She rinsed the rag in the sink, then lifted Mikey's shirt to see how much had soaked through.

Penny's cousin Kate had been killed on the *Windy City*, and somehow that had meant Penny had gotten to be Janet's guide to all things Martian. And when the baby came, Penny had been Miss Go-To for child care.

Now Mikey calls her 'Mom.'

"We're going to have to wash this shirt, mister," Janet said to her son. He didn't seem to care, not surprisingly.

"Okay, Mister," Janet said, picking Mikey up, "let's go."

As Janet walked into the kitchen with Mikey in her arms, a glass, slipped out of Penny's hand. Penny bent down and tried to catch the slowly-tumbling glass, ignoring the ice sloshing out of it. She missed, and as she did, the slab of lasagna from the plate in her other hand slid off, heading for the floor.

The glass hit the hard ceramic tiled floor first, cracking audibly, followed by the wet splat of the lasagna. Red sauce from the slice bounced up and splattered onto the white enamel cabinets.

"Son of a bitch!" Penny said.

"You do it too!" Janet said between laughs.

"Damn it, Janet, grow up!" Penny snapped over her shoulder. "I'm tired of being your Mommy!"

"Oh you are?" Janet said, recoiling as if she'd been struck. "I didn't know you were my Mom."

Penny turned and looked at Janet. "I..."

"No, I get it completely," Janet said, her stomach churning. *All this time I thought she* cared *about me*! "You think I'm some kind of charity case, a Miss Pity that you need to take care of!"

"No, I..."

"Don't bullshit a bullshitter, Penny dearest." Janet shifted Mikey in her arms. "I'll make different arrangements for Mikey by the end of the week." She turned and stomped out, slamming the front door.

Bill Kelly slid into an open bar stool, one of a dozen available. *Grant is definitely my fault. Lieutenant or no, he shouldn't have been first man on that ship. It should have been me with Nomura.*

Yet another screw-up, he thought. Just like back on Earth. On Earth, it wasn't his fault that the damn engine fell off. The Lieutenant was supposed to be covering things for him and make sure everything was tightened up. But the Lieutenant was a General's kid, and didn't have to admit fault. So Kelly took the fall.

"What's your poison?" Scott Moon asked. Or maybe it was Todd. Bill Kelly couldn't tell the twins apart by looks.

"Shot and a beer," Kelly replied. "Red Crown," he added, specifying the brand of whisky.

"Coming up, buddy," Scott said, turning to pour. Being called 'buddy' was the only way he knew to tell the brothers apart. Scott called everybody 'buddy.' His brother Todd, equally bad at names, called everybody 'friend.'

Moon's Base Bar was a dive, with rough concrete floors that were hosed down periodically and mismatched, battered fiberglass and metal furniture. The bar, of glass blocks and a copper top, was about the only attempt at 'décor' in the joint. There were supposed to be colored lights behind the glass, but most of them were burnt out. A few cheap prints, pictures of various moons, sparsely decorated the red brick walls.

Since it was a dive, which made the "pick your poison" remark entirely too accurate. Scott came back, and plopped an amber beer and a shot glass down.

"On your tab?" Scott asked.

"Yep. Bill Kelly." There was another 'Kelly' in their system, a fact he'd discovered last month while trying to settle up. At least that Kelly, Steve, drank vodka, otherwise they'd never have gotten it squared away.

Kelly drained about half the shot glass, and chased it with a large slug of suitably cold beer. Moon's Base was a dive, but unlike The Sparrow, which was closer to his so-called 'apartment,' they served beer at an American temperature.

"Hey," Scott said. Kelly looked up to see him standing with his brother. "We heard about your ship. Sorry."

"We sent flowers to the funeral," Todd added. "Least we could do."

"Oh, and we're buying this round," Scott said.

"Thanks, guys." Kelly said. The brothers nodded and wandered off to take care of the other customers.

Tony Chen deserved a gold watch and grandkids, not a metal box. He took another swig of beer, and shook his head angrily. *I shoulda never let that kid talk me out of going back for them.*

The rational part of his mind argued that the kid was right—a rescue attempt was hopeless. But sometimes you have to do the right thing even if it was hopeless. It was the difference between a real man and a coward. Kelly grimaced. Coward. He didn't like the taste of that word on his mouth. But he'd better get used to it.

Kelly finished his second shot, and was contemplating the last of his second beer - two beers and two shots was usually all he did - when the blonde walked in. Mostly blonde—her hair had clumps of pink in it. She was wearing tight jeans and a tank top, which really highlighted her tits.

She flounced her way up to the bar like she was on a mission and straddled a stool next to him.

"Bourbon on the rocks," she said, tossing a two-Euro coin on the bar.

"Red Crown's on special for two-fifty, friend," Todd said.

"House is fine," the blonde replied. She ignored Todd's attempt to look down her cleavage. Not that Kelly blamed him.

"Another one for you, friend?" Todd asked Kelly.

"I'm done, thanks," Kelly replied.

The girl pretended to sniff her armpits. "I took a shower!"

"Glad to hear it, kid," Kelly replied. "It's not you, it's me."

Her drink arrived, and she drained about half of it in a gulp. *Why'd she bother with ice? The whisky was still warm.*

"Good to hear I wasn't losing my touch," the girl replied. "I've been out of circulation for a while."

"So have I." *What the hell.* "Hey, Todd," Kelly yelled. "I will do another."

"That's the spirit," the girl said. "You a regular?"

"I've been in a few times. Haven't seen you before."

The blonde smiled. "I haven't been in since at least middle of Cancer."

Kelly still hadn't gotten used to the Zubrin Martian calendar. He'd gotten trained by the US Air Force, and they used the Darien calendar. "Mithune?"

The blonde looked at him with mock irritation. "You know, why can't the people on this damn rock pick one fucking calendar and go with it?"

"That would be too easy," Kelly said. Either way, she hadn't been in there for at least 90 days. About the time his divorce finalized.

"So what happened?" The girl asked. "To put you back in the game, I mean."

"Divorce."

"Rough?"

"Are there easy ones?"

"I guess not."

Kelly's drink arrived, and he clinked glasses with the girl. "What's your story?"

Her smile faded for a second. "Let's just say I'm available and leave it at that."

"Works for me."

Chapter 19

Friday, 39 Virgo Year 52 07:45 local (March 9, 2074, 13:40 GMT) Port Lowell, Mars

"LOOKS LIKE YOU HAD A LONG NIGHT," Jack said to an unshaven and rumpled Roger McNally as he walked into McNally's office. It had been a couple of days since that dinner at Vito's. As far as Jack knew, there had been no movement on the negotiations.

Unless McNally had something, of course. Otherwise why ask me to come down this early in the morning?

"I did," Roger replied to Jack's question. "Damn rollalong broke down on the way back. I just got in an hour ago."

"What rollalong?" Jack asked, pouring himself a cup of coffee.

"The one I took to see my contact," McNally said.

The door chimed, signaling the arrival of Sean Yeargan.

"How's the office hunting going?" McNally asked as Yeargan walked into the main area of the office.

"I signed a lease yesterday," Yeargan said making a bee-line for the coffee pot. "The landlord's supposed to get it painted and ready for move-in by the end of the week. How was your trip?"

"Shitty," McNally replied, and gave them both more information then was strictly needed about the rollalong's breakdown.

"Lovely planet," Yeargan replied, sitting down at his paper-strewn desk. He had brought in a brown paper bag from which he produced a box of donuts. "Breakfast, anybody?"

"Don't mind if I do," McNally said. Jack helped himself as well.

"Find anything out?" Jack asked. "From your source, I mean?"

"Our mystery ship was bought out of Bensonville."

"Should I know where that is?" Yeargan said.

"Olympus." McNally waved his hand. "One of the other towns, on the East Rim."

"I thought Turner Springs was the only spaceport," Jack said.

"Need to update your homework, Midshipman," McNally said with a leer. "Bensonville is listed as having a Category Four facility."

Two thirds of Mars qualified as a Category Four facility, Jack thought sourly. Category Four was little more than a flat patch of dirt.

"What kind of ships can you move out of a Cat Four?" Yeargan asked.

"Small, mostly. Why?"

"I got an email from the United States Air Farce, I mean Force," Yeargan said smirkingly. He knew McNally had been in the Canadian Air Force. "Apparently they lost some missiles."

"Lost?" Jack said.

"Well, stolen I presume, but the email was rather vague."

"And?" McNally asked.

"And the Zoomies think our mystery container has them."

"What mystery container?" Jack said, wondering how exactly one went about stealing a shipping container full of missiles.

Yeargan briefly explained about the "Spears and Aguilera" container. "They want us to keep it under our hats," he said at the end. "So, what kind of ship would you need to get a container down to the surface?"

"Nothing that could land on a Cat Four field," Jack said. "Although you could moose it."

"Moose?" Yeargan said.

"Material Out Of Space Easy, or MOOSE," McNally said. "Wrap the container in a heat shield, strap a parachute on it and fire a retro."

"Would you want to do that with ordinance?" Yeargan asked.

"I wouldn't," NcNally said, "but somebody might. Lots of stuff gets MOOSE'd down. You need a big open area to land in, like several square kilometers big, but that's really the only requirement."

The last thing Mars needs is some nut running around with a box full of missiles. He looked at the other two men.

"What are we going to do about this?"

"We?" Yeargan said. "I thought you were just here for the coffee."

"First they kidnap my friends and shipmates, and now they're going to start firing off rockets." Jack took a deep breath. "I can't let that happen. I'm in. All the way." *My parents are going to kill me.* "But it's just me. I can't speak for Space Rescue."

"I don't expect you to, kid," Yeargan said. "We're going to have to do this off-the-books." Yeargan held out his hand. "Welcome to our party."

Jack's cell phone rang. He pulled it out of his pocket and glared at it. The caller ID said 'Janet Pilgrim.'

"Sorry, guys, I need to take this."

McNally waved him on as Yeargan got up to refill his coffee cup.

"Hi Janet," he said, not looking at the video display and not bothering with the ear-piece.

"I'm not Janet," a woman's voice said.

"Penny?" Jack asked. He looked at the screen. Penny Sharpe's face, a mixture of worry and irritation, was staring back at him.

"Sorry to call you so early," Penny said, her face tight.

"That's okay. What's up?"

"Janet's missing," Penny said. A child's chubby hand reached up and started to grab one of Penny's tightly-wound blonde curls. "She didn't sleep here last night."

Penny must have gone over to Janet's to pick up Mikey.

"She left Mikey alone?"

"That's what Mikey said. I found him on the countertop eating cereal."

"Damn that woman," Jack said. "She's got responsibilities."

"Unfortunately a job isn't one of them."

"How so?"

"Marty called just after I got here."

Jack shook his head in disgust. "She didn't show up for work and he finally fired her."

"Yep."

"And you need me to find her so you can go to work."

"My shift at the ICU starts at three."

"I'll get right on it," Jack said.

"Bring her over to my house."

"Okay," Jack said, cutting the connection.

"Can we help?" McNally asked. With Jack's phone on speaker, they had heard both sides of the conversation.

Jack frowned. "Not really. I'll find her."

"Well, let me know if you need anything," Yeargan said. He turned to McNally. "Anything else we need to know?"

"I got a picture of one of the pirates," McNally said.

"I doubt that will do much good," Jack said, standing up to leave. "The four we have in the morgue are all John and Jane Does."

Somebody was pounding inside Kelly's head. Persistent fuck, whoever he was. Also small, a thought which brought a smile to Kelly's face.

Smiling hurt, which woke Kelly up. That and the poke to his ribs from his blonde-and-pink-haired bedmate. "Somebody's at the door."

That made more sense than a little man in his head. He sat up, perhaps a tad too quickly, and waited for a second to clear his head. "I'm coming, damn it!" He shouted. It hurt to shout.

The knocking stopped. Kelly stood up, and started to look for his pants. His 'apartment' had started life as a steel shipping container, and was one of a group of units facing a narrow walkway. The interior finish was decent, and the only way to tell from inside what the place used to be was the narrow size. That and you had to step up to get into the bathroom. The bedroom was in back, with the bathroom separating it from the living area.

Kelly's pants were lying on the floor in the narrow hallway leading from the bedroom. He put them on and padded barefoot to the living area, then put his eye to the peephole in the door.

Midshipman Jack Williams was standing in the hallway. *What the fuck did he want?* Kelly opened the door.

"What can I do for you, sir?" he asked. "It's my day off."

"You seen Janet?" the kid asked.

"Who?"

"Can I come in?" Williams said.

"Sure," Kelly said, blocking the door. "But in my house I'm the boss, Mr. Williams."

"Of course, Chief," Williams said. Kelly stepped aside and the kid walked in and stood just by the door. Kelly walked over to the 'kitchen,' a counter on the wall butting up to the bathroom, and started to make coffee.

"The guys at Moon's said you went home with a girl last night," Williams said.

"So?" Kelly replied. "One of the many things I do without consulting your advice."

"Hi, Jack."

"Janet," Williams said. "Nice to see you."

Things were moving a bit too fast for Kelly's hangover. The blonde he'd taken home, apparently the girl that the kid was looking for, was standing in the hallway to the bedroom, naked. Obviously blonde was her natural hair color. She walked in and wrapped herself around Kelly.

The kid, Williams, was bothered, but tried to play it straight. "How's your son?"

Kelly could feel her tense up, but she kept it out of her voice. "Fine, thank you." She looked up at Kelly. "Coffee on?"

"I'm brewing it," Kelly replied. "My housecoat's in the bathroom if you want it."

"I'm okay," she said, a shit-eating grin on her face.

"Would you mind explaining what the fuck's going on?" Kelly asked of Jack. "Like how you two know each other?"

The kid gestured with his chin at Janet. "You just fucked Peter Grant's girl."

Shit. "How the hell was I supposed to know?"

"I'm not property," Janet said.

"Asking a name was too much trouble?" Jack said, ignoring Janet.

Kelly's head resumed its pounding. "Perhaps more to the point, what fucking business is it of yours anyway?"

"She left her son alone last night," Jack said.

"I'm a big girl," Janet said.

"Mikey's not," Jack said.

Kelly glanced longingly at the coffee maker. This was not a good way to start a day. He then looked at Janet. Left her son alone? "How old is he?"

"A Mear."

Two. She rubbed up against him, sparking an involuntary reaction. What did Dad say? *Don't stick your dick in crazy.*

"So that's old enough to be alone by himself?" Jack barked.

"Don't you raise your voice at me, Jackson Williams," Janet replied, partially detaching from Kelly.

Jack glared at her. "Man's been gone less than a week and you're out trolling shit bars trying to get laid."

"Jack," Kelly said. "My house, my rules." *Not that Moon's Base wasn't a shit bar.* The coffee maker beeped its readiness. Kelly moved toward it as if it were an emergency oxygen tank in a hull breach.

"What difference does it make?" Janet said. "Man's never coming back. You said so yourself."

"I think I know where he's being held, dear," Jack replied.

"So?" Janet asked.

Kelly took a sip of the steaming hot coffee. It didn't help much.

"We're going in to get him," Jack said.

"Who's we?" Janet asked. "And why should you care?"

"I care because it's my fault," Jack said, his voice cracking.

Not entirely your fault, Kelly thought. I left him.

"As to 'who's we,' it's me and whoever else Yeargan can find," Jack said. "He's got his checkbook out."

Janet looked away. "Sounds thin."

Kelly couldn't argue with that assessment. But still, at least the kid was trying to *do something*, not just getting drunk.

"So where is he?" Kelly said, taking a gulp of hot coffee.

"Bensonville. Republic of the White Race." Jack explained about the mother ship and the inside person.

He could be someplace worse, Kelly thought when Jack finished. "You got a plan?" Kelly finally asked.

"Not yet," Jack said. "We're working on it."

"So what information do you have?"

"Location, mostly. We need to gather more."

Kelly thought for a second. It was put up or shut up. "I'd like to see what you have."

"You two are nuts," Janet said. She brushed him aside and poured herself a cup of coffee.

"You want to put some clothes on, dear?" Kelly asked.

"Mind if I use your shower?" Janet replied, ignoring the question.

"Not at all," Kelly said. "Feel free to borrow my robe. Jack, care for a cup of coffee?"

"Sure, Chief, I will."

Chapter 20

Friday 38 Virgo Year 52 09:15 local (March 9, 2074, 13:55 GMT)
Port Lowell, Mars

IF THAT TANK TOP was any tighter it would burst, Jack thought, looking at Janet while they climbed onboard the trolley. Although it was an improvement over her other outfit.

The trolley was mostly empty, and she took a seat as far away from him as possible. It was just as well she was sitting so far away - Jack didn't have a lot to say to her.

As the trolley started to move Jack called Yeargan on his cell phone. "Chief Kelly wants to see what we've got," he said.

"Great," Yeargan replied. "Where are you?"

"On the trolley to Janet's place."

"You found her?"

"Yeah," Jack said, "and just happened to run into Kelly on the way."

"Tell you what," Sean said, "I'll meet you at Penny's house. She's my cousin-in-law."

"Now might not be a good time for that," Jack replied. He'd forgotten that Penny and Kate—Janet's old captain—were cousins. Mars was proving to be a small planet.

"Except it looks like she could use some help with Janet," Yeargan said.

True, Jack thought. The only problem was whether Janet would accept help. "You know the address?"

"Fifth Street, right?" Sean said.

"Yep," Jack replied.

"I'll be there shortly."

Yeargan's office was just a little closer to Janet's than they were, so depending on trolley schedules he might just beat them.

* * *

The trolley stopped at Fifth Street just long enough for the three of them to pile off. Janet and Penny lived on Fifth, within a few doors of each other. As he strolled down the wide hallway that consisted of Fifth Street, he could hear the bells of sheep being herded above him. This section of the city was completely underground. Above his head, at ground level, a long glass dome ran down the length of the street, the opening to the level below bisecting a grassy park.

Must be grass-cutting day, he thought. Better not take Mikey up there later on—the kid will get himself covered in sheep shit.

"Where's Mikey?" Janet asked.

"Penny took him to her place," Jack said.

"Good. I want to stop at my place and change clothes."

"Okay," Jack said. Penny wants to put your ass in a sling—making her wait will just make it worse.

Jack and Kelly went directly to Penny's place. Sean Yeargan opened the door to them, another donut in his hand.

"I brought the donuts," he said, gesturing towards the kitchen / family room in back.

"Thanks," Kelly said. He held out his hand. "Bill Kelly, Chief Astronaut on the *Volodka*."

"Sean Yeargan," Sean replied, transferring the donut to his left hand. "Special Counsel to the North American Insurance Consortium."

"That's a mouthful," Kelly said, a smile on his face. "What's it mean?"

"I fix shit," Sean said. He wasn't smiling.

"Oh," Kelly said, his smile fading.

"Janet's first mate was Sean's son," Jack said.

"Sorry for your loss," Kelly said.

"Coffee in the back," Yeargan said, cocking a thumb.

"Great," Kelly said, walking ahead down the hallway.

"How was your meeting with Penny?" Jack asked.

Yeargan shrugged. "Okay, I guess. Apparently she and Kate were raised together."

I knew they were close, Jack thought as they walked back to the family room, where Penny was putting out some plates on the counter. Mikey was playing with a toy truck in the corner.

"Where's Janet?" Penny asked of the two men.

"She stopped to change clothes," Kelly replied. "I'm Bill Kelly. Mr. Grant was my boss."

"That damn woman needs more then fresh clothes," Penny said. She took Kelly's offered hand. "Hungry?"

"I could eat, but right now caffeine's more important."

"How do you take your coffee?"

"Black, thanks, Mrs. Sharpe."

"I'm divorced," Penny said, "and please call me Penny."

"Okay, Penny."

Jack turned and saw Yeargan slide into the downstairs bathroom.

"Penny, I need to use your upstairs bathroom," Jack said.

"Make yourself at home," she replied.

Jack was washing his hands when he heard the door slam. It had to be Janet—the woman never just closed a door. Penny's "where have you been?" and Mikey's "Mommy" confirmed it.

Jack decided to wait a minute and let Penny and Janet have some privacy. Penny started to talk, too quietly for Jack to hear the words, but the tone was cutting. When he couldn't stall anymore, he walked down the stairs to find Penny and Janet standing at the middle landing.

"Not only did you leave your son alone, young miss," Penny said, "but you just lost your job."

"I'll talk to Marty today," Janet said, her face hung down.

"I doubt it'll do any good," Penny said. "What did Marty say last time? Remember?"

"No more second chances."

"Right," Penny said, pointing at Janet. "Well, I'm about at the same point."

"You leaving?" Janet said, looking at Jack.

"I guess so," Jack replied. "Sean Yeargan and I will bring Chief Kelly up to speed at the office."

"Up to speed on what?" Penny asked.

"They're going to John Wayne some kind of 'rescue,'" Janet said, scorn in her voice.

"This I've got to hear," Penny said dubiously. The group of them walked back to the kitchen.

"Jack says y'all have a plan," Penny said.

"We're working on it," Yeargan replied.

"I'd love to hear it," Penny said.

"Well, why not?" Yeargan replied, standing at the kitchen counter. He pushed aside the nearly empty box of donuts and produced a couple of printouts from his pocket. The rest of them, including Janet, gathered around the counter.

"OK, so Williams here spotted a track near *Price* just before they got jumped," Yeargan began.

"Based on size and capabilities, we decided that the ship had to be a Mosquito," Jack said.

"I think I'm missing something," Kelly said. "What is the significance of the contact?"

"We think it was the mothership the pirates used to get out there," Jack said.

"Think?" Janet said, looking at her son playing on the floor. "Sounds thin."

"We go with what we got," Yeargan said. "At any rate, we tracked down all ships of that type known to be in Martian space."

"As opposed to not known to be in Martian space?" Janet asked. Yeargan ignored her.

"One suspect vessel was recently bought for cash from a very shady character," Jack said, gesturing at Yeargan, who started to unfold a printout. "She's from Bensonville," Jack continued, "and we've got her picture."

"This was hard-to-get information," Yeargan said. "We paid a bunch for it."

"For this?" Kelly said. "A picture and a fake ID?"

"We know the ID is fake," Yeargan said, a note of exasperation in his voice. He folded the printout flat, allowing everybody to see it. "But this 'Richards' woman probably used the same ID for other activities."

"Maybe," Kelly said. "How sure are we she's from Bensonville?"

"She's not," Janet said, taking the printout from Yeargan.

"Maybe so," Yeargan said.

"Her real name is Jennifer Rachel Storey," Janet said, her voice flat. "She was born on Mars, out on the southern fringes of the Utopia Planita, in a place called Florence. Shipped out to Earth at age eighteen standard. Put herself through college in Philadelphia as a stripper and hooker."

The room was very quiet. Even Mikey stopped playing and looked up at his mother.

"She's one of the pirates that took your ship," Jack said.

"Yep."

"How'd she get to Bensonville," Penny asked. "I thought her group worked out of Boxtown?"

"Maybe she decided to lay low after the *Witchcraft* fiasco," Janet said.

"What *Witchcraft* fiasco?" Jack asked.

"Before your time, kid," Kelly said, looking at Jack. "*Witchcraft* was a ship that had been reported missing for months, then she just showed up in orbit. The crew said they'd been pirated."

"As I recall," Yeargan said, "the crew claimed that the pirates had just suddenly left."

"More likely been stuffed out of an airlock," Kelly said. "There were signs of a fight everywhere."

"Whatever," Yeargan said.

"Well, I know for a fact that Rachel's ship attacked the *Witchcraft*," Janet said. "So whatever happened, Rachel got the short end of the stick."

"Apparently it wasn't that short," Penny said, "or the bitch wouldn't be alive."

"Piracy only pays if you don't lose the ship back to the crew," Yeargan said.

"Which would explain why she resurfaced," Jack said. "She's broke."

"Do we know what level of involvement she's got in this?" Janet asked.

"No," Yeargan replied. "I mean, I just found out who she was a minute ago."

"That's not true," Jack said. "She bought the mothership."

"Was she just a bag lady or did she do something more substantive?" Kelly asked.

Janet smiled. "Sounds like y'all got more questions than answers."

"We've got more answers than we did an hour ago," Yeargan said. He sighed. "But not nearly enough. My offer is still open, Janet."

"What offer?" Penny said.

"To be part of his merry band of, what would you call them, mercenaries?" Janet said. "Run off and shoot pirates."

"Are you smoking dope?" Penny asked. She looked at Janet. "You are not going out on some harebrained scheme like that?"

"I really don't need you to mother me," Janet said. "We had this discussion. But no, I'm sitting this one out."

"It doesn't seem like we've got the kind of intelligence we'd need for a rescue," Kelly said.

"Not yet," Yeargan said. "But I don't know how much more intelligence we'll be able to gather from here."

"Six thousand kilometers *is* a long way," Kelly said.

"There's a train to Bradbury," Jack said, "and rollalong service to Bensonville Under."

"Under?" Penny said.

"There's a lift from Under to Bensonville—up the cliff of Olympus." Two kilometers of cliff, to be exact.

Kelly stepped away from the counter and went to the coffee pot. "Anybody need a refill?"

Nobody said anything. "You know," Kelly said, his back to the group, "I have some leave coming up."

"Oh?" Jack asked.

"Three weeks, as I recall, sir," Kelly replied, returning to the counter.

"I can make it worth your time," Yeargan said. "Financially, I mean."

"So you're in?" Jack asked.

"Yes. But it's not for the money."

"We can worry about that later, Chief," Jack said.

Penny glared at Jack and Kelly. "So you two are going to run off and be heroes?"

"It's what we do, ma'am," Kelly said with a smirk.

Judging from the look on Penny's face, the joke fell flat. "This mess is partially my fault," Jack said. "It's my responsibility to fix it."

"You know," Yeargan said, "I think we'll need all sorts of folks before this is done, including administrative support."

"Is that supposed to mean something?" Penny said.

"You told me Miss Pilgrim was recently unemployed."

"You are high," Janet said.

"Administrative," Yeargan said. "Shuffling papers."

"Boys with toys," Janet said with a sniff.

"I take it that's a no," Yeargan said.

"You take correctly."

"You do need a job," Penny said.

Janet glared at her, then looked at Yeargan. "How much does it pay?"

"Twice what you were making at the welding shop," Yeargan said. "Assuming that I can at least pick your brains about Storey."

"In that case," Janet said with a shrug, "Sure."

"Good enough," Yeargan said. "For now."

Chapter 21

Friday, 38 Virgo Year 52 19:45 local (March 10, 2074, 00:25 GMT)
Port Lowell, Mars

SEAN WALKED UP TO THE CASHIER STATION, and placed his tray on the checkout scanner. The place had all the ambiance of a hospital cafeteria, which fit since it was. But it was nearly deserted at this hour. Not a lot of people spend their Friday nights in a hospital cafeteria if they could help it.

Penny's going to try and talk me out of this, Sean thought, as the overhead light for the checkout machine, suspended about head-high, flared brightly for a second. Immediately after, a price flashed up on the screen.

"I got this," Penny said, reaching around him and tapping her hospital ID card against the reader. The machine deducted the cost of the meal from her account, then said "Thank you for using General Food Services" in what was supposed to be a pleasant tone. But something was wrong with the speaker, so what came out was grating.

"Thanks, Penny," Sean said. He looked around the cafeteria. "Plenty of seats."

"Nobody eats in a hospital cafeteria unless they have to," Penny said. "although the Chicken Ala King is usually pretty good."

Sean made a face. "If you say so." They headed to a table in the back.

"Puke on a plate," Sean said, pointing to Penny's plate. "The army put me off of that. Janet recommended the Rueben, although I'm still not sure how 'fresh' this clam chowder can be."

"Clam farm, or ranch as they call it, is at the end of our street. Kid brings a bucket to the hospital every morning."

"Weird planet," Sean said.

"I guess so," Penny said. "So what does the Army have to do with Chicken Ala King?"

"We were in Korea," Sean said. He felt a sudden chill, which always followed that thought. "After we went north, somehow my platoon got two whole skids of nothing but Chicken Ala King MREs. Ever eat that stuff frozen?"

"No. Haiti's not known to be cold."

Sean leaned back. Penny was full of surprises. "You served?"

"Navy corpsman. Got attached to a Marine platoon doing so-called peacekeeping."

"That was after my time." He dipped a fry in ketchup. "They put you through nursing school?"

"GI Bill."

"I heard 'so-called' was an apt description—for Haiti."

"I spent a year there—two deployments." She paused, her fork in mid-air. "There wasn't much peace to keep. We tried peacemaking instead."

"What did that involve?"

"Mostly we hiked up into the hills. If the Skinnies—"

"Local slang?"

"Yeah. If the Skinnies took a potshot at us, we shot back. Mostly by calling in artillery fire from the gunline. Then I got to try and clean up the mess."

"There were days I could kiss those Navy SOBs," Sean said. "God was it cold."

They both ate for a minute. Penny broke the silence.

"You saw combat, yes?"

"Lots."

"But you trained for it, right?"

Sean grinned. "Until we were sick of training."

"And people still got killed, yes?"

I think I see where she's going. "Yes."

"So why are you in such an all-fired hurry to send these amateurs in to play commando?"

Sean took a bite of his sandwich and swallowed before he answered. "Because it needs to be done."

"Maybe."

"Bullshit," Sean said, hearing his voice rise. He took a breath. "This planet is fucked up."

"So you're going to personally un-fuck it? You, a rookie kid and some ex-Air Force wrench jockey?"

"They're going up against pirates, Penny, not NK Regulars."

"Two of my squad went home in bags," Penny said. "One of them put there by a twelve-year-old with a .22 bolt-action. Caught a second-tour sergeant right between the eyes."

"So we keep paying them?" Sean looked at his sandwich, suddenly not hungry. "Your cousin was killed by that red-haired bitch."

Penny leaned back and crossed her arms. "The real reason comes out. Killing Storey won't bring her back."

"No, but it might prevent somebody else getting killed."

"Keep telling yourself that. The real reason isn't stopping piracy. It's about you getting revenge."

Sean picked up his sandwich as if to take a bite, then put it down. "I want justice. Since I can't get that, I'll take revenge. You should understand that."

"Understand is not the same as agree. Sometimes we need to move on."

"Sometimes," Sean said. "But not now. We can do both."

Penny frowned. *I'm not getting to her.*

"So you say. But why do you care about this ship?"

Sean wondered if he should tell her about the missiles. He decided not to. *Hell, I haven't told Kelly yet.* "It's stolen."

"And getting Jack and that Kelly fellow killed taking it back is a good idea?"

"The *Price* is the price I pay." Sean immediately regretted the inadvertent pun. "Like I told you this morning, I got sent here to put the kibosh on this piracy problem. We've got an opportunity to start that work now."

"And you're willing to create some orphans?"

"The attack on the *Price* made five orphans, Ms. Sharpe." Sean looked down at his sandwich, then pushed back from the table. "I hope we don't end with more, but yes, that's a price I'll pay."

He got up and walked out of the cafeteria, leaving his half-eaten food behind.

Chapter 22

Monday, 41 Virgo Year 52 11:00 local (March 12, 2074 17:40 GMT) Space Rescue Headquarters, Port Lowell

JACK FELT ASHAMED, LOOKING AT THE VIDEO, freshly-received from the pirates. With the identification of Rachel Storey, things had been looking up. Now this video. On it Grant, sporting a fresh black eye and hang-dog look, said something about being held in an inescapable location, and asked them to pay quickly. Then the video ended.

"They obviously worked him over," Yeargan said. "He probably tried to escape."

"You think so?" Newindink asked.

Newindale, Jack. Captain Newindale. Better keep that straight or find another job.

They were sitting in Newindale's plush office. Since it was impossible to tell if Newindale's question was rhetorical or not, Jack decided to answer. "Yes, sir. Trying to convince us that they're serious."

"They undoubtedly are, Midshipman," Newindale replied. "I wish Lieutenant Grant hadn't acted so precipitously. This will make my conversations with local leaders more difficult."

"Conversations?" Yeargan asked. "With whom, exactly, may I ask?"

"I hardly think it's relevant," Newindale replied.

"Since I'm conducting ransom negotiations on behalf of the *Price* crew, perhaps I'm a better judge of that." Yeargan seemed to be pretty good at saying sarcastic shit like that in a polite tone. Jack decided he'd have to learn the trick.

"If you must know," Newindale said, "I've had conversations with Spenser Pearce and the European Union legate, among others."

"I haven't had any conversations with them," Yeargan said. "What have they said to you?"

"They are quite concerned, of course, and are reaching out to their sources. Do you have any intelligence as to where these people are based out of?"

"I'm afraid not," Yeargan said.

It was very convincing, and Jack made a note not to play poker with the man.

"Midshipman Williams," Newindale said, swiveling his chair. "I understand you're heading back up to the *Volodka*?"

"Yes, sir, this afternoon." Jack replied. "Now that we've filled our officer slots, Captain Mfume wants to conduct some training workups."

"Very good," Newindale said. "I understand Chief Kelly is not returning."

"Yes sir," Jack said. "He's just taking a few weeks. He was shook up over leaving Lt. Grant and Able Spacer Nomura." As am I.

Newindale nodded. "Kelly's a good man. You've got coverage for him?"

Jack nodded yes.

"Good. Is there anything else to discuss?"

"No sir," Yeargan said. "I will keep you advised as to my negotiations. If your inquiries produce anything, please let me know."

"Of course," Newindale said. He stood and reached across his desk to shake Sean's hand. "Hopefully we can reach a peaceful resolution to this."

Jack waited until they were completely off the base before he said anything. "Who's Spencer Pearce?"

"Only the second-least-influential person on Mars," Yeargan said. He gestured vaguely at a bar across the street from the base. "He's right below the guy who cleans the pisser at that bar."

"Seriously."

Yeragan stopped in the middle of the street. "Seriously. The guy flits around like a fairy, holding 'unity conferences' and similar shit, all attended by a collection of dreamers, has-beens and never-wases."

"The EU Legate?"

"His power ends just past municipal pressure here in Port Lowell."

Jack smiled. "So he's the least influential guy on Mars?"

"No, actually that would be your idiot boss, The Great Dink." Yeargan, apparently realizing that they were standing in the middle of the street, resumed walking. "How long are you topside?"

"Two days for workups," Jack replied.

"You have time to stop by my office?"

"Actually, no. I need to meet with my new captain."

Yeargan offered his hand. "Good luck."

Sean Yeargan smiled as he walked up the stairs to his new office. They screwed up, he thought, reflecting on the pirate video. Grant would only try to escape if he was being held on the Martian surface.

Deep space ships only carried lifeboats in bad movies. Orbit-to-ground shuttles weren't exactly standard equipment on deep space ships either, especially something like the *Price*, a vessel designed to be loaded and unloaded at a specialized orbital port. No, Sean thought. He's somewhere in Bensonville.

Now if I could just get Janet with the program.

Sean arrived at the door to his office suite just as Janet was walking out.

"Going to lunch?" Sean asked her.

"I was," she replied, "but since you're here can we talk for a minute?"

"Sure," Sean replied. They stepped back inside and settled around a small, round laminate wood-toned table Sean used for meetings. The green-upholstered chairs went nicely with the newly-painted green walls.

"What can I do for you?" Sean asked.

"When were you going to tell me?" Janet asked.

"Tell you what?"

She slid a printout over to him. It was an email from Colonel Slevnik.

"Where'd you get that?" Sean asked.

"I file shit, remember?" Janet said. "Clerical support, you called it."

"I didn't think you needed to know." Sean leaned back in his seat. "Hell, I didn't think you cared."

"I don't," Janet said. It was an obvious lie.

"Well, then there's nothing to talk about," Sean said, getting up. "Enjoy your lunch."

"Does Kelly know?"

"Yes," Sean said, making no move to leave. "Part of his brief is to find the container."

Janet was clearly puzzled. "Now, wait a second," she finally said. "He needs to find the prisoners, find the container, verify what orbit the *Price* is on..."

"We got people working on the orbit," Sean said.

"And if the hostages are in the town. . ."

"They are, otherwise Grant's talking about escape wouldn't make sense."

"Figure out how to get our people in without setting off any alarms."

"And back out, yes."

"Isn't that a bit much?"

Sean shrugged. "It's not like we're breaking into a North Korean nuclear silo."

"You don't understand," Janet said. "These Martian towns are tiny. Bensonville's what, fifteen hundred people?"

"More like three kay. Your point?"

"One guy asking that many questions will stick out like a sore thumb."

The hook is set. Now let's reel her in. "I don't have anybody else to send. They'd shove Jack out the nearest airlock."

"We need to find somebody," Janet said.

"Who?"

She sat quietly for an instant. "You son of a bitch," she finally said.

"Pardon?"

"You're setting me up," she replied, waving angrily at the printout. "I was supposed to find this, and come running to you."

Now what? "Well..."

"Don't bullshit me, Sean."

"Okay, I won't," Sean replied, taking a seat. "I need you. I need everybody I can find, but I especially need you."

"Why me?"

"You convinced your pirates for months that you were part of them. Then, when the time came, you turned them inside out."

"I had help."

"And you will now." Sean thumped the table. "But to make this work, I need information, from the inside. A lot of it."

Janet smiled. "I can't hardly waltz in there, slide up to Rachel and ask 'where's the missiles, honey,' now can I?"

"They aren't looking for you, and think you're a blonde."

Janet leaned back, her arms folded across her chest. "What about Mikey? If I don't come back?"

"My daughter Irene can't have kids. She's already adopted a girl, and wants a boy."

"You think of everything, don't you?"

"It's my job." Your move, dear.

She sat for a long minute. "Fine, then. I'm in. But I want twice what you're paying Kelly, half up front."

"You drive a hard bargain," Sean said, even though she really didn't.

That SOB really did set me up, Janet thought as she let herself into her house. And I probably underpriced myself to boot. Yeargan had been entirely too quick to pay.

She flipped on the hall light and tossed her purse in the general direction of the couch. It missed, hitting one of Mikey's toys sitting on the floor. Janet looked at her purse and decided the hell with it. She walked back to the kitchen and poured herself a whiskey.

I suppose I'll want a gun. She took a sip of her whiskey, looking at the empty pistol case sitting in the cabinet, a half-full box of shells next to it. The gun that had been there was at Penny's place.

I do have her key still. She took another sip of whiskey, then glanced at the refrigerator door. A printout of Penny's work schedule was still up there, hanging from a magnet advertising a plumber. *She's at work, or supposed to be. And surely Mikey left* something *at her house.*

She drained her glass at a gulp. *Better do this now, before I pick up Mikey.*

The next morning, Sean let himself into his office to find a brunette woman sitting at Janet's desk. It took him a minute to make the connection.

"What do you think?" Janet asked.

"Do you own any shirts that aren't two sizes too tight?" Sean asked. He touched his chin. "And your face?"

"If they're looking at my tits they're not looking at my face," she replied. "The chin's just a little makeup."

"It works. Mikey settled in?"

"Yeah. Jack's sister does day care. He's having to learn to share though."

"Good for him." Sean closed the door behind him. "Where'd you learn that trick?" he said, waving a finger around his face.

"The Internet."

Sean reached into his pocket, and pulled out a small automatic. It was the same gun he'd given Roger.

"You might need this," he said, handing it to her.

"I prefer revolvers," Janet said, producing a small snub-nose from her desk drawer. She looked at it for a second. "I guess this is a family heirloom, since it belonged to Mikey's dad."

The man who raped her. "You use that to kill him with?"

"No. I took a shotgun to him." There was steel in her voice. "When should I leave?"

"Today, if possible."

"Works for me. Did you get a direct flight?

Janet smiled with what might have been genuine humor. "No such thing on this planet. I change rockets on Phobos."

"Janet," Sean said. "We do need you, and I will take care of your kid, but try to keep your head down."

"No fun that way," Janet said. The smile she flashed would have been appropriate for a wolf looking at a rabbit. "You know something else I found out on the Internet?"

"No."

"Hoof and mouth disease," Janet said. "Ever hear of it?"

"Vaguely," Sean said, wondering what the relevance was. "Nasty animal disease."

"You know how you cure it?"

"No."

"If there's no hoof and mouth disease, there's no hoof and mouth disease. You find an outbreak, you kill any animal that could possibly be in contact with the infected ones and burn their carcasses. In humans, 'hoof and mouth disease' is spelled 'piracy.'" She got up from her desk. "Well, I have a flight to catch."

Chapter 23

Sunday 47 Virgo Year 52 18:00 local (March 19, 2074 04:40 GMT)
Dutchman's Bar, Port Lowell, Mars

"LIEUTENANT ORTEGA, YOU LOOK GREAT," Jack said, greeting her as she walked into the back room of Dutchman's bar. He was going up tomorrow morning for work-ups with *Volodka's* reconstituted crew.

So now's the time to recruit people and go rescue their own.

"Thanks, Jack," she replied with a wan smile. "I've felt better."

Jack followed her to her table, and helped her sit down. Although clearly still sore, she did look good, considering she'd been shot two weeks ago.

"Want a beer, ma'am?" Jack asked.

"Please," she said, waving at a couple of people from another ship. "I'm just off of my pain pills."

Jack fetched a beer for her, and walked over to Yeargan, who was standing at the front of the group.

"Everybody you expected?" Yeargan asked.

Jack looked around. Kelly was sitting at the front table, checking names. Jack glanced at him and got a thumbs-up. "Yes sir."

"Good. Let's get started."

Jack closed the door, and walked in front of the nearly life-sized reproduction of Rembrandt's *The Night Watch*, which covered the back wall of the party room at the bar.

"Thanks for coming on short notice," Jack began, "and I appreciate you giving up part of your evening." The group, mostly crewmembers from the *Volodka* but a couple of others, looked at him expectantly. "Before I begin, I need to warn you. What I'm about to propose could get people killed."

That got everybody's attention.

"I want to go rescue Lieutenant Grant and Able Spacer Nomura," Jack said. "An armed rescue."

The room was dead silent.

"But I need you to understand," Jack said, his stomach tight, "that this is *not* a Space Rescue operation. We can't use any of their equipment, at least not officially."

"What are we using?" Carla asked.

"We've got some financial backing," Jack said, gesturing at Yeargan, "which I'll cover in a minute. But before I get into that, I want to be clear. Even if what I propose succeeds, it is in direct contravention of Space Rescue policy, so you could get fired. Anybody who doesn't want to get fired, please leave now."

"I assume we can back out if your 'proposal' is too much for us," Cameron Lewis said. He was one of *Volodka's* astronauts.

"As long as you keep your mouth shut about what you hear here, Cam," Kelly said.

"I can do that, Chief."

"Good," Kelly said. He gestured at Jack to proceed.

"OK," Jack said, as his stomach did a flip-flop. "Here's what we have. We have solid information on who hijacked the *Price* and kidnapped Nomura and the Lieutenant."

"What kind of solid information?" asked a female, vaguely Asian-looking, from one of the back tables.

"The kind you can base an action plan on," Jack said. "You are?"

"Sandra Kim. Comms officer on the *Hines*."

The *Jim C. Hines* was one of the other Service ships. She was at Carla's table, obviously a friend.

"A known pirate," Jack continued, "one Jennifer Rachel Storey, purchased the mother ship used in the attack."

"Okay," Kim said, sounding a bit dubious.

"She's based at Bensonville," Jack said, "and that correlates with the last known course of the *Price*."

"So we just assume that our people are at Bensonville?" Kim asked sarcastically.

"We've got somebody on the ground there," Jack said. "She arrived two days ago via the Bradbury train. Based on her reports and other information, we're quite confident that our people are there."

"Who is this 'somebody'?"

"Her name is Janet Pilgrim," Yeargan said, standing up. "Chief Kelly's going to join her."

"And you are, sir?" Kim asked. Several other people were trading looks and whispered questions.

"Sean Yeargan," he replied. "I work for Zurich North America Insurance. I'm also Special Counsel to the North American Insurance Consortium." He paused for a second. "To translate that into English, I've got the checkbook."

"Okay," Kim said, "so you're the moneyman. Why are you paying?"

"We're taking it in the shorts with piracy losses," Yeargan said. "We've decided to do something about it."

"Also," Kelly said, "Mister Yeargan's son and daughter-in-law died on the *Windy City*."

The room got very quiet. Sandra Kim broke the silence. "That was Janet's ship, yes?"

"Yes," Jack said.

"I heard she'd crawled into a bottle," Kim said.

"She crawled out," Yeargan replied.

Rather recently. Hope she's staying out.

"If you say so," Sandra said. "So what's the plan? We go in guns blazing?"

"Hopefully not," Jack said. "We've got a plan, and if the operation follows the plan, we shouldn't be shooting."

"If not?" Cameron asked from the back.

"That's why we're going to do some training first," Jack said. "But let me lay out the plan in broad strokes." Jack took a sip of his water and continued. "We have two teams. One will go to Bensonville, and there, assisted by our inside people, including the Chief here, will bust out both our guys and the *Price's* crew. A second team will capture the *Price* in orbit."

"Who cares about the *Price*?" Kim asked.

"I do," Yeargan said, "Or rather my bosses do. Getting the *Price* back is, well, the price I pay to keep them all happy."

There was a nervous titter at Sean's bad pun. Jack decided to strike before the crowd's mood changed. "So we're going to need two tactical teams, somebody to locate the *Price*, and some logistical support. All from people we can trust to keep their mouths shut."

"There's only a thousand or so ships in orbit," Kim said, "so we're going to have to visual ID them all?"

"No," Jack said. "We only need to get a visual on ships that can be reached by a VTL rocket from Bensonville. Bensonville just has a Class Four strip." Class Four was graded dirt with a steel mesh overlay, and one step over unimproved.

"Turner Springs has a full spaceport," Kim said. "They could be there."

"They're not going to use Turner Springs," Yeargan said. "For two reasons." He held up two fingers. "Politics and greed. The folks at Turner are trying to seem respectable, so that's politics. If the pirates did operate out of there, somebody'd want a cut, so that's greed."

"Not a lot of rockets can fly out of a Class Four strip," Carla observed. "None of them are exactly high performance. That puts the *Price* in a narrow orbital lane." Carla tapped Kim's shoulder. "The skywatchers should be able to find that easy."

Some people geeked out about trains, others spaceships. There was a whole subculture of folks who kept records of ships they'd seen.

"OK, so we find this ship," Kim said. "Then what?"

Jack took a deep breath. "Then we re-take the *Price*."

"Who's leading that detail?" Kim said.

"I am," Jack replied. "I'm looking for shooters and ground-to-orbit transport."

"How many for the boarding party?" Chief Krauss asked.

"At this point, we're guessing six to eight," Jack said. "We have no idea how many folks are guarding the ship, if any."

"Somebody's guarding it," Kelly said. "Janet is working on that number, and I will be when I get there."

"Bombardier makes some nice light shuttles," Krauss said. "I've got a full instrument license, assuming we can rent one."

"I'm sure that can be arranged," Yeargan said.

"You thought about weapons?" Lewis asked. "For the space assault, I mean."

"No," Jack replied.

"My brother owns a gun store and range just outside of town," Lewis said. "I work there occasionally, and we can keep it quiet."

"You volunteering to go or just cheerlead?" Kim asked.

"I'm going," Lewis said. "Somebody's got to keep Mister Williams there from getting his head blown off."

"We'll need an assault team for Bensonville," Jack said.

"We're getting a little ahead of ourselves," Kelly said. "First question is who's in. Hands up if you're in, please."

Everybody's hand went up except Sandra Kim. She glanced around. "This is bullshit, us trying to freelance an operation like this."

"You got any better ideas?" Carla asked. She looked at Jack. "I'll go, if you'll have me."

"You need to get healed up," Jack said. "We'll find somebody else."

Kim scowled. "Oh fuck," she said, raising her hand. "I'm in. But just for the record," she said, "this is a harebrained idea."

"Thanks, Sandra," Carla said, patting her on the shoulder.

"Well, now that that's settled," Sean said.

"Also for the record," Kim said, "I can fly and own a Cessna Two-Jay jumper."

The Cessna 2J was considered one of the best rockets for Class Four strips, and had the largest passenger capacity. For short suborbital hauls, it could carry up to eight spacesuited people.

"Would you be willing to lead the ground assault team?" Jack asked, pressing his luck.

"You. . ." Kim said. She looked around, then heaved a deep sigh. "I guess so."

Chapter 24

Tuesday 49 Virgo Year 52 11:45 local (March 20, 2074, 23:45 GMT)
VSRSS Volodka, Stickney Base, Phobos, Mars

JACK TOOK A DEEP BREATH, then knocked on Captain Mfume's cabin door on the *Volodka.* He'd only been topside for two days.

"Midshipman Williams, reporting as ordered, sir," he said.

"Enter," Mfume said, his voice clearly audible through the thin fiberglass.

Jack pulled himself in and closed the door behind him. The *Volodka* was moored at Stickney Base, Phobos, which meant that there was a definite 'up' and 'down' in the cabin, just very little gravity. Williams stood in front of the Captain.

"You wanted to see me, sir?" Jack said.

"Just how long did you think you could give me the mushroom treatment?"

"Sir?"

"Don't 'sir' me, Jack. This half-baked rescue you and that traveling salesman are cooking up."

"I'm not sure I know what you mean, sir," Jack said.

"Don't. I just got off the phone with your buddy Yardman."

"You mean Yeargan?"

"Whatever. He tried to give me some song and dance about 'duty' and all that, and even let slip that somebody was smuggling missiles in." Mfume glared. "But I think that what's really happening is Yeargan is looking for a private army he can rent cheap, and found us."

"Sir, we have people being held prisoner,"

"Damn it, son, do you think I don't know that!" Mfume barked. "But we don't go off on some private vendetta!"

"Regarding the missiles, this Colonel Slevnik,"

"Mike Slevnik?" Mfume asked, suddenly curious.

"I believe so, sir. He was investigating a General Mandrake."

"Larry Mandrake?" Mfume asked.

"I don't know," Jack replied.

"Stay put," Mfume said, turning away to his cabin's phone. He punched in a number, and a few seconds later Sean Yeargan's face appeared on the screen. "I'm going to put you on speaker—Jack's here."

"Hi Jack," Yeargan said. "Sorry—I just got off the phone with the Captain here..."

"Stow it," Mfume said. "What did Mike Slevnik tell you about Mandrake. Exactly."

"We've traded several messages," Yeargan said. "On the last one, the Colonel said these missiles were in relationship to something called 'Rhode Island Red.'"

Mfume shook his head in disgust. "Coops. The idiot that put Mandrake in charge of coops should be shot."

"Sir?" Jack said.

"A Rhode Island Red is a chicken," Mfume said, disgust dripping from his voice. "Chickens live in coops. 'COOP' is the military acronym for 'craft of opportunity.'"

"And?" Sean said.

"The plan was, in time of war, to impound and arm merchant ships. Deep spacers, obviously."

"So these missiles would arm pirates," Jack said.

"Ha," Mfume replied. "No, that idiot Mandrake was up to his eyebrows in the Manifest Destiny Movement."

"Who are?" Jack said.

"A bunch of crackpots who think that the Solar System is God's gift to America. My guess is that they'll use the missiles to try and seize control of Mars, and hope that the US will annex the place."

"I hardly think that China and India would just sit back and watch that," Yeargan said.

"'Think' and 'Mandrake' are words that don't go together," Mfume said. "The only reason he got a star, hell the only reason he got in the Air Force Academy in the first place, was because his mother was a Senator and his Grandmother a President."

"Seems like we have a problem, sir," Jack said.

"Yes we do!" Mfume said, glaring at him. "And, Midshipman Williams, if you expect to get very far in this organization, you'll learn to bring those problems up the chain of command."

There was nothing else to say. "Sir, yes sir."

"So how do you know Mandrake?" Yeargan asked.

"Mike and I were in the Academy together. Mandrake was two years ahead." Mfume looked at Sean. "Send me everything you've got on this." He turned and looked at Jack wearily. "Have a seat, Mister Williams. Tell me everything you know."

"Does that mean you're officially in?" Yeargan asked from the video.

"If Mike Slevnik's worried about this, then the shit is about to hit the fan," Mfume said. "So, yes, I'm in."

"I'll email you everything," Yeargan said.

"Good," Mfume said, "I'll call you after I've reviewed it." He broke the connection and looked at Jack. "Proceed."

Jack sat down. "First, sir, we believe that the hostages are being held on the ground."

Mfume rolled his eyes. "This shit gets better and better."

Sunday, 44 Virgo Year 52 14:00 local (March 26, 2074, 05:20 GMT)
Orbital Training Facility, Phobos, Mars

Jack blinked as a bead of sweat ran down from his forehead into his eye. It was one of the joys of gravity. It also made his spacesuit not just bulky but heavy.

He had been in orbit for a week since the meeting with Captain Mfume, a lot of that spent training here on the *Dahlia Mars CGM*, a member of Mars' 'broke fleet.' The *Dahlia Mars*, like the *Price* a Daewoo Type 15, had arrived at Mars to discover that CGM Shipping, their owner, had gone bankrupt. The various shippers and their insurance companies had stepped in to get the cargo offloaded, but were now wrapped up in a court battle with CGM over compensation. Until matters got sorted out on Earth, *Dahlia Mars* stayed put, moored in an out-of-the-way spot on Phobos.

The ship, pitch dark, creaked. *Probably thermal contraction. Or it could be a gunman at that corridor junction shifting his weight.*

There was only one way to find out. Jack crouched down as low as he could get in the confines of his spacesuit and shuffled along the deck, ghostly green through his night vision goggles.

At least these have a good field of vision. They were almost as wide as a pair of regular glasses, and only marginally heavier. Jack shifted his pistol to his right hand as he came to the end of the bulkhead. It was a flimsy fiberglass interior partition, certainly not bulletproof, but it at least obscured his body's outline. *Show time.*

Holding on to the bulkhead rail with his left hand, Jack pivoted on his left foot, trying to keep as much of his body behind the dubious cover as possible, and swung his pistol into the cross-corridor. He fired twice, the heavy revolver barking loudly in his hand, shooting at what would be waist height to a standing man.

The goggles blanked out most of the muzzle flash, but Jack waited a second before peeking out to see what, if anything, was waiting there.

"How come your MILES gear isn't buzzing?" Jack asked, standing up.

"I silenced it," Derek Lewis said, leaning back against the bulkhead. He looked quite comfortable in jeans and a T-shirt, with the harness of the Miles gear over it. The harness had several sensors, and when any of them were hit by an infrared laser, the device was supposed to emit a very annoying buzz as well as a strobe light. Jack's pistol had been modified to fire blanks, and every shot emitted a laser burst which would trigger the gear. It allowed for very realistic training.

"Why?"

"If this was a real ship you were clearing, would dead bad guys buzz?"

"Of course not."

"And you don't want to be suckered into something by listening to somebody moan, right?"

"Right," Jack said. He tapped a button on his sleeve, switching his radio to voice-activated. "Sector Charlie cleared."

Derek pulled a hand-held unit out of his back pocket. "Fin-ex, fin-ex," he said into the unit. "Faith, lights please. Everybody in the mess deck for hot wash."

A wash would be nice, Jack thought, but that's not what we're going to do. He holstered his pistol and turned off his goggles as the lights came up. Derek turned and walked back down the corridor to the mess deck with Jack following.

The ventilation had started by the time they arrived at the trio of booths that served as mess deck. Jack paused under a vent and let some cooler air blow down the back of his neck.

"Water?" Derek asked, standing next to a cooler they'd brought.

Jack nodded, and Derek tossed a plastic bottle at him, its flight path curving due to the centrifugal force of the hab deck's spin. Jack managed to get a hand on the wet bottle and hang on.

"Nice catch," Fencl said, walking into the space.

"Enjoy your nap?" Jack asked. She'd been 'shot' just inside the airlock when they arrived.

"Not really," she replied. "Do the heads work?"

"No," Derek said. "There's some piss-bags under the table."

Somebody, probably an insurance company, was paying Direktor Shipyards a small fee for maintenance. Frau Martinka Direktor, the shipyard's manager, let Space Rescue conduct 'non destructive training' on the ships in her care, for a small fee. Neither fee included providing working toilets.

"I'll hold it," Fencl said.

Jack glanced at her. She was somewhat famous for having an iron bladder. He unholstered his revolver and started to unload it. Like everybody else, he was carrying a six-shot Ruger, chambered in .357 Magnum, with an integrated laser sight. Rule 9.5 of the US Marine Corps "Rules for Gunfighting" was "Use a gun that works *every time*."

They'd tried five different types of semi-auto pistols, all with problems. The gas-operated types couldn't handle the sudden temperature and pressure changes from vacuum to ship normal. The blowback and recoil types worked once, but if the energy from the recoil was allowed to move the shooter, which happened nearly every time in zero gee, they jammed. So a revolver it was.

"We going to start this debrief?" Fencl asked.

Jack looked up. "Where's Cameron?"

"Coming, sir," Cameron said from behind Jack.

"Attention on deck!" Fencl barked.

"At ease," Captain Mfume said, walking into the room. "Proceed, Mister Williams."

"Aye, sir," Jack said. "Cameron, hit it, please."

Cameron shrugged. "Nothing to hit."

"What do you mean, 'nothing to hit?'" Fencl asked.

"I mean that you didn't do anything wrong," Cameron said. "Well, other than you getting shot, but that wasn't because you did anything particularly wrong."

"Somebody's got to be first in the door," Jack said.

"And sometimes the first guy in the door gets killed."

"So we're ready?" Jack asked.

"As ready as we can make you, sir," Derek said. He gestured at Captain Mfume. "Unless he has some other ideas."

"I don't," Mfume said. "But you're correct. Even if you do everything right, chances are somebody's going to get shot."

It was a sobering thought. "Yes sir," Jack finally said. He looked at Derek. "They haven't moved *Price* yet?"

"No sir. Any lower orbit and they'd get turbulence from Olympus Mons."

Jack looked at Captain Mfume. "Any news on the ground assault team, sir?"

"They are ready to go."

"Good." Jack looked around at his tired crew. "Clean guns and back to the ship. Twenty-four hour stand-down."

That got a few cheers, but only half-hearted. *They know that the real thing's on the other end of the stand-down.*

Chapter 25

Monday 48 Virgo Year 52 17:49 local (March 20, 2074, 00:49 GMT)
Bensonville, Republic of the White Race, Olympus Mons, Mars

WHAT A DUMP, Kelly thought. The windowless room was small, with barely room for a single metal bedstand and a fiberglass night table.

"Best room in the place," the landlady, a hard-bitten old woman, said. "Fifty a week, cash American."

Bensonville used American dollars, despite the fact that many of its residents had been kicked out for various crimes, racial and otherwise. Kelly did the conversion in his head. Twenty Euros. "What about meals?"

"That's extra. A dollar a day for breakfast or six a week, and two dollars a night for dinner. Lunch we'll talk about."

Well, Yeargan did say get a cheap place. Surely this was the cheapest flea palace in Bensonville. "I'll take it," he said. "Put me down for a week's breakfast and I'll be down for dinner shortly."

The old woman held out her hand. "That's cash in advance, please."

Kelly counted out three twenties from his front jeans pocket. "Mrs. Rybak, you can owe me another dinner."

"We eat promptly at six," she said, pocketing the money while nodding at an ancient clock on the bedside table. "Washroom's down the hall. Shower takes quarters, which I bet you don't have."

"Actually no, didn't think to ask at the currency exchange."

"I'll give you your change in quarters at dinner."

Once she left, Kelly tossed his duffle bag on the bed. He'd packed light. The only thing that might get him into trouble was the nine-millimeter automatic, which he'd wrapped up in a towel with a spare clip. He was a spy, not an assault team, and if he needed more than twenty rounds he was in very deep shit.

He put the pistol under the mattress near his head. Janet had been in town for a week now. She'd confirmed that Rachel was in town, and also thought she knew where the hostages were being held.

It was one thing to sneak around in the periphery of town. Even if they were on the lookout for Janet, the description would start "look for a blonde" but she couldn't very well walk up to Rachel Storey and start asking questions.

That was where Kelly came in. He had two jobs. First, figure out how to sneak a team into town, and more importantly, out. Second, figure out exactly what security they had around the hostages. Janet's last report had given him a lead.

"Rachel has a sister," the message had read. "It looks like the sister is involved."

Kelly needed to find the sister.

Dinner was served buffet-style, with Mrs. Rybak putting out food on the kitchen counter, and everybody sat at a dinette next to it. The food left much to be desired. Dinner was a tasteless and overcooked stew. He filled a plate, and joined his fellow boarders, expecting to be politely grilled.

Kelly's cover story was simple enough—he'd just had a nasty divorce (true) and his ex had cleaned him out (also true). She'd shacked up with a black man (true, but then he'd met his ex in Cuba and she was quite dark) at which point Kelly had blown a gasket and beat up the man (untrue, but not because of any great love for the prick). Finding himself the object of law enforcement interest, he'd left town. Clean, simple and explained why he didn't want people calling back to Port Lowell about him.

To his surprise, nobody asked him much of anything. His fellow boarders, a pair of ex-cons judging from their crude tattoos, barely spoke at all. Rybak's most profound question was about which "tee-vee" shows Kelly liked. Apparently that was what she called video serials, and Kelly wasn't surprised that her tastes were much different than his. As far as his efforts to gather information went, about all he learned was that one had to check 'yes' or 'no' for dinner by noon the next day. He doubted he'd be so lucky as to be rooming with the pirates, but you'd think in a small town like this gossip would get around.

Not that Kelly spent much time gossiping. His trip had been exhausting, so he went to bed early. When he came down the next morning, Kelly discovered that the breakfast menu consisted of toast, jam, coffee and juice. The dinner menu of roast pork was posted, written on a chalkboard, and Kelly noticed that his fellow boarders had both checked 'no' for dinner. Figuring that they knew something he didn't, and considering that he hadn't thought it possible to overcook stew but knowing you could overcook a roast, Kelly also checked no. After taking a fifty-cent shower, consisting of barely two minutes of lukewarm water, Kelly made a point of announcing that he was going out to look for work.

The advantage of 'looking for work' was that it gave Kelly an excuse to wander all over town. Not that there was much of town to wander around in. Bensonville was a small place. The figures Kelly had seen before leaving had suggested a population of just under three thousand, which actually made it fairly large by Republic standards. Turner Springs, the big city on the mountain, was barely over ten thousand.

Kelly's first stops were up and down the main retail street in town, Charles Street. There were a handful of businesses, standing in little forlorn clusters between rows of empty storefronts. There were more than a few residences on the main drag as well. He'd been in half a dozen such stores, glad he wasn't really in need of work, when he came to the town's bookstore. As he walked up, a portly older woman arrived at the front door, key in hand.

"Good morning," Kelly said to her.

She glanced up and squinted at him, a lock of graying hair falling over her face. "Morning. I'll be open in a minute."

"No hurry," Kelly replied.

She unlocked the door, putting a bit of body English into the frame to take pressure off of the lock.

"Looks like the frame is bent," Kelly said.

"You think?" She replied. "I spoke to the landlord last week about it, but he's not gotten back to me." She stepped inside, and Kelly followed.

"Just give me a second to get the lights on," she said, walking towards the back.

"No hurry, ma'am." Her reply, if any, was lost in the click of electrical switches. She came back up front, and stood behind a fiberglass counter that was trying to masquerade as wood.

"Now, sir, can I help you find something?"

"A job, actually."

"Oh, I'm sorry," she replied. "I barely make enough here to pay myself."

"What do you do when shipments arrive?"

"Shipments?"

"Of books."

She smiled. "We print on premises." She gestured at a plastic counter card. "Print on Demand."

"Oh," Kelly said. "Bookstores I saw in Port Lowell got shipments in."

"Probably less then you think," the lady said. "It's much cheaper to print them up locally. No returns, and no shipments from Earth." She gestured at a large metal rack in the front of the store. "Some of our bestsellers are right there. They're mostly display copies, of course. But if there's not a second copy there, I can print up anything you want. Now if you'll excuse me for just a minute, I need to put some coffee on."

As she headed towards the back room, Kelly decided to check out the selection, starting with the bestseller lists.

Number one on the list was "A True White Man; The Story of Charles Benson Senior." She had two copies, shelved face out. Second on the list was a single copy of "The Turner Diaries" with a cover of a white man bayoneting a black man while a white girl cowered in a corner. The rest of the selection apparently went down from there.

Kelly had decided to buy the Benson book as cover when the front door opened. A young girl, high school aged with straight black hair, walked in. Her jeans were low-cut, and between the jeans and her skimpy T-shirt, there was a good hands-breath of exposed skin around her waist.

She ignored him and went straight to the counter, where the owner was standing, a mug in her hand.

"You get my book printed, Mrs. O'Malley?" the girl asked.

She scowled as she put down her mug. "You know, I don't agree with your reading material, Miss Storey."

Storey? Not that common a name. Kelly, the Benson book in his hand, stopped at another rack closer to the counter and tried to listen in.

"What's wrong with it?" the girl asked.

"This Obama fellow was black," O'Malley said.

"So? He was a President too."

"I still think you shouldn't be reading his book," O'Malley said. "I've got a biography of him I can print out for you."

"You mean the one by Kellogg?" the girl said. "I read that in the library. It's a hatchet job and the guy's a crap writer."

"I realize Miss Rachel is more, well, free-thinking," O'Malley said, somehow making 'free-thinking' sound dirty, "but you're just a child."

"My money's green," Storey said. "You got my book or not?"

"Actually no, but I can print it up for you in a minute."

"I'll wait," Storey said, in a tone used by put-upon teenagers everywhere.

O'Malley gestured over the girl's shoulder at Kelly. "Are you ready to buy? That book I keep on inventory."

"Take care of the girl," Kelly said. "I'm still looking."

"A liberated man, are we?" the Storey girl asked as O'Malley walked into the back room.

"Pardon?"

The girl pointed at the bookshelf where he was standing. Kelly realized it was labeled "Women's Interests," which couldn't have been more inappropriate for his cover. He grinned and tried to hide his embarrassment.

"Research on the opposition," he said.

"Oh," the girl said. "I haven't seen you around, have I?"

"Probably not," Kelly said. He held out his hand. "James Connor. Call me Jim. I just got into town last night."

"Jim," the girl said, taking his hand, "I'm Minty."

"I'm sure you are," Kelly said.

"No, that's my name. Arminta Ann Storey. I go by Minty."

"Nice to meet you, Minty," Kelly said.

"What brings you here?"

"Work," Kelly said. "Well, trying to find work."

"Oh. What do you do?"

"I can do just about anything," Kelly said. "Last job was in construction, dome-fitting." It was the first job he could think of, and one that he'd actually done. The fact that it didn't fit with his cover was a problem. Kelly gestured at the back room, hoping to change the subject. "If she gets mad at you, does she do stuff like print pages upside down?"

"She would if she knew how to operate her equipment," Minty replied. "But it's really an automated black box. She just selects a title and it prints. You'd have to get into system settings to muck it up."

"Oh," Kelly said. "Shouldn't you be in school today?"

"We're on break for a half-month," she said. "So what does a dome-fitter do?"

Obviously Bensonville followed one of the Martian calendars with sixty-day-long months. "Takes panes of glass for agri-domes and schleps them around, installs them in the dome framework, then makes sure they seal up."

"Not much call for that around here."

"I've done other stuff."

"I'd tell you to try the warehouses, but with school on break a lot of kids picked up jobs there."

"Well, they'll need somebody when school goes back," Kelly said. "Your mother's okay with your reading?"

A cloud passed over the girl's face. "I wouldn't know."

Kelly gestured at the back room, confused. "She was talking about 'Miss Rachel'..."

"Rachel's my sister."

"Oh," Kelly said. *Contact made.* "Say, you know if anybody's hiring? I'm new in town..."

Chapter 26

Tuesday 49 Virgo Year 52 10:15 local (March 21, 2074, 06:15 GMT) Bensonville, Republic of the White Race, Olympus Mons, Mars

After Minty went on her way, Kelly, armed with his book, checked out the other half dozen businesses on Charles Street. He made a note to go back to the Eagle's Lair, a bar-restaurant, that evening. It wasn't open for lunch yet, but besides promising better food then Rybak's burnt offerings, it appeared to be a community hangout, and a likely place for information. Pirates had friends, and friends liked to have a drink once in a while.

Charles Street ran east-west, and there were eight or ten cross streets, more on the south of Charles then north. It made sense. What little economic activity that took place in Bensonville was transshipment of stuff to the interior of Olympus. This took place via the road and warehouse network on the north side of town. People lived on the south side, and worked on the north.

Kelly had reached the east end of Charles Street, closest to the elevators which were the only overland way off of the mountain. He'd come in that way last night. It might not be a bad way to get a team into town, but everything he saw from the street end confirmed that forcing an exit out that way would be disastrous.

To get from the street to the elevators, one had to walk thru a metal gate, protected by a ticketing booth. Kelly couldn't tell for sure if the glass there was bulletproof or not, but there was no obvious way to quietly force your way past it.

Calling the thing he'd ridden up in an 'elevator' was like calling a whale a fish. The mountain Olympus, more like a plateau, rose out of the Tharsis plains in a ring of cliffs. Bensonville was at the top of the cliff on the east edge of the mountain, a good two kilometers of near-vertical drop down to the Tharsis plain. There were two massive elevators, each more like Staten Island ferries than 'elevators,' running up and down on an exposed steel frame parallel to the cliff face. Vehicles were driven on to the lower level of the elevators, arriving and leaving through a vast enclosed and pressurized marshalling area, while pedestrians and drivers could make the ride in a pressurized upper level.

Hell, there was a snack bar in the upper level of the elevators, unsurprising since each lift took twenty minutes or so. A long time for an alarm to be raised and the elevator brought back up. Assuming you got past the ticket booth and timed it to arrive when a lift was scheduled. More to stay in cover than anything else, he walked up to the ticket counter.

"Do you know if they're hiring?" he asked the clerk, a gray-haired lady who could be a twin to Mrs. Rybak.

"Don't know," the woman replied, "but you can fill out an application."

"What's the web address?" Kelly asked.

"We do it by paper," she said. "Got a pen?"

Kelly took the paper form, a bad photocopy, from the lady and filled it out on a nearby bench, using the book as a clipboard.

When he returned the application, the lady looked at it and said, "So you're staying at my sister's?"

"I am?"

"Yessir. Candice Rybak, used to be Hornfeldt, is my sister. We're twins."

"Oh," Kelly said. "Nice to meet you."

Cindy Robards proved to be moderately more talkative then her sister, but that wasn't saying much. Kelly took his leave of her when a couple of paying customers came up, reminded of what a small town this place was.

Kelly walked down the second street going south from Charles, named creatively enough Second Street. About three doors down there was a storefront, closed, with the name "Joe's Import & Export" painted on the glass window. A handwritten note on a piece of paper next to the door handle said "Moved to 221 Second Street."

"Might as well see if Joe's hiring," Kelly said under his breath. Actually, Joe's place was being used to hold the prisoners, according to Janet. But somebody looking for work would certainly try there, right?

He continued south down the dimly-lit and deserted street. *Everybody's at work.* Like most of the town, only every other overhead light was on. The street itself, rough-cut volcanic rock, was dark, and seemed to suck in the light. Posting street numbers didn't seem to be high on anybody's priority list, nor were there obvious block breaks. Still, it *was* a small town.

He walked down the center of the street. To his right was a narrow alley, and as he walked, a door just north of the alley opened and a very short man with a bad comb-over stepped out. The man, with the bleached skin and hair of somebody who spent a lot of time out in the hyper-oxidized sands of Mars, had a large pistol strapped to his hip, which looked gigantic on him, and was wearing a paint-stained T-shirt. He was carrying a folding chair in his hand, which he sat down in front of the door. Minty Storey walked out of the same door immediately behind him, still carrying her book.

"Hi Mister Connor," she said with a half wave.

"Call me Jim," Kelly said, walking up to her.

"Who the hell are you?" the short man asked.

"David," Minty said, "this is Jim Connor. Jim, this is David Eggman."

The short man, Eggman, eyed Kelly suspiciously. "What are you doing here?"

Kelly had a bad moment trying to remember his cover. "Looking for Joe's Import & Export," Kelly said, gesturing back towards the main street. "It said he moved here. I was hoping he was hiring."

"Joe was my brother-in-law," Eggman said, "and he's been dead for a couple of mears now."

"I'm sorry," Kelly said. Eggman didn't seem too upset about his brother-in-law's death. "I saw the note in the storefront that he'd moved..."

"To here," Eggman said, craning his neck back. "But we're not hiring either."

"Oh, sorry. You wouldn't know who is?"

"Do I look like a placement agency?" Eggman asked.

"No, just a fellow white man."

A bit of the gruffness faded. "You know anything about fueling rockets?"

"I did that in the Air Force, back on Earth."

"Now that Locklin's dead, I hear they're looking for a fuel man at the 'port."

"What happened to him?" Kelly blurted out. Maybe I'm not cut out for this spy business?

"Accident," Minty said. "When he was on vacation."

"Oh," Kelly said. "I'm sorry." He looked around. "Where's the spaceport?"

"Other end of town, off of Ninth Street," Minty said, pointing. "You'll probably want your 'suit."

"It's at Mrs. Rybak's," Kelly replied. "I'm staying there. I guess that's on the way."

"It is," Minty said. "Got plans for lunch?"

"Something cheap," Kelly said.

"Can't beat the Eagle's Lair," Minty said, "especially since I'm buying."

That earned her a raised eyebrow from Eggman.

It also simplified Kelly's life. A job at the spaceport would be very helpful for smuggling people in, and lunch with Minty would get him in with the pirates.

"What a bitch!" Minty said. Kelly and Minty were sitting in a booth in the back of the Eagle's Lair, and he had told her the cover version of his divorce. It had just opened for lunch when they arrived, and Minty had grabbed the booth. She finished the beer she'd ordered with lunch as punctuation.

"What exactly is the drinking age here?" Kelly asked.

"Old enough to reach the bar, I guess," Minty replied. "Nobody seems to have asked."

"I guess I'm still used to Earth," Kelly said. "You say that like you're not from here."

"I'm not. Rachel and I moved here a Mear ago."

Right after the *Witchcraft* and *Windy City* attacks, Kelly noted. I wonder what went south.

"What brought y'all here?"

Minty grimaced. "Don't ask."

"That's not fair. I told."

"You could have said 'don't ask.'"

She has a point. A few more customers had dribbled in, but the place was at best half-full. The waitress breezed by and put a piece of paper on the table. It took Kelly a minute to realize that it was the bill for lunch.

"Any kids?" Minty asked.

"No. You know, I probably ought to get a move on."

"The port here's not very busy. Locklin spent a lot of time hanging around at the store."

"The store?"

"My sister runs an art gallery," Minty said, reaching for the check, "and before you ask, no she's not hiring."

"I'm surprised that a town this size can support an art gallery."

"It can't," Minty said. "But don't tell my sister."

"So Locklin was an art fancier?"

"Actually, I think he was putting the moves on my sister. Funny thing about a small town—it's like playing Monopoly. Eventually, you land on every property. But I wouldn't be asking around about him."

"Why not?"

"Just because," she said. She pulled out a wallet from her back pocket, like a boy, and counted out cash. Kelly noted the check was even handwritten.

"Thanks for lunch," Kelly said. He pointed at the bill. "Not to look under the hood of a gift car, but why?"

"Let's just say I wanted to scope you out."

Kelly smiled. "I guess I'm flattered."

"You should be," Minty replied with a straight face.

Kelly didn't know how to take that, so he forced a grin.

After lunch, Kelly suited up and headed west on Charles Street then south on Ninth. Ninth Street ended in a large vehicle airlock, flanked by a smaller pedestrian lock. A sign pointed up a flight of stairs to 'Spaceport Terminal.'

At the top of the stairs was a large waiting area, empty, but with large glass windows looking out over the Martian sands. Kelly walked in, and headed down a narrow hallway running over the airlock and parallel to the bank of windows. He came to what was obviously a prefabricated control room, the metal pressure door propped open by a pair of spacesuit boots.

"I've heard of sleepy spaceports," Kelly said, popping his head into the control room.

The sole occupant, a sandy-haired man in his late forties, woke up in mid-snore. He looked at Kelly with one eye, feet still propped up on a console.

"Radio volume's full up," he said, jerking a thumb in the general direction of a bank of speakers. Kelly could just hear the hiss of static. "And so is the contact alarm on the approach radar."

"You have approach radar?"

"Why wouldn't we?"

Well, Class Four strips didn't usually have radars, and technically weren't required to have a controller on duty. Neither of these things were something Jim Connor would know. "It seems like an awfully small port for something expensive like radar," Kelly improvised.

"Radar's not that costly," the man said with a smile. "Besides, ours fell off of a truck."

Stolen, in other words. "You in charge?"

"For now. Who's asking?"

"Jim Connor," Kelly said, sticking out his hand. "A guy in town named Eggman said you might be needing a fuel man."

"Dean McIlhaney," the man said, offering his hand. "Director of Operations here. Shorty's right—I do need a fuel man."

"I did that in the Air Force, back on Earth," Kelly said. "I might be a bit rusty."

McIlhaney waved out the window. "We're not that busy." He swung his feet off of the console. "You ready for an interview?"

McIlhaney idea of an interview consisted of locking out to the surface, where he quizzed Kelly on the operation of the fueling equipment and general refueling procedures. Fueling was accomplished by dragging flex-hoses from a standpipe and making the necessary connections. Pumping and valve operation was handled from the control room via a fueling console, although there were a set of manual cutout valves in a room under the passenger waiting area. It was, in short, pretty simple.

"Your rig here's pretty standard," Kelly said, "but I don't know a lot about these type of ships." He gestured at a pair of Bombardier VTLs, but McIlhaney's back was to him.

"Well, there's only about a dozen ships based here, so you'll learn those soon enough. As far as visitors, we don't get a lot of those, but we've got the standard databases. If you get a new bird, just print out the checklist."

He'd seen a printer and PC in the valve room, right next to a small airlock to the surface. "Sounds reasonable."

"So, when can you start?"

"Now. I suppose I should ask about hours and pay."

They quickly reached agreement on those details, and McIlhaney put Kelly to work fueling one of the Bombardiers for a late afternoon launch. Kelly was just finishing up when he saw the crew for that rocket step out of the airlock. One of the figures was a very short man with a very big gun, worn in a holster on his hip. The man's suit had a picture on his chest of an egg with two human legs sticking out.

After work, Kelly stopped at Rybak's to change and shower. There was a shower, with free water even, at the spaceport, so Kelly planned to use it in future. After getting cleaned up, he headed out to the Eagle's Lair.

The 'worker's special' dinner there wasn't half bad, which was a marked improvement over Rybak's. The Lair had a long table set up next to the kitchen, and for three dollars served meatloaf, mashed potatoes and green beans, coffee or lemonade and a piece of apple pie. One of the ex-cons from Rybak's sat across the table from Kelly.

"Always come here on Wednesdays," the guy said. "Wednesdays is meatloaf and apple pie." It was more then he'd said at dinner and breakfast combined.

"Thanks, I will," Kelly told him. He speared the last bit of apple pie and washed it down with his coffee. Leaving a small tip, Kelly walked up to the bar area. A small cluster of people, mostly serious drinkers by the looks of them, had gathered.

"I'll take a beer," Kelly told the barmaid.

She flashed him a gap-toothed smile and said, "Dark or light?"

"I'll try the light," Kelly said.

She walked away and returned with a light yellow beer. It wasn't Budweiser, but it was drinkable. Kelly took his beer and headed into a side room. A fake wooden sign, probably plastic made on Earth, advertised it as the 'Fun Side.' There were a pair of ancient arcade game consoles on the wall, and a trio of dingy pool tables in the middle.

He walked up to one of the game consoles, occupied by a woman, brunette, wearing tight jeans and a long-sleeve T-shirt.

"Not going to happen tonight," she said as he approached. "Don't really care what you tell your boyfriends." It was a shooting game, and she pointed a plastic pistol at the screen.

"Can I at least get a minute so it's not so obvious?"

"Sure," Janet told him. "But don't make me lose this game."

"I won't."

"Where are you staying?"

"Rybak's boarding house on Fourth." Kelly looked over his shoulder. They were alone in the room. "I ran into Rachel's sister today."

"Minty? Yeah, I saw you two at the bookstore."

He hadn't seen her, which for some reason bothered him. But he pushed on. "Looks like she's got some information."

"Oh?"

"Yeah. I saw her walking out of the prison."

"Good. So how many guards?"

The woman was nothing if not single-minded. "I haven't asked yet."

"Well don't, stupid. Get her to talk about all the exciting stuff in town."

"How do I do that?"

"Tell her this place is boring." The game console played a mournful tune, and Janet made a face at it. "I died."

"Like she doesn't know that?"

"She's fucking sixteen. Every sixteen-year-old thinks that they're the only people in the world who get it." Janet fished in her pocket and produced another dollar coin out. "Got a job yet?"

"The spaceport. I'm working there as a fuel man. They got a radar with an automatic alarm."

"Cool," Janet said, restarting the game. "That radar needs to go off. You tried to check in with the folks back home?"

"No. I'll do so tonight."

"Okay," she said. In a louder voice, she said, "hey, dude, clean the crap outta your ears. I'm busy here!"

"Suit yourself, babe," Kelly said. He strolled off, taking a gulp of his beer.

Chapter 27

Tuesday 49 Virgo Year 52 18:15 local (March 20, 2074 02:15 GMT) Bensonville, Republic of the White Race, Mars

"ASK ME HOW MY DAY WENT," Minty said, putting the platter of baked chicken back in the center of the table, having taken two pieces. Rachel had no idea how she ate so much without blimping out. Tony Lords had joined them, since his wife and daughter had gone to Turner Springs for a baby shower.

"How'd your day go?" Rachel said.

"Met Bensonville's newest resident," Minty said.

"Dolores' baby drop?" Tony asked.

"Don't be crude," Rachel said.

"No, Dolores did not have her baby," Minty said. Rachel was surprised - the woman looked ready to burst. Dolores was a tiny woman, and the local betting pool had Ed Prell as the odds-on favorite for baby daddy. He was a big man. "So who else is due?" Rachel asked.

"Not a baby," Minty said around a mouthful of chicken. "Man moved into town."

"Why?" Tony asked.

"That's what I asked him over lunch," Minty said. "Considering that he'd been sniffing around outside the hostages' barracks."

"We're calling that dump a 'barracks' now?" Tony asked.

"You have an amazing ability to go straight to the capillary, Tony," Rachel said. *Probably nothing. Strangers wander up here all the time.*

"Shouldn't that be 'jugular?'?" Tony asked.

"Not in your case. What exactly were you doing at the barracks?"

"Shorty,"

"Mister Eggman to you," Rachel said.

"Has me tutoring his son," Minty said. "I stopped by to get paid. Speaking of paid, aren't Class B folks supposed to get paid in advance?"

"No, actually," Tony said. "So, Minty, who is this mystery man?"

"Calls himself Jim Connor." Minty told them about Connor's divorce. She ended by saying, "and he got a job as fuel-man at the 'port."

Fuel man. Locklin's old job. McIlhaney was supposed to keep that open for Locklin's son when he got back from Turner Springs.

"Why was he at the barracks?" Rachel asked.

"Supposedly looking for Joe's Import and Export."

"Guy had to be really hard up to move here looking for work," Tony said.

"It's the part about being from Port Lowell that worries me," Minty said. "I mean, the Space Rescue guys are from there, right?"

Well, the girl's not a complete idiot.

"It is the biggest town on Mars," Rachel said.

"Sending one guy doesn't make much sense," Tony added.

"Unless they want somebody to scope out the place," Minty said.

"How would they know to send somebody here?" Tony asked.

Damn good question. "They wouldn't," Rachel said.

"Question," Minty said, reaching for another biscuit, "how trustworthy is our cut-out man?"

"Bryce?" Rachel said. "He doesn't get paid unless we get paid."

"More likely this Connor guy's just a drifter," Tony said.

"And if he's not?" Minty asked, looking over her water glass at her.

"Picking him up will tip off whoever sent him," Rachel said. "Besides, I'd like to get some more information."

"Such as?" Minty asked.

"Part of running an interrogation, sis," Rachel said, "Is being able to ask questions that you already know the answer to."

Minty chewed on that thought for a second. "So you can catch him in a lie?"

"You're learning, dear."

Minty had the grace to blush. "I'm trying, sis."

"Sounds like a plan," Tony said. "I'll keep it under my helmet. Chuck gets kinda reactionary sometimes."

He meant 'reactionary' in the sense of 'over-reacts' which was common usage in the town.

"I took some notes," Minty said, fishing out a piece of paper from her back pocket. "I figure Rachel can have somebody check out his story."

Rachel almost looked around for her phantom 'somebody' to help.

"Did you get enough to eat?" Rachel asked as she walked Tony to the door.

"Yes, thanks," Tony replied. "You heard about Junior's latest brainstorm, right?"

"No," Rachel said. "I thought you needed a brain to have a brainstorm."

"Be careful," Tony said, "Junior's the type to cut out somebody's tongue but not kill them."

"It's just us two."

"Yeah, well anyway, Junior's decided that those missiles must be worth a lot of money."

"They probably are."

"Yeah, well, he's going to try and get the investors to trade us—their cut for the missiles."

Rachel felt a chill down her spine. "That might get dangerous."

"You think so?" Tony took her arm. "Our mystery man might be looking for the Space Rescue dudes. He could also be scouting us out for the investors."

"I'll be careful."

"Please do."

I wish she'd wear a robe, Rachel thought as Minty came into the kitchen, her dark hair matted from sleep. Minty was wearing an old t-shirt as a nightgown.

"You're up early," Minty said, stifling a yawn.

"Tony called—his wife's back from the shower."

"Finally, huh?"

There'd been a sandstorm, which had delayed Mrs. Lord's return for two days.

"So," Rachel replied. "You sure this guy's name was Connor?"

"Yes. Your guy finally get back to you?"

Minty had Chuckle's understanding of time zones, which was to say none. Rachel decided to ignore that problem.

"Well, nobody named 'Connor' got a divorce in Port Lowell for the last mear."

"I guess we need to have Chuckle's boys pick him up," Minty said.

"Have some coffee," Rachel said, offering the pot to her.

"I'm good."

"Well, you're not," Rachel said. "So he lied."

"Yes."

"And we didn't? If half the folks in town knew my previous employer was a damn African country they'd space us."

"Your point, sis?"

"Just because he's lying about his past doesn't mean that he's got anything to do with our piracy."

"A coincidence?"

"Maybe. Or maybe you're inventing spooks out of thin air."

"If you say so, sister."

"I do." Rachel took a deep breath. "You need to pay him another visit. We need more information."

"That's going to be a problem," Minty said. "I'm flying up for a shift guarding the ship."

"When?"

"Lift at five."

"Maybe I should take our mystery man out to dinner?"

"Just dinner," Minty said. "If he's legit I got dibs on him."

"He's too old for you."

Minty stuck her tongue out. "He's experienced, not old."

Rachel knocked on Minty's door later that afternoon.

"Come in," Minty said.

Rachel did. Minty's room was a mixture of little-girl pink and dark teenager, and even more of a mess than usual. Minty was sitting on the floor, cleaning her AR-15 while using a bed sheet to catch the oil.

"Can we talk?" Rachel asked.

"Sure," Minty said.

"I don't think you'll have any problems up there," Rachel said.

"I hear a 'but' coming."

"But if you do, I want to give you something."

"Your Glock?" Minty looked up, her eyes gleaming with avarice.

"No, something more useful," Rachel said. "Cash, for one." Rachel handed over a small roll of bills. "For emergencies, and it's a loan, so I want it all back."

"Got it," Minty said, stuffing the bills into the back pocket of her jeans. "That it?"

"No," Rachel said. "A name and a number." She handed over another piece of paper.

"Who's Steve Bryce?" Minty asked, reading from the paper.

"A lawyer. Not the most honest one, but he'll do."

"What's this for?"

"If, if things go to shit and we get separated, don't try and call me here." Rachel pointed at the paper. "Call him."

"Why not you here?"

"If things go to shit, I may not be here."

Chapter 28

Monday 55 Virgo Year 52 18:15 local (March 27, 2074 16:15 GMT)
Bensonville, Republic of the White Race, Mars

"SO, MISTER CONNOR," Rachel asked from across the table, "what exactly are your intentions regarding my sister?"

They were sitting in the 'side garden' at The Lamp Post, the other restaurant in town. It wasn't much of a garden, more of an empty lot on Third Street behind the main restaurant. The stone roof of the habitation dome was still three stories above them, although it had a skylight cut into it. It was the height of summer and the sun was still out, causing a wan gray light to drift down into the space.

"My intentions?" Kelly asked with a smile. "That's a rather old-fashioned way of speaking."

Rachel shrugged. "Sometimes the old ways are the good ways."

"Well, ma'am, you can relax. My intentions are limited to buying her lunch." *That and figuring out what the internal security arrangements are like at the jail.* He smiled reassuringly at Rachel. *Maybe you can help me there?*

"Lunch?"

"I owe her one—she bought the first day I was here."

"Oh," Rachel said. "So, is Mrs. Rybak's cooking as bad as I've heard?"

"Worse," Kelly replied. "You wouldn't believe the goop she served Monday." Rybak had served a tasteless mess of noodles and tomatoes with a few flecks of chicken she'd called spaghetti. At least she hadn't been able to burn that, although it might have been better used as fuel than food. "What she doesn't overcook has no taste at all," Kelly added.

"So why eat there?"

"Nothing's open on Monday," Kelly said. He gestured at their salads. "Besides, the price is right. I wouldn't be doing this if I hadn't just got paid."

"Well, since I asked you to dinner," Rachel said, "I should pay."

"Thank you. Now I owe a lunch and a dinner."

"Nonsense," Rachel said, waving her hand at him. "You're a single man. You don't owe us anything." Rachel took a bite of her salad, then said, "I hear you're working at the port. How is it?"

"Okay. It's a full day."

"It seemed like Locklin had more time off."

"He probably did. I only fueled two rockets yesterday, but McIlhaney's got me doing other stuff too. Painting and handyman crap." Kelly leaned over the table. "I think he's just trying to keep an eye on the new guy."

Their main courses arrived, interrupting the conversation for a minute.

"So where'd you say Minty went to?" Kelly asked after cutting his chicken.

"Band camp in Turner Springs," Rachel said.

Which was funny, Kelly thought, since I could have sworn I saw her get on a rocket this afternoon.

"Do you need to be kept an eye on?" Rachel asked.

"No," Kelly said, talking around a really tasty bite of grilled chicken. He swallowed. "You know, I'm confused. What brought you here?"

Rachel smiled. "What do you mean, 'brought?'"

"You don't seem like you're from around here originally."

"No, I'm not a White Power forever chick," Rachel said. She reached for her glass of wine. "You know, that's what they call the women's sports teams here. 'White Power Chicks.'"

"Then why are you here?"

She sat her wine glass down carefully before answering. "Some things aren't fit for discussion."

"Like why Eggman's sitting outside a supposedly unused building with a pistol on his hip?"

"Shorty always carries that pistol. Hell, he probably takes a shower with it."

"You didn't answer my question."

"Show me yours and I'll show you mine."

"I'm simple," Kelly said. "Wife ran off with a black man. Your turn."

"I came for my health. The waters."

"What waters? This is a volcano."

"I was misinformed," Rachel said.

No, you're playing me.

"You talked to your brother lately?" Rachel asked.

"Who?" Kelly said. "Oh, yeah. Called him last night." He didn't have a brother, actually. The call was to Sean Yeargan.

"Everything okay back home?"

"I guess. Tamara is bitching about money." Tamara was his ex-wife, and she probably was bitching about money.

"I thought she was shacked up with a guy?"

"She is. He's broke and she didn't get as much from our split as she thought she was owed."

"Sounds like a good reason not to get married."

"Oh but I loved her dearly once."

"Now, is your brother older then you or younger?"

"Younger," Kelly said.

"Only one brother, right?"

"Only one. Why?"

"Curious. Doing anything tomorrow night?"

"Working."

"Huh?"

"Boss says he's got some overnight flights scheduled."

Rachel gave him a disbelieving look. "Overnight flights from here? Who's flying?"

"No idea. I just fuel them." It was actually the truth. He wouldn't know who was on the ship until it left.

"Oh. Sucks to be you."

"It's overtime," Kelly said with a shrug.

"Then I'll bring you a plate."

"Thanks, but don't bother," Kelly said. "McIlhaney's covering us both."

"If you say so," Rachel said.

Well, this meeting's a bust. She's not giving me anything.

* * *

When Rachel got home she called Bam Bam.

"I was just about to call you," Bam Bam said when her face popped up on the screen.

"About what?" Rachel asked.

"Supposedly the money's coming through day after tomorrow," Bam Bam said. "You and I need to be upstairs. We're supposed to be on tomorrow night's flight."

"That flight was why I was calling. What's going on?"

"Somebody's got to move the ships," Bam Bam replied, an exasperated look on her face. "The crew and I handle *Price*, while you take care of *Cranston*."

"The special container?"

"Chuckles said that the investors have a self-loader."

A ship with its own crane to move the container. "Are the crew still buying that bullshit about you being a hostage?"

Bam Bam shrugged. "They should. They were told I'm being held on the *Price*. Besides, I'll be gone as soon as we hit Phobos."

Rachel hoped so, because Bam Bam's story didn't hold much water. But that wasn't why Rachel had called. "Did your dad tell you about this Connor fellow?"

"Yes. He's cute for a guy."

Rachel glanced at her, eyebrows arched.

"What?" Bam Bam said. "You're the only chick in town who can go both ways?"

Rachel ignored the comment. "Connor can't seem to keep straight whether or not his brother is older or younger than him," Rachel blurted out. "Or whether his brother lives in Port Lowell or Earth."

Bam Bam reflected for a second. "So he's a bad liar?"

"It all makes sense," Rachel said, feeling a bit desperate. "Tell us they're going to pay, so we relax our guard. Then they hit us."

"We need to tell Chuckles," Bam Bam said.

"I wouldn't," Rachel said. "He might blow the deal. And what if this Connor dude is just some flake?"

"You're right, of course," Bam Bam said. "But we're all supposed to be upstairs."

"I'll delay my departure," Rachel said. "Unless you're taking up the crew tomorrow."

"No, not until the cash is in the bank," Bam Bam said.

"Good. Tell Chuckles that I'm feeling under the weather and I'll go up with the prisoners."

"Okay, then what?"

"I'll bring 'Connor' over for dinner," Rachel said. "I do have a pair of handcuffs, you know."

"I seem to recall that," Bam Bam replied, rubbing her wrist with her hand. "Be careful."

"I always am."

Chapter 29
Monday 55 Virgo Year 52 17:15 local (March 27, 2074 9:15 GMT)
Stickney Base, Phobos, Mars

"YOU LOOK A LITTLE GREEN AROUND THE GILLS, sir," Sandra Kim said, a smug look on her face as she sipped a soft drink from a metallic foil packet.

"I feel a little green," Sean said. Actually, he felt more than a little green. Phobos' gravity was practically zero, so most of the manned spaces were in one or another spinning pressure vessel buried under the surface. This tiny conference room on the Space Rescue base, featuring a window facing an angry red Mars, wasn't spun for gravity. Sean's head was never good for freefall. To make matters worse, he'd had to transit three or four spinning sections to get here. The quick transitions from fake gravity to no gravity just made his head worse.

"You want a pop?" Jack said, another soft drink packet in his hand.

"No, thanks," Sean said. Jack was upside down to him, and just looking at Jack almost caused him to lose his lunch. "Let's get started."

"Sure thing," Jack said. He pulled himself right-side up next to the stand-up conference table.

"Let's go over Jack's part first," Sean said. He nodded at Jack, who called up an orbital track chart on the display which served as the top of the table.

"The *Price* is in a low orbit, and marks on top of Olympus every sixty-one minutes. Leaving in two shuttles from Phobos base..."

"Why not depart from the *Volodka*?" Sandra asked. "She could get you a lot closer."

"She's technically still in workups," Jack said.

"So?"

"So," Sean said, "If she were to suddenly leave the docks, somebody might make a call."

"At any rate, we've got three windows in every 24 hour period," Jack said. "Each window is roughly eight hours apart. We want to launch at 0715 hours Martian Prime tomorrow. With flight time, that puts us on target to the ships at 2315 Olympus time."

"But you're not launching until Chief Kelly calls in, right?" Sandra asked.

"We'll launch before he calls, but not attack," Jack said.

Jack clicked through the display, graphically showing the proposed flight path. "Besides arriving at night local time, Olympus will be just falling below their horizon."

"They won't be able to talk to their base for thirty minutes, during which you should be able to secure the ships," Sean said.

"Assuming they're not paying for a satellite relay," Sandra said.

"Janet checked that out," Sean said. "The only satellite relay is to CIAM-Sat-4."

"That's a commercial Internet access link," Sandra said. "It can do a secondary feed to anything within a light-second of Mars."

"Janet checked. They are using a directional array for orbital comms."

"Wonder how many pirates she fucked to get that information," Sandra asked.

"As many as it took, dear," Sean said, letting his irritation show. "Let's move on."

Jack changed the display to a trio of their best telescopic photos of the *Price*. "As you can see, the *Price* is docked with a Bombardier Mosquito."

Mosquito is a good name for it, Sean thought. It looked tiny attached to the dorsal docking port on the *Price*.

"Since Mosquitoes' only have a single docking collar," Jack said, calling up a schematic on the display, "they must be using one of the *Price's* collars for resupply. The way the ships are configured, we'll fly our approach on the *Price's* ventral bow, and attempt to gain access via the ventral service airlock at this junction."

Jack changed the display again to a line drawing of the ship with a flight path. He was basically flying 'under' the bow of the ship, and attaching to the bottom. "Given where the pilothouses of the two ships are, this approach will be invisible."

"Radar?" Sandra asked.

"Off," Sean said. "One of our hams checked."

"I assume one of these boats will stand off while the other docks?" Sandra said, pointing to the schematic, which showed two shuttles.

"No, actually," Jack said. "Neither ship will dock. We'll cross via suitjets and attack both ships at once."

Jack's team had eleven people all told—two pilots, a medic and eight for the boarding party. Per Kelly, the pirates had "four or five" people guarding the ship.

"How are you getting in the Mosquito?" Sandra said.

"There's a two-man airlock just aft of the centrifuge," Sean said, reaching over to call up a schematic. "Cameron and Derek will go in there first, with two more shooters following."

"It might work," Sandra said. "What's the fallback plan?"

"Just that," Jack said. "Fall back."

"I'd still like to wait on my assault until the *Price* is secured," Sandra said.

"We've been over that," Sean said. He wondered if she was getting cold feet. "For all we know, they check in with the ground every time they regain signal."

"Doubtful," Sandra said.

"But if they do," Sean said, "and the orbital crew's missed a check-in, your group could be flying into an alerted town. Do you really want to try to shoot your way through three thousand white supremacists?" He took her silence for a no. "Okay, Lieutenant, your turn."

Sandra changed the display to show a split screen, one part an orbital photo of Bensonville, the other part a rough map hand drawn by Kelly and Janet. "After we get Kelly's all clear call, we launch from Bradbury in three Cessnas timed to arrive at Bensonville at 2315 local."

"What's your flight time?" Sean asked.

"Thirteen minutes," Sandra said. "Then, once we've landed and assuming that Kelly gets the radar off..."

"He will," Jack said.

"I hope so, because I'll have no way to tell," Sandra said. "Assuming the radar is in fact off, nobody will know we're there. Kelly or Janet will get us into the station, and lead us to the hostages." She paused. "I'd feel much better landing even an hour later."

"These small towns roll up the sidewalks after dark," Sean said.

"Moreso an hour after the bars close," Sandra said. "Which per Janet is midnight." Sandra sniffed, suggesting that Janet would be all too well aware of bar closings.

"Orbital mechanics is a bitch," Sean said. "We go for the assault at eleven-fifteen their time or seven AM. Which time do you think we'll have more people awake?"

"Can't Janet take out the comm link?" Sandra said.

"With what?" Sean replied. "Good looks and charm? Besides, once the link goes down, everybody knows something's up."

"If you say so," Sandra said. "At any rate, we extricate the hostages as quickly and quietly as possible..."

"Quiet is better than quick," Sean said. "Remember that."

"Got it," Sandra said. "Once we bust the hostages out we beat feet back to the ships and go to Bradbury."

"What's your plan for that?" Jack said.

Sandra looked up at him. "I'm worried about that. According to Kelly, there's a guard sitting outside until 'around eleven' and we don't know how many guards are inside."

"The guard will be gone by the time you get there," Sean said. At least I hope so. "I might yet have an answer on the inside arrangements."

"That would be nice," Sandra said. "But if this guard's not gone, we'll have to shoot him."

"You have a shooter designated? With a silencer?" Sean asked.

"Yes," Sandra said. "Me. So what are you bringing to the party?" Her face suggested she didn't like the idea very much. Neither did Sean. From what he'd heard, the outside guard was just a kid looking for some extra money.

"Besides the checkbook?" Sean said. "I had a meeting with Bryce this morning, at which I told him that we've agreed in principle to pay. But since they haven't opened for business in Chicago, I can't confirm that until this evening."

The Martian day was forty minutes longer than Earth's day, a fact that tended to push the two calendars way out of sync with each other. It was more of a problem on Mars than Earth, Sean noted ruefully, chiefly because the folks on Earth didn't give a damn about Mars' problems.

"Sounds like a plan," Jack said. "I've got to get back and get ready."

Sandra nodded. "So do I." She reached across the table and took Jack's hand. "Good hunting."

"You too," Jack said.

"Now we wait for Kelly to check in," Sean said. *We can't attack until he does.*

Chapter 30

**Monday 55 Virgo Year 52 20:01 local (March 27, 2074 12:01 GMT)
Bensonville, Republic of the White Race, Olympus Mons, Mars**

KELLY POPPED THE FACEPLATE OF HIS HELMET. He was standing in the fuel manifold room of Bensonville port, and it was just past 2000 hours. Things were going to shit already.

First, there was the ship he'd just gotten finished fueling. Chuck had personally ordered them to go up, and now Jack's crew would have eight guns to fight instead of four. *Eight guns that Jack didn't know about.*

Well, if they figured out their fuel problem, he thought, taking off his gloves. He'd popped loose the primary control board for pump logic. It would take a while to diagnose, and more time to physically get to the board, but that kind of thing happened all the time, so nobody would be terribly suspicious.

More troubling was the decision to post McIhaney's son in the radar control room. That decision also came down from Chuck in person. For some reason, the man was mighty jumpy tonight.

"Hey sailor, wanna get some dinner?" Rachel asked.

Kelly's head jerked up to see Rachel walking in from behind a fuel manifold.

"Nervous?" She asked.

"You startled me," Kelly replied. "Thanks for the invite, but Rybak's got a plate for me. How'd you get in here?"

"Nobody locks their doors in this town."

"Apparently not," Kelly said. Except I did lock that door.

"That ship leave yet?" Rachel asked.

"No. You can hear them, faintly, from in here." Nor would they be leaving for a while.

"I thought you hated Rybak's food?"

"I do, and thanks for the offer, but after wrestling fuel hoses, I smell like a goat."

"I like goats," Rachel said, a fake-looking smirk on her face.

"I don't, Rachel." Tonight's burnt offering at Rybak's was on the altar of meat loaf. By now, sitting out on the counter, it would be brick-like, not that he had time or inclination to eat - he had calls to make.

"I'd be glad to let you take a shower," Rachel said. "No quarters needed."

"Generous of you, but I've got a free shower here and calls to make."

"Oh?"

"One of my nephews is feeling ill."

"I thought you said your brother didn't have any kids?"

"I did?" Kelly said. He wondered why Rachel was wearing a tan blazer over her jeans. It wasn't that cold in the dome. "You sure?"

"Positive," Rachel said, pulling back her tan blazer and producing a full-sized black semi-auto pistol. She pointed it at him.

"Hey, you shouldn't be kidding around with a gun like that."

"I'm not kidding," Rachel said.

"You know, there's enough liquid methane in these pipes to blow half this town into orbit," Kelly said. "One wrong bullet..."

"I'm the best shot in town," Rachel said. "Besides, with hollow points, there won't be too much over-penetration."

No, but they would penetrate me just fine. His pistol was in his suit's thigh pocket. It would look funny fueling a rocket with a gun strapped to his hip. He looked at Rachel. She was a proven killer.

"I really don't know what game you're playing," Kelly said, "but having guns pointed at me makes me nervous."

"It should, Connor, or whatever your real name is," Rachel said.

"Connor's my real name."

"Well, let's just say I've got my doubts," Rachel said.

"Okay, so how do we resolve those doubts?" Kelly asked.

"Let's drop by my place," Rachel said. She smiled, like a wolf looking at a trapped rabbit. "Call it dessert."

* * *

She didn't pat him down. Kelly hoped that would be her last mistake, although it didn't look like it would be immediately helpful. Bensonville was a working town, and went to bed fairly early, but right now there were still folks out on Charles Street. The new guy pulling out a gun and popping a local woman on the street would surely create a stir.

Not that it looked good for Kelly to do that. Rachel was on his left, holding his arm casually. Her hand was in the pocket of her tan blazer, fist surely wrapped around the automatic. It was doubtful that Kelly could even get to his gun in his right thigh pocket before she got hers into play.

I've got time, he thought. As long as I'm clear of them by ten-thirty I can meet up with Janet and get the radar down. Kelly cleared his throat. "You must think I'm a real desperado."

"How so?" Rachel asked.

"This little frog-walk."

"I'm just enjoying a stroll with a gentleman friend, that's all," Rachel said. "After all, we were seen having dinner."

They turned onto Second Street, and walked past the jail. A young kid, barely older then Minty, was standing outside the door. He had a pistol on his hip, suspended from a black nylon belt, and was wearing a tan shirt over his faded jeans.

"Always wondered what was going on in there," Kelly said.

"You may be getting a personal tour," Rachel replied.

Just on the other side of the jail was a large overhead pressure door. It was halfway down, and a tiny old woman wearing a faded blue ball cap with the white letters VPA on it was waving at them.

"Gotta set Yankee," she said to them.

"We're coming, Mrs. Green," Rachel said.

Most towns, especially one-stoplight places like Bensonville, closed selected interior pressure doors at night. It was called setting Material Condition Y or "Yankee" and usually fell to members of the Volunteer Pressurization Association.

It wasn't so much loss of pressure that they were worried about as fire. Smoke in a confined space, and a pressure dome was the definition of 'confined,' could kill you dead. Closing selected doors and vents at night when fewer people were about helped prevent the spread of these problems. One could still move about in the dome via side airlocks, but those were supposed to be kept closed when people weren't in them.

The important thing about Yankee for Kelly was that Mrs. Green and the gunman at the jail were on the other side of a solid pressure door. They came to the front door to Rachel's place just as the big door behind them stopped rattling.

"Open it," Rachel said to Kelly.

"Gladly," Kelly said. With his left arm, Kelly pulled Rachel towards him and brought his right fist up, driving it into her face, then spinning her body away.

But as he did that, her foot came up and made solid contact with his crotch. A wave of pain and nausea shot through him. Struggling through the pain, he reached down to his pocket and grabbed his pistol.

Pistol in hand, Kelly looked up to see a black blur moving at his face. He thought to duck but couldn't move fast enough as he caught a mouth full of metal. Dazed, he brought the pistol up and thumbed back the hammer, but something hard crashed on his wrist.

"Drop that fucking pistol or you're dead!" Rachel barked.

Kelly shook his head, and put his hand to his face. He tasted salt in his mouth. He blinked and found Rachel staring at him, her gun in his face.

"I said drop it!"

"Fuck, woman," Kelly said. His mouth felt thick. "I'm doing it." He eased the hammer back down with his thumb and tossed the gun away.

"Nice try, shithead," Rachel said. Her nose was bloody if not broken.

"Now what?" Kelly asked.

"Loose the spacesuit," Rachel said. "Right fucking now."

Chapter 31

Monday 55 Virgo Year 52 23:00 local (March 27, 2074 15:00 GMT)
Approaching CCS Charles S. Price, Mars orbit

"TIME?" CHIEF KRAUSS ASKED. She was in the pilot's seat of their rented Bombardier B-16 shuttle. It, like the other rented vehicle following directly behind, was sleek and streamlined with oversized wings for Mars' ridiculously thin atmosphere. It would be a shame to put bullet holes in it, Jack thought. They'd never get their deposit back.

"Twenty-three hundred in three, two, one, mark," Jack said from the co-pilot's seat. They'd all set their clocks to Olympus' plus eight time zone.

"We should be getting a visual on the *Price* any minute now," Krauss said.

Jack saw a glint out the window, to his right and slightly 'above' the planet's horizon. He looked at it through his binoculars.

"Contact twenty right and ten up," Jack said. "Looks like our bogey."

"Estimated range?"

Jack pushed a button on his binoculars and the display was overlaid with a series of hash marks. Using a thumb wheel, he adjusted the scale to where one mark was on each end of the pair of ships. He'd pre-programmed the length of the two ships into the binoculars' computer in meters. By pressing another button, the device would do some geometry and calculate the distance in kilometers.

"One nine nine eight," Jack read off.

"We're in the slot," Krass said. "Always nice to know the geek squad on the ground got it right for once."

Jack was too busy to comment aloud, but she'd been bashing their amateur ground-based spotter for days now. So far, they'd been dead on, although 'dead' was maybe not the right word.

"One nine zero zero," Jack said. It was a good rate of closure. Not fast enough for anybody to worry, but they'd be alongside in a few minutes.

"Quit playing with yourself, you pre-vert!"

"You wish I was playing with myself," Minty said. "And it's pervert, not *pre*-vert."

Minty looked over her shoulder to see Russ Nelson drifting up the central corridor of the Mosquito. His bullet-shaped and shaved head loomed in the light from the bridge access tube. Apparently Russ's nap-time was over.

"Whatever," Russ said. "What's the traffic picture?"

"Traffic?"

"Yeah, traffic. You know, ships and shit flying around up here."

Minty gestured at the confusing display. "And I would know about traffic how?"

"Jesus Christ, save me from these tadpoles," Russ said. "Don't you know anything?"

"If you want me to learn something," Minty said angrily, "then show me!"

"I don't have time for this shit, girl!" Russ glared at her. Finally, with an effort, he said, "Ya got eyes, right?"

"I do. Haven't seen a thing."

"Well that's no good," Russ said. "Call Bensonville and find out what's the hold-up. Assuming you can find the radio."

"I can and already did," Minty said, a smile on her face.

"Figures. First thing a girl does is find out how to gossip to her friends."

"I haven't been gossiping, for Christ's sake!"

"Well," Russ said. "What did you find out in your non-gossipy conversations with B-ville?"

"They said they'd call me when they launched."

"What's the malfunction down there?"

"Do I look like a rocket repairman?"

Russ glared at her, clearly trying to come back with a retort, when the overhead speaker crackled. "Romeo this is Bravo, over."

Minty picked up the mike, which looked like an old-style telephone handset. "This is Romeo, over."

"Romeo, this is Bravo. Bird is away, call-sign Charlie."

"Copy that," Minty said into the mike. "What's the ETA, over?"

"Three zero mikes, over."

"Roger, Romeo standing by." Minty put the handset back into its cradle. "Thirty minutes," she told Russ. "About ten minutes after loss of signal from B-ville."

"So I heard. I gotta take a dump, then I'll be back to relieve you. Think you can handle things here?"

Handle what? Minty wondered. It wasn't like he let her handle anything. *Except the stove and the mop.* She could use those all she wanted. *I might as well play with myself.* "I got it, boss."

"Good."

Russ left, the hulking man doing a credible imitation of stomping in zero gee. Wonder why he's always pissed, Minty thought, as she looked around the tiny control cabin. For about the thousandth time, she wondered who 'Randal Cranston' was and why he was important enough that this ship was named after him.

It had been luxurious once, but that was twenty years ago, and the previous owners hadn't kept things up. She looked outside, and saw a glint of metal. The *Cranston* was docked bow-to, so from her perspective it was port forward, but from the perspective of the combined ships it was ventral or below. It was way too early to be seeing the bird from B-ville, and the contact was too far east of Olympus to be their shuttle. She rummaged through a storage bin mounted on the side of her seat, looking for her binoculars.

"I got it visually from here, sir," Krauss said. "Go hook up with the team."

The *Price* was almost directly dorsal to the shuttle, so much so that Jack had to crane his neck back to see. The ship looked tiny, like something you'd carry on your keychain.

"I'm gone," Jack said. He pulled himself over the seat and hand-over-hand through the cramped compartment to the tiny airlock. The rest of the assault team had already locked out, and were hanging on to a few straps they'd rigged on the shuttle's exterior.

Jack went on internal air, then cycled the lock. By the time he was outside, the *Price* was visibly larger, but still maybe ten kilometers away. The forward nozzles puffed, cold gas shooting out silently in white clouds.

The *Price* was above them, relative to the planet. Things in higher orbits moved slower, so their approach had been to go low and overshoot, then brake while adding an up vector. It was tricky flying, but neither ship's bridge could see them.

He plugged a wire from his suit into an exterior comm jack, secured to a hand strap with a liberal amount of duct tape. "Williams online," he said.

"Alpha copy," Otarski said. He was the squad leader for this group under Jack.

"Two minutes to attack," Fencl said. She was inside the ship, monitoring the radios while keeping herself in reserve for medical emergencies. "All units report manned and ready."

"Any word from the Chief groundside?"

"Negative," Fencl said.

"Wonderful," Jack said. He looked at the *Price*, a rapidly-growing ship above him.

"Do we go or abort?" Fencl asked.

"We go," Jack said. "Signal Two." He looked at the other launch, which blinked its running lights, acknowledging Fencl's signal.

They said that in war the plan was the first casualty on contact with the enemy. It looked like they were right.

Monday 55 Virgo Year 52 23:05 local (March 27, 2074 15:05 GMT)
Ryan—Daley Field, Bradbury, Mars

Lieutenant Sandra Kim looked at the clock in the cockpit of her Cessna light rocket. "Damn it, Chief, call me!"

Chief Kelly was supposed to call and report that the radar at Bensonville was out before she launched. He should have called hours ago, before she even loaded the ships.

He hadn't. the scrambled fleet-tac radio warbled, then synced up. "Group Whisky is commencing attack."

Group Whisky was William's group in orbit. They were launching their attack on the Price. The fleet-tac crackled again.

"Group Kilo, status, over."

She was Group Kilo. Kim flipped her mike to the fleet-tac channel. "Any update from Bravo, over?"

"Negative, over."

No news from Bensonville. She looked at her co-pilot. "Tell the tower and Bird Two we're launching."

"But..."

"But nothing. We gotta go, and go now. Three should guard fleet-tac and come when we call them." *If we call them. If we don't get in a firefight on the landing field.* Kim keyed up fleet-tac. "Lead and two are launching now. Three will launch once the Lima Zulu is secured, over."

"Mike copies. Good luck, out."

We're going to need it.

Monday 55 Virgo Year 52 23:00 local (March 27, 2074 15:00 GMT)
Yacht Randall Cranston, Mars orbit

"See anything?" Russ asked on his return.

"No," Minty said. By the time she'd gotten her binoculars out, whatever it was she'd seen was gone.

Probably a meteor hitting Mars' upper atmosphere.

She'd been told that you could even see them skip over the atmosphere like stones tossed over a pond. The Martian atmosphere was supposedly even worse than Earth's for that. It was thin but tall, and even on the surface it could be clumpy.

"Okay, then, I've got it."

"I stand relieved," Minty said, and pulled her way out of the captain's chair.

Minty walked into her cabin and pulled her shirt off over her head. She tossed it in the direction of her bag on the floor, but miscalculated the spin and watched it curve away.

"Wonder if I can get a shower in before the next shuttle arrives," she said aloud. Russ was surely going to want "all hands on deck" for the incoming ship.

The general alarm croaked for a second, like it was clearing its throat, then started to sound loudly.

"What the hell?" Minty said. Then Russ's voice boomed over the intercom. "We're being boarded!"

Oh shit! Minty looked around for her rifle. Her eyes landed on it and her space suit. *If bullets start flying I'll surely need a suit.*

Chapter 32

Tuesday 56 Virgo Year 52 00:10 local (March 27, 2074 16:10 GMT)
Yacht *Randall Cranston,* Mars orbit

MINTY FINISHED ZIPPING up her suit as the intercom barked again.

"Boarders attempting access on aft maintenance lock!"

"You think so?" Minty said aloud. She grabbed her pink AR-15 and racked a round into the chamber, then stuffed the spare clip into a suit pocket.

Only an idiot would attack with one launch. These people were not idiots. They must be attacking both ships at once.

Minty stepped out of the cabin and saw Sammie Deschamps climbing up the top of the ladder from the centrifuge to the main core of the ship. Sammie's shotgun was slung on her back.

"I'm right behind you!" Minty shouted. She tried desperately to swallow around the massive lump in her throat.

Jack thumbed back the hammer of his pistol as he locked his feet under a hard-point. With his free hand, he counted down on his fingers from three. When he clenched his fist, Lewis tripped the Jaws-of-Life. The hydraulic jaw silently ripped back the metal of the hatch. Air rushed out, the moisture condensing in the glare of a floodlight from the shuttle, their only source of light on the ventral side of the *Price.*

The lock was empty. *Amateurs.* During their practice sessions, a suited shooter in a lock, especially squirreled back in a deep one like this, could kill two or three people.

At Jack's gesture, two strike team members pulled themselves into the airlock with him. Once the three of them were in the airlock, Lewis activated a temporary inflatable patch which sealed off the ruined hatchway. Petty Officer Diep tried the latch on the inner hatch. She gave an okay sign. Not locked.

Jack opened the manual valve to pressurize the airlock as he braced up, ready to shoot. A quiet fart, growing louder, was the sign of air returning. Diep braced up, and as soon as she could, she tripped the hatch and pushed it in slightly, using her shoulder and legs to overcome the residual pressure differential. Eric Reed, their third team member, shot a flash-bang-puke grenade into the space with a spring-loaded gun, and then Diep let the door slam shut.

Jack heard the bang of the grenade clearly despite his suit helmet, the hatch and the low pressure. Anybody on the other side would be deaf and blind. Good thing, too—the spotlight from the shuttle outside was shining through the temporary patch, silhouetting them in the airlock. He gave a thumbs-up to Diep, who re-opened the hatch.

The access corridor on the other side of the hatch was dark except for a cluster of green lights, probably from a control panel. Then the space was illuminated by muzzle flashes, accompanied by the bark of a rifle. Jack fired several shots blindly into the space as the temporary cover behind him suddenly sprouted holes. A low-pressure alarm sounded, competing with the bark of gunfire, somewhat muffled by Jack's still-closed helmet.

Shit! Where's the shooter? Jack wondered if he'd fired three or four shots. Between the damn spotlight outside and the muzzle flashes, his dark vision was gone, and he hadn't had time to activate his night vision goggles.

Then he saw one of the green lights wink out. Got you, you son of a bitch. "Two o'clock!" Jack yelled, indicating where he thought the shooter was. He aimed and pulled the trigger on his pistol three times rapidly. The third time the hammer fell on an empty cylinder.

"Sound off!" Jack said, rapidly flipping the shells out with a wrist movement, then fumbling with his speed loader.

"I'm hit," Reed said, his voice strained.

"I'm okay," Diep said. "I'll evac Eric."

"Clear the corridor first," Eric said. "I can wait."

"Light coming up," Jack said, snapping closed the cylinder of his pistol. He broke a trio of amber chemlights and tossed them down the corridor.

One of the chemlights bounced off a body drifting in the corridor. Half of the man's head was gone.

"One pirate down, Reed's hit," Jack said. "Corridor clear. Lewis, patch the lock and evac him, then send the follow-on. Diep and I are moving in."

"Copy," Fencl's voice said over the link. "We're attached to the hull. I'll meet casualty in the airlock."

Casualty. Fencl was trying to be professional. Maybe it helped. "Copy, we're moving. Interrogative status Bravo team?"

"Entering now," Fencl said. Bravo team was taking on the crew in the Mosquito. Jack looked at a counter running on his heads up display, projected inside his suit. They had twenty minutes to clear the ship and set an ambush for the team coming up from the surface.

Minty pulled herself up into the zero-gee central corridor of the centrifuge. In her haste, she pushed off too hard, and bounced glancingly off of the far corridor. She found a handhold and pulled herself aft, while trying to chamber a round in her AR-15 with her free hand. A live round popped out of the chamber, spinning away in the gravity-less space. *Focus, bitch!*

At the first junction she turned and looked to port to see Sammie and Ian move into the side corridor leading to the main lock.

"You're too close!" Minty yelled. "If they blow the lock you're screwed!"

"Get your ass in here, girl," Sammie barked back.

There was a blinding flash of light from the corridor, and a cloud of smoke. Sammie's shotgun barked once, the shot clattering against metal. Minty got a whiff of the acrid gas and immediately felt nauseous. She closed her helmet visor and hit the button for suit pressure.

As she did, Sammie's shotgun barked again, followed by a flurry of pistol shots. Sammie's body, streaming blood, flew out of the corridor and slammed into the far wall.

"I give up!" Ian shouted.

A glob of puke floated down the corridor, mixing with the globules of Sammie's blood.

Shit! I need to get out of here! Minty kicked back and started scrambling for the central corridor. As she did, she heard more gunshots, hollow-sounding, coming through the docking collar from the *Price.*

We've already lost this fight.

Chapter 33

Monday 55 Virgo Year 52 20:19 local (March 27, 2074 12:19 GMT)
Bensonville, Republic of the White Race, Olympus Mons, Mars

"DON'T GET ANY IDEAS, DUDE," Rachel said, poking 'Connor' in the back with her pistol.

"Dark enough, isn't it?" the guy asked.

Most of the lights were off, except for a single floor lamp at the far end of the room. The switch for the overheads was at that side of the room. It usually wasn't a problem since she rarely came in this way.

"Not your problem," Rachel said while trying to keep from swallowing blood. Careful to keep her gun away from him, she reached out and grabbed his arm. "Sit on the box facing the wall." She pointed to a large wooden crate.

He sat down, facing the side wall to her left. *Well, I didn't say which wall.* Not that it mattered.

Rachel walked over to a metal desk she used when she made the occasional sale and opened a side draw. She'd put her handcuffs in there, as well as a pair borrowed from the jail. As she did this, she wiped a handful of blood from her nose. It certainly felt broken.

"I think you broke my nose," Rachel said. She wiped her face, and with the gun pointed at 'Connor' she walked over to him slowly.

"You got me pretty good too," Connor replied.

"Hands behind your back."

"Hey, let's not get crazy here," he said. "And I'm sorry about your nose."

"You can do what I say or I'll just shoot you now."

He put his hands behind his back. Rachel cuffed his hands with her set, a bit awkwardly working with one hand, and used the jail's set to connect that to a pad eye on the crate.

"Happy now?" the dude asked.

"Getting there," she said. She walked across the shop and ducked into a bathroom, stuffing her gun in the waistband of her jeans as she did. She grabbed a clean towel, one of the older ones, from under the sink and wetted it, then tried to stop the bleeding from her nose.

A couple of minutes later, she ditched the blood-soaked towel and grabbed a dry one. She walked into the front room, walked up to her prisoner and slapped him open-handed on the face. "That's foreplay, shithead."

"That all you got?" he asked. It was a bluff—there was blood in the man's mouth from her gun.

"No," she said. "I got pliers and you got a nut-sac. Do I need to draw you a picture?" She grinned at the man. "You're going to regret breaking my nose."

"Look, you psycho bitch," he said, "I told you I got nothing to do with the damned Space Patrol!"

Rachel fiddled ostentatiously with the pliers. She could see beads of sweat popping out on the dude's forehead.

They'd been at this for at least an hour, maybe more. She'd had to take another break to get her nose to stop bleeding. It still hurt something fierce.

"You've lied to me once, David or whatever your name is," Rachel said. She clicked the jaws of the pliers together underneath his nose. The thin fabric of his suit liner would offer little protection. "How do I know you're not lying now?"

He looked away. "'Cause I'm scared shitless."

He should be scared. She noticed his eyes wander, and followed them to see he was looking at a wall clock, mounted in the hallway to the back rooms.

"Got a hot date?" She asked.

"No," the man said. "Could I please get some water?"

"Later. Tell me your story again, Dave," Rachel said.

"My real name is David Philpot," the dude said, looking at the floor. His face flushed, a reaction Rachel didn't expect. "I robbed a bank back on Earth."

"Where?" Rachel said. She made a show of referring to a pad of paper where she'd been keeping notes.

"Colorado Springs. A branch of the Bank of Earth."

"Why?"

"Banks is where they keep the money."

"No, smartass, why that branch?"

"Small bank, in the out lot of a shopping center. Easy in and out."

"What happened next?"

David, if that was really his name, sighed. "Some black cop, off-duty, was there. The newsnets said he was banging a teller. When I walked in, he was on the can. He came out with a gun, and I shot him."

"So you ran to Mars?" Rachel asked. She immediately regretted it. You never asked a leading question like that.

"Eventually. I mean the local cops, the state cops, everybody was hot on my ass."

"You know," Rachel said, "The problem I got with this story is that if you'd capped a black cop, half of this town would buy you a drink." And why would capping a cop cause embarrassment?

"How many of the other half would turn me in for the reward?" He asked. "Besides, even if they didn't turn me in, if Interpol found out I was here, I'd be stuck on this rock."

Kelly struggled not to cry. He jerked on the handcuffs for what had to be the fifteenth time. They weren't going anywhere. *Lord, I do not want to die here*. It was his most fervent prayer in years.

It was fifty / fifty whether Lieutenant Kim's group would even get out of their ships. They didn't know about the watch, and the radar's proximity alarm would give McIlhaney's kid plenty of warning. Once they got on the ground, half-a-dozen militiamen could be set up and waiting for them.

Kelly jerked on the handcuffs again. Young McIlhaney was a strapping big boy, and apparently played nose guard on the high school football team. Kelly was trying to figure out how to quietly neutralize him when the Storey woman showed up.

He stared at the blank stone wall. Janet didn't know about McIlhaney. If she came looking for him there—well he'd be a handful even for two people. *I've got to be the world's shittiest spy. Stick with rescuing.*

Even if she did somehow deal with the kid, Janet would have no idea where he was. Besides, there was no slack in the plan for people to conduct another rescue. This was where he died.

"See, here's my problem," Rachel said. "It's all too pat for me."

"Check my story out," Kelly said, looking at the floor. "I got all night." Even though I really don't. "Look, lady, I'm really sorry about your nose."

"Who were you calling in Port Lowell?"

"Calling when?"

Rachel stepped up to him and slapped his face open-handed. It was more insulting then painful. "The other night. Minty said you kept calling people in Port Lowell."

Shit. That wasn't in the Philpot cover story. He racked his brain. "Look, I couldn't just walk up to a ticket agent, say 'hi I'm Dave Philpot, wanted murderer, and I'd like a ticket to Mars.'"

"Continue."

"So I had to pay a guy for a false identity."

"That would be the Connor paperwork?"

"Yeah. Some Russian dude."

"I thought they got out of the organized crime thing," Rachel said, stepping away from him. "It's now Brazilian mobsters."

"Could be. All I know is that the guy I paid on Earth was Russian. Ivan Ivanovich. What money from the robbery I hadn't blown I gave him."

The bitch faked a yawn. "I'm sure this has a point, yes?"

"When I got to Mars, a dude said I owed the mob more money. I could either pay in cash or 'jobs.'" Kelly looked at her, trying to look sincere. "I'm done with this criminal shit. So I said cash, and now *he's* after me for money."

The heartless bitch laughed. "Oh you are a sad sack, Philpot." She turned off the laughter just like a light switch. "What's the name of this supposed Russian mobster in Port Lowell?"

"Feodor Denisovich." Kelly vaguely remembered hearing that name in the local news in conjunction with organized crime. "Goes by Felix Dee. Check it out."

"Check it out," Rachel said mockingly. It was clear she wasn't buying a bit of this. *Then just kill me*! "I will," she said.

He looked up to see Janet Pilgrim step out of the darkened back area of the room. She'd put on a skimpy pink tube-top, and if the waistband of her pants were any lower she'd be arrested for indecent exposure. Janet had a snub-nosed revolver in her left hand, which she pressed to the back of Rachel's head.

"Don't bother," Janet said, her voice calm. "Philpot got caught last week in Mexico, and somebody pushed Felix out of an airlock without a suit."

I just might live. Kelly jerked on his handcuffs. *But the mission will fail.*

Rachel felt something hard press against the back of her head. *I knew I should have locked that damn door*, she thought. *If whoever this was wanted me dead, I'd already be on the floor.* She put up her hands slowly, fighting the urge to pee.

"Don't bother."

"Janet Pilgrim," Rachel said, "what brings you here?" *I just might make it out of this alive.* A cold sweat hit her. *Minty! They've got to be hitting the ship*!

"You wouldn't really kill me, would you Janet? I thought we had something."

The other woman snorted, pressing her gun harder into Rachel's head. "You're not that good of a lay, you murderous bitch."

Rachel looked down to see Janet wrapping a hand around her pistol, the butt sticking out of her blazer pocket. Rachel's mouth worked, but suddenly she couldn't get any words out.

"Where's that brat little sister of yours," Janet asked. "The one with the cute pink gun?"

That's why I'm still alive. "Upstairs, waiting," Rachel said.

"She went to the Price," Connor / Philpot / whatever-his-name was said.

"You sure about that?" Rachel said.

"Not many people carry a pink AR-15," he said.

"Rachel, meet Bill Kelly, Chief Astronaut of the Volunteer Space Rescue Ship *Volodka*."

Volodka. The damn ship Chuckles tried to take.

"What the fuck are you doing here?" the man, Connor, Kelly, Whatever-His-Face, asked.

"I thought it was obvious," Janet said. "Rescuing you."

"What about the spaceport?"

"Don't worry about that now," Janet said.

Rachel heard what sounded like a gun's hammer being thumbed back. "Where's the key?"

"Fuck you," Rachel said, trying but failing to prevent her voice from breaking.

"I'm sure I can find it," Janet said. "Last time."

"You're going to kill me anyway!" Rachel wailed.

"Of course I am."

Rachel looked up with her eyes, and saw a picture of Minty and her together.

"When are you hitting the ships in orbit?" Rachel said.

"Why do you care," Janet said mockingly. "Minty's 'just upstairs.'"

"I can help," Rachel said.

"You can provide the key, or I can just find it off your body," Janet said.

"No, I mean after. With Sam at the spaceport!"

"Funny the things a man, or rather a boy, will do when you flash them some tit. He's out like a light."

"You lie," Rachel said.

"Don't need to," Janet said. "I got the guns, remember?"

"She could help with the prison guard," what's-his-face said.

"Bill Kelly, would you please just shut the fuck up!" Janet said.

"He's right, I could," Rachel said.

The only response was a gun pushing harder at Rachel's head.

"We're wasting time," the guy said.

"Fine, you bitch," Janet said. "Rachel, uncuff him and help us with the guards. If you do that, I won't kill you."

"Deal," Rachel said.

"But remember what Gus said?" Janet asked.

Gus? Gus who? "No?"

"Captain Gus, your buddy," Janet said. Rachel could just hear the smirk on Janet's face. "If anything goes wrong, your fault, my fault, nobody's fault, I will kill you first. No matter who else dies, you die first. Got it?"

"I understand," Rachel said. "Now should I uncuff the Space Patrol dude?"

"My name's Kelly," the man said, "and you should."

Chapter 34

Tuesday 56 Virgo Year 52 23:15 local (March 27, 2074 15:00 GMT) Yacht Randall Cranston, Mars orbit

MINTY ARRIVED IN THE CENTRAL CORRIDOR of the *Cranston* just as another cluster of shots echoed over from the *Price.* She fumbled with her suit radio, turning on to be rewarded by random tones on all channels. Somebody was jamming.

"Hey, dude, I'm bleeding here," she heard Ian say, his voice echoing in the hallway.

"You'll be bleeding a lot more if you don't do like you're told," somebody else said. "We're going to the bridge."

Shit! That meant they were coming here! Minty glanced around, looking for a place to take cover. There was nothing.

"Move, damn it!" the stranger shouted.

Good idea. Minty pulled herself to the ladder going down from the central corridor into the spinning crew area. She half climbed, half fell down the ladder, ending up in a heap at the bottom.

Now what? She stood up in the one-sixth gee and looked up. *Sooner or later they'll do a sweep of the ship. But do they know a relief crew is coming up?*

Her suit radio was still being jammed, not that it had enough power to reach anybody. *But the cargo tug had a standard bridge-to-bridge unit.* She looked up to the central corridor. That would be the quickest way, unless they had a guard posted. *Can't risk it.* There was another way...

Tony Lords took in the view of space from the window. He was sitting in the co-pilot's seat in a Cessna 15 rocket. They had just finished their boost phase, and his daughter, Brenda, was sitting beside him, piloting their launch up to the Price. Everything looked peaceful.

Since Brenda had rolled the ship so that Mars was 'below' them, or as she said, ventral, there wasn't that good of a view of the planet. Most of what they could see was in darkness anyway. He felt a flush of pride, though. Girl was becoming a real spacer. It was a shame she'd had to get mixed up in Junior's bullshit plan for interplanetary domination. The boy should try sobriety first, then conquest.

"Dad," Brenda said, "When you open the hatch, make sure your gun is ready."

Tony Lords gave his daughter a weird look. "Why in the world would I do that?"

"Something's not right, dad. Just trust me."

"I do trust you," Tony said, gazing absently at Phobos. "But it would really help if I knew what the problem was."

His daughter sighed, just like when she was a little girl and he caught her hand in the cookie jar. Not that he had been around that much to catch her. Keeping Charles Benson Senior out of jail and preventing his many rivals from killing him had been more than a full-time job.

"Rachel may have found a spy back in town."

Tony's head jerked over to look at his daughter. "That Connor fellow?" *Your turn to be surprised.*

"You've heard already?"

"Rachel and Minty mentioned him days ago."

"Oh. I just found out."

"Too damn many secrets in this operation," Tony said. "But that's why I suggested to Junior we post a few extra guards. Any reason you're telling me this now?"

Brenda's head bobbed, vaguely in the direction of the *Price.* "Russ is too busy to come to the radio, and Ian wants us to dock at a different hatch."

Russ not being front and center was a bit worrisome. The man was a real control freak, and Ian was so green at this you could hear the kid photosynthesize.

"So what? I mean, if Connor was a spy, what could he do?"

"That control board—the one that was loose?"

Finding and fixing it had cost them over two hours, and then they'd had to wait for the next window. "What about it?"

"That's a new board. I put it in this morning."

"So it being loose was no accident." It was a statement, not a question. But still, was it really possible that somebody had taken the ship back? "I talked to Russ before we were supposed to launch," Tony said. "Everything sounded fine."

"When exactly was that?" Brenda said.

"1930."

"Have they been checking in since then?"

"They were supposed to be," Tony said. Supposed to be was the operant phrase. When he'd left the town's communications center, which doubled as the emergency monitoring and police dispatch office, the shift was just changing. He smiled ruefully. The overnight shift was one guy, Fat Tommy Thompson, a man not noted for enthusiasm or independent thinking. It was entirely possible he'd not gotten a check-in and not done much about it.

"That's just not a lot of time," Tony said. "And it would be one hell of a coincidence that they would try to retake the ship tonight." *Whoever they were, which was another good question. It wasn't like there was a Martian Police Force or anything.*

"Would it be? I mean, is anybody expecting trouble."

No. Why would they? "The ship's owners are paying."

"But the money's not in the bank."

Good point.

"Look at it this way," Brenda said, adjusting something on the control panel. "If everything's okay, then the worst that could happen is Nelson's a bit pissed off."

"You're right," Tony said. Besides, Russ was perpetually pissed off anyway. "So how we gonna play this?"

Jack looked around the zero-gee access tube on the *Price*. It was halfway between the main hub, which allowed access to the centrifuge, and on the same plane as the access to the *Cranston*.

"Good place for an ambush," Cameron Lewis said, floating beside him.

"Us or them?" Jack said, trying and failing to be funny. There were at least two pirates still running amuck on the ships, hiding in one of dozens of cubby-holes available on any manned platform, and an unknown number of people coming in from Bensonville. Searching a ship, especially for a moving target, was hard. They'd spent an hour once in the training ship before they found their bogey. Or in other words, twice as much time as he'd had.

The kid they'd captured, Ian, claimed not even to know how the radios worked, let alone if Bensonville had been warned. He just might be green enough, but Jack couldn't take the chance. Especially not spread as thinly as he was.

"I was thinking them, boss," Cameron said, pointing at the port airlock that the pirate supply ship was supposed to dock.

"I know," Jack chided. Cameron could be very literal-minded sometimes.

"Lights on or off?" Cameron asked.

"On, I think," Jack said. "On the off-chance that they don't know we're here, we want them to let their guard down."

"Okay, sir," Cameron said. "Where do you want to set the ambush?"

Jack gestured towards the central hub. "Reefer deck."

"Put them on ice, huh?" Cameron said with a grin.

"I hope so."

The two men moved back a couple of meters, passing a round hatch leading to the refrigerator equipment room. The hatch was marked with a red X in chalk, signifying that the room had been cleared. They then came to the actual reefer deck, where Diep was waiting for them. This deck was really just where the access tube widened into a square compartment. All four sides of the square were lined with refrigerator doors, most with paper printouts slid into plastic holders. The *Price* had a greenhouse which produced some fresh vegetables, but the primary function of the greenhouse was for oxygen generation. Most of the crew's food was either frozen or canned.

Jack's plan was simple. They'd hide out in the reefer deck, blocked from view of anybody coming in through the airlock. Once the first man arrived at the reefer deck, Jack would grab him while Cameron and Diep would hold the rest of the relief party. Chief Krauss would bring her bird, with Pacht as a doorgunner, around from an empty slot on *Price's* cargo deck to prevent the launch from leaving.

"Derek, this is Williams," Jack said over the suit radio. He hoped that on its lowest power setting it would not be detectable outside the ship. "Any luck, over?"

"Negative, over," Derek Lewis said.

Wonderful, Jack thought. Derek and another Rescueman were looking for the pirates, while the last boarding party member was sitting on the bridge of the Mosquito. *Thin. Hopefully not too thin.*

Jack's left ear was set to a bridge-to-bridge radio frequency. In that ear, he heard their captive pirate say. "I've got you on visual, Charlie." It was the signal to get ready.

"Copy, Romeo. Making final approach. Be advised we're using the small docking collar, over."

Why in the hell would they do that? Jack wondered. He took a deep breath. It was too late to change anything now.

Tony pulled his way through the cabin, heading to the small docking collar.

"Hey," Eggman yelled to Tony's back, "why are we using that damned small collar?"

"What, can't fit through it?" Tony said, trying to keep a light tone to his voice. "It's quicker, that's why," he added.

"Brenda got a hot date or what?" Fritz, the fourth man on the team, yelled.

Or what, Tony thought. He ignored the other men.

The Cessna 15 looked like a squat cylindrical pyramid, and had two main access docks. There was a large rectangular one, which doubled as the upper hatch, on the side, and there was a small tubular Soyuz-standard collar dead on the nose. This hatch was accessed from the main cabin by a tube and ladder system, and Tony was in the tube, just behind their hatch. He was using the ladder to brace up, so he could shoot if he had to, but he'd also clipped a steel cable from his suit to a tie-down.

It was in fact quicker to fly a rendezvous to the nose collar, simply because the pilot had better visibility. The other reason was that the collar would only support one person at a time, limiting the chance of somebody rushing in.

"Dock in ten," Brenda said, using the ship's internal loudspeakers.

A few seconds later, the docking collar seated with a solid thump, and began automatically pressurizing. Once the green telltale light went on, Tony manually cranked open the hatch and pulled himself down a meter-or-so long tunnel to the *Price's* hatch. He paused there for a second, making sure he was braced up and that the muzzle of his assault rifle was pointing into the ship, and pushed the button to open the hatch.

"What's the hold up?" Eggman yelled, standing behind him in the tunnel.

"Don't piss your pants," Tony said, as the round steel hatch slid into its pocket on one side. Using it as cover, Tony peeked around. The corridor was empty.

"Where the hell is everybody?" Tony shouted. The lights were on, but somebody should be in the corridor to meet them, if only out of boredom.

"Quit jerking off," Eggman said from behind him.

Tony pulled himself into the cylindrical corridor. The gray walls and white padding on various corners showed no signs of a problem.

"Hey, Eggman," Tony yelled. "Have Brenda call and find out where everybody is."

"Hey, man," Eggman replied, "I actually gotta take a piss. Would you mind stepping this up?"

Suddenly a hatch in the corridor a few meters in front of him opened up. Tony grabbed for a handhold to stop his forward motion and tried to plant his feet on something.

"Man am I glad to see you guys," Mel Morris said, his head popping up out of the hatch, flashing them his too-perfect smile.

"What are you doing?" Tony said.

"We got jumped," Mel said, his face turning dark. His body was halfway out of the hatch. "I think they got Russ."

"Shit," Tony said. Just then, a trio of faces popped up down the corridor, and gunfire rang out deafeningly.

"It's an ambush!" Tony shouted, his feet flailing. "Back back back!"

He fired several rounds wildly in the general direction of the bad guys, letting the recoil walk him back. Mel, between him and the gunmen, caught at least a couple of rounds in the back, which sent his body jumbling towards Tony, blood spurting out everywhere.

"I'm hit!" Eggman shouted, still in the docking tunnel.

"Get into the ship!" Tony fired another burst, letting the recoil walk him towards the hatch. Mel's body bounced into him with a sickening thud. Tony blindly pushed Mel's body down the corridor, and scrambled towards the hatch.

He pulled himself in and jammed his shoulder against Eggman's foot, pushing the man down into the main cabin. "Goddamnit move you little shit!" Tony yelled, hearing something ricochet behind him.

Tony suddenly felt heavy, like the nose of the ship was now the bottom, and a great wind blew past him. It got very quiet and cold. Holding on with one hand, he reached up and closed his suit helmet's faceplate.

A wave of hot air filled his helmet, and he took a deep breath which burned in his lungs.

"Close the hatch, dad," Brenda said, her voice sounding tinny in his earpiece. He pulled himself into the main cabin and back up the docking tube. Visible out the end of the tube was the *Price*, already getting noticeably smaller.

Tony wrapped his hand around the hatch and pulled it shut, nearly losing his grip as the ship swung violently. He dogged the hatch and, struggling for air, said "Secured."

"We got company, Dad," Brenda said. "Get up here."

Tony pulled himself back into the cabin, noting that both men inside had their faceplates down, and headed to the flight deck, where he slid into the co-pilot's seat.

"Pressure's coming up," Brenda said over the radio. She tapped him on the arm and pointed outside.

"This shit just keeps getting better," Tony said. A sleek Bombardier aerospace shuttle was closing on them. There was some dude hanging out the hatch, a big gun in his hands.

"Land now," Tony said.

"I think I need a hospital," Eggman said, his breathing heavy over the radio link. "It don't look good."

"We can't get back to B-ville for another fifteen minutes," Brenda said.

Tony gritted his teeth. "Fuck Bensonville. Get us in some atmosphere now before that fucking idiot starts shooting at us."

"Brace for re-entry," Brenda said, rolling the ship violently to get the main engines in line with their orbital motion. "Dad, pull up a nav screen and tell me where we're going."

Tony did as she asked, fighting the sudden sensation of gravity. "Best field is Roarke's Drift," Tony said, reading off the screen.

"They got a hospital?" Eggman asked.

"Yes," Tony lied. Actually, it had a Class Three medical facility, according to the nav computer, which meant one doctor. Better than nothing.

"We need to warn Bensonville," Brenda said, busily setting up for a re-entry.

"I'll work on that," Tony said, calling up a help screen for the communications system. "You just get us down in one piece."

Chapter 35

Tuesday 56 Virgo Year 52 00:19 local (March 27, 2074 16:19 GMT) Yacht Randall Cranston, Mars orbit

I*'VE GOT TO WARN off the relief party,* Minty thought. To do that she needed something more powerful than her suit radio. Like what was in the cargo tug. Getting there without getting shot was the trick.

Minty walked approximately a third of the length of the central corridor of the crew area until she came to the repair locker. It was a tiny space, like everything else on the ship, but it had one advantage—an airlock. She pulled three bags of emergency repair gear out of the way and dumped them in the corridor to clear a path to the airlock.

She had just finished that when the radio jamming stopped. *The relief team is coming.* She reslung her rifle so that it was in front of her and made sure the safety was on, then she slid sideways into the airlock.

Minty pulled the inner door closed, feeling suddenly claustrophobic in the tiny space, barely big enough for her. She started to reach for the pressurization valve, then stopped.

Alarm. Changing pressure in the airlock will trip an alarm in the bridge. That's where the attackers are.

She looked around the cramped space, trying to figure out where the sensor was. Only when she craned her head back (Causing her helmet to hit the back wall with a solid thump) did she find the sensor—nestled in the overhead next to the light.

"How do I disable you?" she asked.

As she did, Ian's voice came over the radio. "Russ wants you to use the side airlock," he said, apparently talking to the relief ship.

"Must move faster," she said. There were two visible wires feeding into the small disk-shaped plastic unit. She went back into the repair locker and found a pair of wire cutters, which she used to cut both wires into the unit. No alarm sounded, so she dropped the wire cutters on the floor and clambered into the airlock, then used the manual emergency valve to depressurize.

Once the airlock was down to vacuum, she opened the outer door. She was on the aft side of the saucer-shaped centrifuge, which meant it was pitch dark. Thanks to the spin, there was a definite down—and if she fell off, the spin would send her flying out into space.

Minty reached down to turn on her suit light, then caught a glimpse of something shiny. She looked up and saw an aerospace plane glinting in the sun. She jerked back inside and fumbled for the airlock light, quickly turning it off. She waited until the spin hid her from sight.

Thirty seconds. I have thirty seconds before they can see me. She clicked on the light and searched for the ladder. It wasn't much—some bent bars sticking out—but it was just close enough to reach.

Minty turned off the light and carefully felt out into the dark. Her suit gloves robbed her of much of her sense of feeling, but she eventually grabbed a rung and pulled herself over, her rifle clicking against her helmet.

Shooting my faceplate off would be really shitty. She heard Ian's voice on the radio again, apparently talking to the relief flight. *Don't talk until you can hear them.*

Climbing was difficult in her suit, even though the spin-generated gravity was half of what she was used to. The rungs were small, and not very well spaced, and she dared not let go.

Then the ladder ended, a good two meters from the main stem-like hull. *Now what?*

Suddenly she heard Mr. Lord's voice on the suit radio, asking where everybody was. *Shit. They're entering the ship!*

Minty toggled her suit radio to transmit, but as soon as she did that, Lord's voice screamed "it's an ambush!"

I'm too late. She put her suit radio back into receive only. *Now it's everybody for themselves.*

Jack let go of his pistol, trusting the lanyard to keep it attached. He needed a free hand to get his faceplate closed. His other hand was busy trying to hold on as the wind roared past him out the open airlock. As he got his suit sealed up, he heard a slam behind him—one of the automatic pressure doors was closing.

"Status!" Jack shouted in the suddenly quiet environment of his helmet. Ice was forming everywhere as the last molecules of air rushed out of the space.

"Diep good!"

"Otarski good!"

Jack toggled his transmitter to the bridge-to-bridge frequency. "Bravo 2 report!"

"Pirate launch is running fast. Should we pursue?" Krauss's voice sounded surprisingly calm.

So much for the fucking plan. Well, this one sure bit the dust hard. He looked around. *Although we still hold the ship and nobody's hit.*

"All units this is Mike Foxtrot actual. Fourth pirate down, no casualties. Break off engagement and make preps to change orbits."

The various subunits started to acknowledge as Jack switched back to suit frequency. "Diep, get that hatch dogged. Otarski, secure the body then both of you lay to the bridge. We're changing orbits before they decide to come back."

"Boss, what about the Mosquito, over?"

That would be Derek, who was still working on this whole chain-of-command thing.

Derek had called on suit-radio frequency, so Jack replied on the same channel. "Go help Feldman. Detach and fall in on our stern."

"Roger, out."

Jack pushed off in the direction of the bridge. The dead body banged against the far bulkhead silently. *Must have heard the audible alarm from the airlock.* He toggled back to the ship-to-ship frequency. "Fencl, what's the status on our casualty?"

"He's okay, but I'd feel better if he were in a hospital, sir, over."

"Your shuttle is detached, proceed as a medivac, over."

"Roger, out."

He looked at the mission clock. They were an estimated two minutes overdue to check in with the pirate base in Bensonville. Hopefully Sandra Kim's team was already on the ground.

Chapter 36

Monday 55 Virgo Year 52 23:15 local (March 27, 2074 15:15 GMT) Bensonville, Republic of the White Race, Olympus Mons, Mars

"FIGHT THE ENEMY, NOT THE PLAN," Sandra Kim said. *God I should have my head examined.* She checked her watch—23:15 local on the dot. *Thirty minutes to get in and out.*

"Pardon, ma'am?" Denise Morris asked. Girl was a rookie, on her first mission.

"Figure out what the enemy is doing and fight that," Sandra said. "Don't assume the enemy is doing what you planned they would do."

"I thought this was a rescue service," Morris replied. "Every time I turn around, people are talking about enemies." 'Even in training' was left unsaid.

"Rescue and war have much in common," Sandra said. "The difference is who the enemy is." She was standing in the crowded main cabin of the Cessna, looking out a porthole at the desolate gravel strip, forlornly illuminated by a couple of lights mounted on the side of the station. The plan was for Kelly to meet them at the landing strip. He wasn't there.

"Morris," Sandra said, gesturing at Denise Morris, one of the two white people in the team. "You're on point. Let's get in there and see what we got." She tapped her co-pilot's shoulder. "Keep her running until we find out what's up."

She went on suit pressure and tripped the switch to depressurize the cabin. As soon as the telltale went red, she opened the outer hatch and took a covering position with her rifle while Morris and Weaver climbed down the side of rocket.

Once the two of them were on the ground and in position to cover her, she followed on the exterior ladder. The climb in the dark didn't bother her nearly as much as the fact that her back was to the station. It felt like she had a big neon target there, flashing "shoot me first."

On the ground she took a prone position under the rocket, waiting for three more people to climb down. It was a shitty place to take cover—the main methane fuel tank was directly above her—but there weren't a lot of alternatives. One of her team, Steve Lorman, would accompany her inside, while two would provide security on the ground. The other rocket, which wouldn't launch until she sent an all-clear signal, carried just four people for local security.

Once the last team member was down, Kim signaled Morris. She and Weaver then dashed across the open space to the airlock.

Kelly had told them to use the small maintenance lock instead of the main passenger lock. Airlocks had pressure sensors, so if they were cycled or just sprang a leak there were audible and visual alarms, both local and at a central monitoring station. In a dinky one-airlock place like this, that central monitoring station was probably the cop shop, absolutely the last place she wanted alerted. Since Kelly was the only person who used the lock, he'd been able to turn off the alarm without anybody knowing about it.

Morris opened the airlock and swept it with the light on her gun, since with all these artificial lights, NOGs were useless. Morris gave the 'all clear' gesture, so Kim and Steve moved up. Morris and Weaver climbed into the lock and cycled through.

It seemed like forever, but after a few minutes her suit radio crackled. "Clear," Morris said.

She didn't want to use radios at all, but a brief transmission like that was inescapable. Besides, by using a digital link, anybody with analog gear would just hear a burst of static. Kim took a deep breath and climbed into the lock with Lorman.

The maintenance airlock was small, and tight for two. Kim took a knee as the lock cycled, her rifle pointing towards the door. As soon as the telltale went green, somebody—Weaver—opened the door from the inside. Kim and Lorman stepped through.

"What do we have?" Kim said, popping open her faceplate. She was rewarded with a strong whiff of lubricants and an undercurrent of old socks.

"This level's clear," Morris said, "but the door to the main gallery was unlocked."

"Anybody out there?" Kim said.

"Nobody we could see."

"Okay. Let's clear the upper level."

Morris walked around a large manifold to a metal staircase leading up. A fiberglass door at the top of the stairs led to a dark hallway lined with offices. Kim gestured at Morris to go right, and sent Weaver with Lorman left. She followed Morris, able to look right over the petite woman's head.

They walked past a couple of glass-walled offices, clearly abandoned or never used and lacking even furniture. Just before arriving at a staircase heading back down, they came to a solid metal wall, with a door cracked open, light spilling into the darkened hallway.

Must be the control center, Sandra thought. She tried to get some saliva flowing in her mouth, and noted her hands were sweating inside her spacesuit gloves.

The door opened out into the hallway. Sandra grabbed the door and flung it open while Morris went in low.

"Clear," Morris hissed.

Sandra stepped inside. "What the hell?"

There was a cot jammed into a corner of the space, and some guy was sprawled out on it face-down, his pants around his knees exposing his large white ass, a prominent mole on one cheek. The man's hands were tied over his head to a conduit with some rope.

Morris popped off her suit glove and checked the guy's pulse. "He's alive."

Sandra gestured at a syringe taped to the side of the cot. "Drugged."

"Clear east," her suit radio crackled.

"Copy, clear west," Sandra replied. "Base, call for Two."

"Copy," her co-pilot said. The second rocket would be there in fifteen minutes.

"Rally," Sandra said. Time to go get their people.

At least whatever happened at the ambush caused the aerospace plane to leave, Minty thought, looking at the cargo tug from her perch on the spinning crew compartment. Despite the near-lack of gravity, her heart was pounding, and her breath sounded ragged.

And once I let go there'd be none. Except momentum was a bitch, and all my momentum is going the wrong way—out into space.

She patted her gun while trying to catch her breath. It wasn't exactly designed for maneuvering in space, but a reaction was a reaction. Minty carefully squirmed around to get her legs in a position to push off. Once set, she got a hand on the pistol grip of her gun, and loosened the sling up so she could point the weapon.

When the centrifuge's spin brought her around to the side of the ship with the cargo tug, she pushed off with both feet. As expected, her momentum started to pull her out away from the hull.

She twisted around her body, and with the gun pointing in the direction she was going—opposite of where she wanted to be - she fired, once, twice, feeling the kick and seeing a huge flash but not hearing anything.

The recoil pushed her back, too hard, and she slammed against the hull of the ship, then bounced out before she could grab anything. She fired another round, which pushed her back but also put her body in a spin.

With a flailing hand, she grabbed a hold-fast and stopped her spin, moaning as the sudden jerk hurt her arm. It wasn't graceful but it worked.

Minty took a minute to get oriented. The cargo tug was only a few meters away, and a series of hand-holds led directly to it. She put the rifle on safe and started to approach it, using both hands.

It wasn't until she got to the tug that the next problem presented itself. The tug's crew area was too small for an airlock. There was just a hatch, which opened in. But with the crew area pressurized, it would take the strength of several men to open the door.

She was stuck.

Chapter 37

Monday 55 Virgo Year 52 22:19 local (March 27, 2074 14:19 GMT)
Bensonville, Republic of the White Race, Olympus Mons, Mars

"WHY?" RACHEL ASKED. They were standing outside the door to her house. Janet finished putting on a small backpack into which she slid her gun before answering.

"Why what?"

Rachel gestured at her. "Why are you here?"

"You kidnapped my boyfriend," Janet said. "Among other things."

Kelly, now wearing his spacesuit, emerged from the house with the pistol he'd taken from Rachel. He'd also produced a large-frame service semi-automatic, which was stuck in a suit strap. "Let's move."

"How long have you been in town?" Rachel said.

"Going on two weeks. Got a job at the laundry." They arrived at the side airlock door. With the big rollup door down, they'd have to use the side door.

"I'll go in first," Rachel said.

"Like hell," Janet replied. "All three of us together. Move it."

Janet took her arm and pulled them together as soon as they were on the other side of the door. To an outsider, it might look like they were an item. Kelly hung back, fiddling with the door or something.

Not wanting to get her arm ripped off, Rachel walked right up to Wilkerson, Janet standing next to her, a stupid smile on her face. *Walt. His first name is Walt.*

"Hi, Walt," Rachel said.

"Walt's my dad," he replied. "I'm Bill."

"Sorry, Bill. Hey, I need to go in and talk to the prisoners."

"Why?"

"Because Charles Junior told me to. The folks paying want another video."

"Now?" Bill said. "Hell, they're asleep." He gestured with his chin at Janet. "Who's your girlfriend?"

Janet let go of her arm, and with a surprisingly swift motion pulled the gun out of her backpack with one hand while grabbing Bill's still holstered gun with the other.

"Don't be a hero!" Kelly shouted. Rachel backed away to see Kelly covering them with both pistols.

"Do you want to die?" Janet asked, the barrel of her snub-nose shoved into Bill's chin. She thumbed back the hammer.

"No," Bill said, barely above a whisper.

"Good," Janet said. She took his gun. "Open the door and don't say a word."

"Rachel?" Bill asked.

"She'll kill us all," Rachel said. "Please?"

"Okay," Bill said. "Key's in my pocket."

"Take it out, real easy-like," Janet said. She stepped away from him. Moving slowly, he produced the key and walked to the metal door, which opened out into the corridor.

"Unlock it and hold it open," Janet told him. "Rachel, you go in first. I'm right behind."

Rachel stepped into the dingy jail, Janet close behind her. *Close enough to use me as a shield.*

She stepped into the space to see Fred, one of the guards, bleary-eyed from sleep, standing behind the desk with the phone. He put the handset down and said to the other guard, "Hey, should we kick Bill loose?"

"Huh?" came a voice from a mound on a cot.

Fred looked up at her. "What are you doing here?"

Rachel felt a hand in her back violently shoving her at Fred.

"Jailbreak, boys!" Janet said, as Rachel caught herself against the desk.

"What the fuck?" Fred said. He looked at his gun, sitting in a holster on the desk, and thought better of it.

"I'm getting too old for this shit," the other guard moaned from the cot.

* * *

Rachel twisted her hands, trying to get comfortable. Janet had handcuffed everybody to a long pipe running along the wall of the jail at about head height.

"I swear to God," Fred said under his breath, "when we get out of here I'm going to kill you real fucking slowly, you traitorous bitch."

"Not like I had a choice," Rachel said, talking carefully around the handcuff key in her mouth. There had been plenty of time while the prisoners' spacesuits were located and Janet had a sloppy reunion with her boy-toy for Rachel to mouth it. "She had a gun to the back of my head."

"You should have let her shoot you," Bill said.

"I didn't see you volunteering to die out there," Rachel said.

"Just shut the fuck up!" Janet yelled at him. "You're all a bunch of pussies."

Yeah, Rachel thought, but these three guys all got a history together. I'm the outsider, so when the story gets told, it will be my fault.

"Senora, we're ready," one of the prisoners said.

"*Vamos*," Janet replied.

Rachel looked over her shoulder as the group walked out. She noted that somebody locked the prison door from the outside after the last person left.

"We got a key to get out?" Rachel asked.

"Of where?" the other guard asked.

"The fucking outside door!" Rachel said.

"Yeah, it's in the desk drawer," the old guard said. "Why?"

"'Cause I'm leaving," Rachel replied. She removed the key from her mouth and used it to unlock herself. It was harder than it looked in videos. The key was wet, for one thing, and the handcuff lock stiff, but she got it. She dropped the cuffs and the key on the floor.

"Good trick," Fred said. "Now unlock us."

Rachel looked around. Apparently they'd taken all the guns with them. She went to the battered metal desk and opened it. As promised, there was a metal key next to a deck of cards.

"I said," Fred said, "unlock us."

"I heard you," Rachel replied. She walked to the door and unlocked it, then carefully opened it and peeked around. Apparently the group had moved off.

"Hey," Bill said, "are you going to unlock us or what?"

"Or what," Rachel said, stepping out of the door. She locked the door and tossed the key away into the street. Sooner or later they'd figure out that the three of them could pull that pipe right out of the wall.

And I need all the time I can steal to get the fuck gone. She looked up in the direction of space. *Minty, if you're still alive, don't be a hero*!

Chapter 38

Monday 55 Virgo Year 52 23:30 local (March 27, 2074 14:30 GMT)
Bensonville, Republic of the White Race, Olympus Mons, Mars

"SHOULDN'T WE LEAVE SOMEBODY HERE?" Morris asked.

"Who?" Kim replied. The original plan was for Chief Kelly to stay behind. Since he worked at the facility anyway, he could keep people out discreetly. It begged the question, "*Where's the Chief?*"

Pilgrim's absence was easy to explain—she was probably passed out drunk on some guy's bed. *I hope she's got a ride out of town.*

"Well, somebody," Morris said. "At least until the second rocket arrives."

Kim glared at her, but bit back her retort. It was the kid's first mission of any kind. "I'm not splitting my forces, and *Price* will be missing her update in," Kim checked her watch, "ten minutes. I'd really like to be gone by then. Besides, we've got three guards to neutralize."

Neutralize. Nice way to put "kill." Kim turned and looked at Weaver. "Let's move—you're on point."

It was just like a rescue mission, Kim told herself as they moved off through the dimly-lit gallery. Well, except on a rescue mission, she'd be carrying a Halligan tool to force open hatches, not a semi-automatic carbine.

At least there was nobody walking about. The long gallery, over two hundred meters as per Kelly's sketch, was broken up into several smaller lengths by the long pressure doors, rolled down for material condition Yankee. It was actually to their advantage. Somebody couldn't just look down and see a bunch of armed strangers wandering around. Each time they came to a man-door, Weaver could crack it open and see if there was a problem before they went through. Kim doubted the doors were completely bulletproof, but if they had to fall back the doors would provide some cover.

Weaver came to yet another door and popped it open. He looked out into the other side, then closed the door.

"Main drag," he said in a quiet voice.

"Anybody out?" Kim asked. *Charles Street. The main drag here was called Charles Street.*

"Didn't see anybody," Weaver said. "But there's a bar or something open on the far side of the gallery."

That would be the Eagle's Lair, a bar named for Hitler's summer house. It was supposed to be about midway between them and the street to the jail. Kim kept her face impassive. "Guns down at your sides, stick to this wall, move briskly but don't run. Got it?"

Everybody nodded. This side gallery was ten meters wide, and the Charles Street gallery was supposedly wider. Hopefully, all the barflies would see would be a few people walking down the street. Coming back would be more problematic. Damn it - Kelly was supposed to find a secondary lock out to the surface.

"Let's do this," Kim said.

Weaver held his rifle down along his right side and stepped through the door. Morris followed, then Kim.

Charles Street was in fact better lit then the side street they'd stepped out from, but not by much. The overhead lights were dim and half of them were off, but most businesses and residences had a wall-mounted exterior light. She looked at the first such light, noting that it was an old-fashioned corkscrew fluorescent. The door next to the light had a sticker on it that read "Charles Street Neighborhood Watch." She hoped they weren't watching now.

The Eagle's Lair had a sign out front, cheap neon, and a couple of fairly bright exterior lights. It was like an island in the middle of the darkness. As they drew even with the place, the front door opened, spilling more light and noise, raucous bar-talk, onto the street.

"Just keep walking," Kim said in a low voice. "Nice interval." They were spread out about two meters distance from each other, and despite what she said, the urge to sprint and catch up with Weaver or Morris in front of her was great. She felt like they were all wearing neon signs that flashed 'shoot me.'

The door closed, and somebody, hard to tell man or woman, lit a cigarette while standing under the sign. They waved in a vague way at Sandra, and she reflexively waved back. The smoker, apparently satisfied, sat down on a park bench next to the door.

"What was that?" Morris hissed.

"Welcome to small town Mars," Kim replied. Morris was from Port Lowell, Mars' biggest city.

As they walked, Kim heard the door to the Eagle's Lair open again. *Quick cigarette.* Then she heard footsteps clicking on the stone.

"Following," Lorman said.

Kim took a quick glance back. Whoever it was, they weren't out for a stroll, and were definitely walking with a purpose.

"Take him out?" Lorman asked.

"No," Kim said. "Not on the main street." Unless they had to.

Kim looked for a street sign. Just crossing Fourth, the roll-down pressure door gray and cold to her right. We get off at Second. *If he keeps coming, we'll take him there.*

They got halfway to the Third Street junction when their tail got to Fourth Street. She heard him stop, and looked over her shoulder to see him fumble with the latch to the man-door. *Just some drunk going home. Probably has to piss.*

They quickly came to the Second Street junction. By that time, the lone smoker at the Eagle's Lair, a good hundred meters away, had gone back inside, leaving the street deserted.

"Let's do this," Kim said, conscious of them all becoming bunched up outside the door.

Weaver grunted and popped the hatch. As he stuck his head in, a hand with a pistol attached to it rested against his head.

"Rumple?" a man, presumably at the other end of the pistol, said.

"Mint," Weaver said. "And nice to see you too Chief."

"Get your ass in here," Kelly growled, retracting the pistol.

"Lorman, hold here," Kim said. She followed Weaver and Morris in, leaving the hatch open.

Inside the space, she was greeted by the crew of the *Price*, all in spacesuits, and Peter Grant.

"I thought we were supposed to spring them," Kim said.

"Janet beat you to it," Peter said. "Nice to see you Sandra."

"You too." She turned and looked at the Chief. "We find a back door?"

"Yes, but we're not taking it," Kelly said.

"Why not?"

"When I got popped, Janet had to leave her suit at the terminal."

"What do you mean, 'when you got popped'?"

Just then Janet walked up. "He means Rachel grabbed him. You want to explain that, chief?"

"Not right now."

"And you're telling me you rescued Chief Kelly?" Kim said.

"As well as popped us out of jail," Peter said. "She's been busy."

"Apparently." Kim decided that she just might be underestimating this woman.

"Sounds like a plan," Kim said. Then she noticed what Kelly was carrying. "Two-fisted shooter?"

He blushed. "Took it off one of the locals."

"Okay then." She looked at Peter. "You guys armed?"

Peter held up a pistol, as did Janet.

"Let's move." Kim said. "Weaver, you're back on point with the Chief." Morris spoke decent Spanish. "Morris, you're on rearguard with the survivors. Let's roll, people."

Chapter 39

Monday 55 Virgo Year 52 23:45 local (March 27, 2074 15:45 GMT)
Bensonville, Republic of the White Race, Olympus Mons, Mars

KELLY LICKED HIS LIP, tasting salt where it had split. Thank God for Janet. He looked at his watch. They were late, but not badly. Hopefully by the time anybody woke up to the Price's problem they could get out of here.

Charles Street was even darker then during the day. The city was partially solar powered, and totally underpowered. The Eagle's Lair was an inviting oasis of light, unless of course you were trying not to be seen.

Janet and Dex Weaver, the lead pair, had just about gotten even with the bar when a man came walking out.

"Hey there," he shouted, pointing at them. "Where you taking them Mexes?"

"Charles Junior wants them moved upside," Janet said.

Somebody else came out of the door, clearly drunk. "I do?" he said. "Who the hell are you?"

Of course Charles Junior would be in the bar. The guy next to him reached for something on his hip. Weaver and Janet both turned to fire, but Dex's gun barked first, a round hitting the lighted sign over the men's head. Both men dove for the ground.

"Run!" Kim shouted.

Nobody needed any encouragement, least of all the *Price* crew. They must have taken off as soon as the man had spoken because they were now even with Kelly, having started behind him. Weaver fired another couple of rounds. Kelly couldn't tell if he was aiming high or just scared, but the end result was bullets hitting the bar's lights, creating showers of sparks.

"Keep yer head down!" the man yelled at Charles, trying to push his head down with one arm while sprawling on the floor and struggling with his holster.

"Get the militia!" Charles shouted. From inside the bar, somebody fired a couple of rounds out through the window, showering glass on the two men's backs. Janet, shooting a pistol she'd taken off of the guard, fired in return, although it didn't look like anybody was scoring any hits.

Kelly found that he was the first one to the door going into Ninth Street. He pulled the man-door open and quickly popped his head in, half-expecting to get shot. Nobody.

"We're clear!" he shouted, then stepped in. He moved into the space a few meters and took a knee against the wall. Its bulk was comforting. The rest of the group came running in. Lieutenant Kim and Janet were the last two in. Janet used the door as cover and fired a couple of rounds into Charles Street then dumped the gun while Kim calmly swapped magazines on her carbine.

"You don't want to be against that wall, Chief," Morris told him. She was breathing a bit hard, but seemed otherwise calm.

"Why?"

"Supposedly they're bullet magnets," she said.

"Lorman, Morris," Kim shouted. "You're rearguard. Everybody else let's move. Weaver, take point."

Lieutenant Kim took a position just behind Dex. There were two man-doors, one each on the east and west side of the main roll-down door, and the two of them ran to the east door in the corridor.

When they got there, Kim opened the door and Dex checked in the space, then he stepped in with Kim coming behind him in a crouch. Kelly followed behind, sticking close to the wall, bullet magnet or not.

By the time the group had gotten through the third and final pressure door leading to the port, they were pretty well strung out. Somebody was doing construction, and had left two pallets of cut stone in the east side of the street a few meters from the base of the ramp leading to the upper level and departure terminal. Kim and Weaver were in the lead, about even with the pallet closest to the ramp, while Janet was maybe two steps behind. Kelly was about twenty meters behind with the faster members of the *Price* crew. Peter was about twenty meters behind him with the Mexican Chief Astronaut. Morris and Lorman, the two rear-guard Rescuemen, had just pulled back from the airlock door.

"We're going out the upper level," Kim shouted. It made sense—that was where the biggest airlock was.

"My suit's in the lower level," Janet said. "I'll meet you outside."

As she said this, Dean McIlhaney stepped out of the terminal on the upper level, a pump shotgun in his hands.

"Look out!" Kelly shouted.

Weaver and Dean fired at the same time. They were both moving to cover, and both missed. Kelly tried to crouch behind a support column, but skid right past it and landed on his ass.

"Hold your fire, Dean!" Kelly shouted, backpedaling furiously.

"Go to hell!" Dean yelled back, punctuating the remark with a blast from his shotgun. The pellets sparked off of the stone floor where Kelly's legs had been a second ago. He looked up to see Janet crouched behind the pallet of stone closest to him. She reached up over the pallet and fired twice blindly, sending Dean back behind his column.

"Dean, this is stupid!" Kelly shouted. "Do you really want to get killed for Junior?"

Dean pumped the shotgun and fired again from behind the column, the shot gouging out rock just above Kim's head.

Maybe so. Kim and Weaver both poked their heads up and fired, accomplishing nothing except putting pockmarks in the column.

"Your boy's just drugged," Janet said. "He'll be fine."

"Go to hell you damned bitch!" Dean shouted.

"We need to get past him like now," Kelly hissed at Lieutenant Kim.

"No shit!" she replied.

Bullets hit the column Kelly was trying to shield himself behind, but they came from the wrong direction. He rolled onto his stomach to see a man shooting at them from the cover of the west airlock door behind them.

"We're trapped!" Lorman screamed.

It does look like that.

Chapter 40

Tuesday 56 Virgo Year 52 00:19 local (March 27, 2074 16:19 GMT)
Yacht *Randall Cranston*, Mars orbit

MINTY LOOKED AT THE DOOR to the cargo tug with frustration. Her suit only had six hours of air left, so she couldn't stay outside. Going back in the ship meant a gunfight against long odds or surrender.

She looked at her pink rifle. *All I need is a hole.*

Life support in the tug was off—actually everything was off—so if the tug lost pressure no alarms would sound. The air would just flow out. And there had to be a patch kit in the tug. Besides, a 5.56 millimeter hole was easy to patch.

She attached a suit tether to an exterior holdfast, allowing her to use both hands to line up her shot. The trick was to not hit anything important inside the tug. Lining this up took a minute or so, but when she thought she was good she pulled the trigger.

Nothing happened. *Take the safety off!*

She lined up again and pulled the trigger. This time the gun jumped in her hand, and a small round hole appeared in the hull of the tug. She held her hand up to the hole, and could feel air rushing out.

The tug's cabin was barely big enough for one person to sit, but evacuating that much air through a smaller than six millimeter hole took a while. Actually two holes, she determined once inside.

Patching the holes was a matter of a few minutes using the emergency patch kit, and she quickly brought up pressure and basic systems. It wasn't until she turned on the radio that she noticed the ship had changed orientation.

"Two, this is one," a voice, male, said over the radio.

"One, go."

"Two, what do we do with our prisoner, over?"

"What's his medical condition, over?"

"He's been shot, but bleeding is under control, over."

"Copy. Stand by, over."

Minty couldn't see where they were going, as the saucer-like crew area blocked her view. But since Mars was now on the port side of the ship, clearly they were shifting orbits.

"Two, one. We're sending over the launch for your prisoner. He'll be medivac'ed to Phobos General, over."

"Roger. Which lock, over?"

"Your bow lock. Bird Two will be there in five mikes, coming from your stern, over."

"Copy, prisoner will be waiting in the lock, over."

"One out."

Minty, having nothing else to do, looked around. She was able to see the aerospace plane fly up alongside them and then cut in front of the *Cranston.*

There was another brief set of conversations as the bird docked and picked up their prisoner, one of her friends. The key piece of information came as Bird Two was undocking."

"Bird Two is clear. We'll see you at Stickney, over."

"Copy, we'll be there shortly, over."

"Bird Two out."

Stickney was a crater on Phobos. They'd rented the tug on Phobos. The tug had an 'auto return home' feature. All you did was push one button and the tug flew itself back to the rental yard.

Minty pulled up the computer help screens. *This can't be that hard.*

Jack took a sip of water, then placed the container in a cup-holder on the captain's console. He was in the *Price's* maneuvering bridge. Although that part of the ship wasn't spun for gravity, they were accelerating to a new orbit at the *Price's* not-very-fast best speed, so objects left floating would eventually collect at the aft bulkhead.

"Sir," Derek said from his improvised position as communications officer, "shuttle one on scrambler."

"Okay," Jack replied, picking up the hand-held mike for the portable radio scrambler unit. "This is Mike Foxtrot, go ahead, over."

"Mike, this is Sierra One. Birds are still in their coop, over."

They hadn't moved the missiles. Good. "Roger, copy, over."

"Also, be advised that we have some unusual heat signatures from the cargo tug on Papa's hard point, over."

"Looks like we found our fifth pirate," Derek said. "Want me to call Papa?"

Papa was the call sign for the pirate's mother ship. Jack thought for a minute. "If you were outgunned a bunch to one and sitting in a cargo tug, what would you do?"

Derek chuckled. "Before or after pissing my pants?"

"After."

Derek's smile faded. "Probably wait to see where I was going, then make a break for it."

"And that's a rented tug, yes?" It was a rhetorical question—the damn thing was a flying billboard screaming 'rent me.'

"So when our pirate figures out she's going back to where it's rented from..."

"She'll let it fly itself home." And then get out, thinking she was home clear. Easier than trying to go in and get her. Jack looked at Derek. "We'll tell Papa, but get me Port Lowell first. We'll have them pick her up on Phobos."

"Copy that, sir," Derek said.

Chapter 41

Tuesday 56 Virgo Year 52 00:05 local (March 27, 2074 16:05 GMT)
Bensonville, Republic of the White Race, Olympus Mons, Mars

KELLY REFLEXIVELY SPUN BACK and fired both pistols at the man behind them, not really aiming. By the time he pulled the triggers, the man shooting at them from behind had ducked back behind the pressure door. Kelly shot anyway, noting that at least one bullet went high. The man reached around the pressure door and returned fire, peppering the wall above him. Kelly tried to get lower to the floor while still being able to shoot, but there was only so far to go. The only thing in their favor was that the shooter behind them was firing from a good forty meters away.

"We need a plan here!" Peter shouted. Kelly looked to see that he was crouched in a slightly recessed doorway.

"No shit!" Kim replied heatedly. The main pressure door started to go up slowly, apparently by a manual crank.

"They get that door up we're fucked!" Peter said.

"They won't," Weaver shouted. She fired blindly with one hand at the shooter in the door and half-ran, half-scrambled to the large airlock door. When she got there, she produced a large utility knife from her spacesuit and used it to jam the tracks of the main door.

The handle of the quick-acting man-door started to move up. Morris saw that, and jumped on the handle, pulling it violently down. "Steve, duct tape!"

Steve Lorman scrambled to her. Using a roll of duct tape, the two quickly secured the handle, rendering the door inoperable from the other side.

"That won't last long, bastards," Dean shouted from behind his column.

"How many bullets you got in that gun?" Janet shouted back.

"Enough to kill you!"

Kelly looked to see Janet send something in sign language to Kim. Like most spacers, Kelly had a few words of sign language, mostly in case of suit radio problems, but he hadn't seen what Janet had sent. He did catch Kim's reply, which was a clear "okay."

"They're coming!" Peter shouted. The group behind the pressure door must have gotten impatient, because three people, two men and a woman, were streaming through the man-door. The lead guy was running towards the space terminal, not even stopping to shoot.

Kelly tracked him, trying to get a lead. He fired, barely noticing the recoil. The first couple of shots went behind the man, but he caught up and hit the man in the hip. The man went down face first, falling slowly in the low gravity.

"Go now!" Kim shouted. Kelly looked to his left to see Kim and Weaver both stand up and fire at Dean. Janet dashed out from behind her pallet and started to run at full speed towards the ramp.

To his right, Kelly saw Morris stand up and run towards the west man door. The other pair of shooters were crouched around just in front of the door. Kelly fired, his shot going high.

Morris's carbine barked, catching the man square in the chest. He went down, but the woman next to him fired, hitting Morris. Morris kept firing, knocking the woman back on her heels, but she kept shooting, hitting Morris again. Both women suddenly collapsed, like puppets after you cut the string.

Kelly stood up and swung to his left to cover Janet. She reached the top of the ramp just as Dean peeked around the side of his column. Sandra Kim's gun barked, and the side of Dean's head exploded like a melon.

The space was suddenly silent. It seemed like everybody was frozen in place, like some picture in an old-fashioned book.

The silence was broken by a moan coming from the running man.

"Drop that gun!" Kelly barked.

The man pushed his rifle away.

"Anybody hit?" Kim yelled.

"Denise is real bad!" Steve Lorman yelled.

"Secure that door!" Kim shouted. "There's a first aid kit in the terminal. Bring her and let's get moving!"

Lorman scooped up the wounded Morris with two hands, letting his carbine dangle by its sling. He ran towards the terminal while Kim's group took covering positions on the upper level where Dean had been firing.

"Meet you outside!" Janet shouted, running into the terminal.

"Hell of a way to run a railroad," Kelly said to nobody in particular. Keeping an eye on the wounded townsman, he waved the hostages ahead of him and up the ramp.

By the time Kelly got into the terminal, they had Morris's suit half open and a Rescueman in a corpsman's suit was working on her.

"We need to move now," Kim said.

Kelly peeked around Kim as the corpsman turned to look up, his face flush with anger. He'd rarely seen that much blood. "She's in a bad way, El Tee!"

"And she'll be in a worse way if we get pinned down in a firefight!"

"Do what you can, kid," Kelly said in a calm voice. "Ma'am, we've got several groups to move."

Kim gathered herself with a visible effort. "Right," she said. "We're dusting off in ten," she said to the corpsman. "Chief, get the hostages loaded on the one-four bird."

"Aye aye," Kelly replied. He grabbed the Mexican Chief Astronaut. "Pajaro uno cuartro, immediatamente!"

"Si," the man replied. He turned to his crew and started barking out orders in Spanish too rapid for Kelly to follow.

Kelly and the hostages crowded into one of the airlocks and cycled out to the Martian surface. Even through his suit, Kelly could feel the cold seeping in. A pair of Rescuemen, armed with carbines, were standing just outside the lock, waving them on.

Rocket One-Four was a large squat Cessna jumper with a blue and white paint scheme. Somebody had pushed one of the moveable stairways up to the bird, making it easy for the group to clamber up to the main compartment at the top of the squat cone-shaped vehicle.

"We fly in style," somebody with a Mexican accent said over the group radio channel. The seats had been removed, making space that would have been tight for eight barely adequate for the dozen or so with Kelly. He secured his feet to the deck with some straps, and used another floor-to-ceiling strap as a handle. It would be a two-gee burn up, but for only a minute or two. Uncomfortable but do-able.

"Clear weapons and report," Janet said over the radio.

Kelly unloaded his pistols. "Kelly clear!" he said.

"All clear, hatch secured, go for lift," Janet said.

The reply came in the form of rocket ignition, followed by thrust. Gravity landed on Kelly's shoulders like a rock.

"Short flight," Janet said over the radio. "Engine cut in one minute."

We'll be on the ground at Bradbury in five.

All hospital waiting rooms look the same, Sandra thought. This particular one was in Bradbury, the closest hospital to Bensonville. "I'm surprised they didn't have a group waiting for us outside." She blew at her paper cup of coffee, sending steam rolling off.

"They weren't able to respond fast enough," Kelly said. "I mean, it's not like they had a plan in case of invasion."

"True," Kim said. A tall black man in bloodstained hospital scrubs stepped into the door of the waiting room.

"I'm sorry," he said. "We did all we could."

"Thank you, doctor," Kim said. "When can we take Denise's body home?"

"That's up to the Bradbury County Sheriff, I'm afraid," he replied. "They investigate any gunshot injury."

"I understand," Kim replied. She turned to Kelly. "I'll stay in town until her body's released. Head on back with the rest of the team."

Chapter 42

**Tuesday 56 Virgo Year 52 17:45 local (March 28, 2074 10:25 GMT)
Space Rescue Headquarters, Port Lowell, Mars**

CAPTAIN SAM MFUME WALKED down the hall to Ed Newindale's office. The rescue mission to Bensonville had happened during the early morning hours Port Lowell time, and he'd spent the entire day dealing with the various fires started by that.

It could have been worse. Only one dead—Denise Morris—and one relatively minor injury. They'd retrieved the missiles, which were under guard until they could be destroyed, and only had one live pirate—some kid named Ian—to deal with.

Mfume reached Ed's outer office. The Rescueman on duty stood up behind his desk and said, "He's on the phone, sir."

"I'll be quiet," Mfume replied. He quietly opened the door to the inner office, noting the newly-added sign on the door which read "Flag Officer Commanding" over the Volunteer Space Rescue Service logo. The man's rank is Captain, Mfume thought. Yeah, he's the senior captain, but this 'Flag Officer' hoo-ha was a bit much.

Ed was sitting at his desk, a massive expanse of wood only lightly dusted with paper. "Yes, ma'am," he said to his phone's video pickup, "I will be at the funeral." He was wearing a headset, so Mfume didn't hear the reply. Ed gestured at the guest seat, keeping his hand out of view of the phone pickup.

Mfume sat down. Calling the relatives was always the hardest part. Back when they'd first started, the senior captain's desk had been a piece of sheet metal held up by stacks of bricks. Jim Hines had been in charge then, and it was a wonder Jim ever found a clear spot to write on for the piles of stuff there.

"I expect your daughter's body will be back late this evening," Ed said.

He was talking about Morris. Mfume glanced at his paper, remembering a time when he not only knew everybody's face but what they drank. Astronaut Recruit Denise Morris, her face frozen for her ID card picture, looked back up at him. A stranger's face, that he'd seen only once before. She'd been in the Service for less than two months, and had just graduated from boot camp two weeks ago.

"The Service will work with you to make all funeral arrangements, Mister Morris," Ed said. "At our expense, of course."

He looked at the picture again. She'd been on the honor guard for Tony Chen's funeral. Now she was getting one of her own. Mfume was getting tired of burying his friends.

There had been five of them, back at the beginning. Jim Hines, Luidas Volodka, Tony Chen, Ed and him. The Boy's Club, they'd called it jokingly.

Jim had been the first to die, back during the fire on the *Dread Buckell.* Then Luidas. He'd gone jogging, stopped to see his girlfriend, and went home to drop dead.

"I am truly sorry for your loss," Ed said. "I'll call you when your daughter's body is back in town." He hung up the phone.

"Captain Mfume," Ed said, "please tell me you knew nothing about this fiasco."

"Don't 'Captain Mfume' me, Ed. I'm the one who got your pants back from those two hookers, remember?"

"Okay, Sam," Ed said, holding up his hand. "Sorry." Ed smiled wanely. "They were built like brick shithouses, though."

"Yes they were." Oddly enough, he'd seen one of them the other day. Now there was enough of her to build two shithouses, maybe even three.

"To answer your question, of course I knew about this."

Ed had a pained look on his face. "Why, Sam? Why would you approve of something like this?"

Mfume wondered, not for the first time, why Ed ended up in charge of Space Rescue. As a ship driver, Ed was competent enough, but Tony was better. Of course, Ed was always good with paperwork. *I just answered my own question.*

"Didn't you stand up for Tony Chen at his wedding?"

"No, the other groom. Ken Yamashita."

"How is Ken?"

Ed looked away. "Heartbroken. So are their boys." He looked back at Mfume. "But revenge is a lousy way to run a business."

"Who said we were running a business?"

"Don't quibble, Sam. You know what I meant."

It was Mfume's turn to pause. "Look, Ed, back when we founded this outfit, what did Tony always say?"

"That the most dangerous thing in the Solar System was a Boeing L-type."

Boeing L-types had more ways to go wrong then any three other ship types. They were also sorely lacking in redundant systems. "How many L-types you seen recently?"

"Other than that one converted into a bar on Phobos? None."

Mfume gestured at the massive wood table with his chin. "You're the stats man. What's the wreck rate?"

"One in three hundred."

"One in three hundred trips to Mars suffer a major catastrophe. What was it when we started?"

Ed looked up for a second. "One in forty."

"And of those one-in-forty disasters, what was the mean survival rate?"

"Just under thirty percent."

One in forty trips to Mars suffered some kind of major disaster, and seventy percent of the people on the ship died. Not only had the number of disasters gone down, but thanks in part to Space Rescue, fatalities were down to twenty percent. Even if a ship did have a major problem, eighty percent of the people lived.

"Sounds like we've gotten a good handle on accidents, Ed. You agree?"

"Your point, Sam?"

"How many hijackings have there been?"

Ed shrugged. That was part of the problem. Nobody was doing centralized tracking.

"Piracy is fast becoming the biggest threat to shipping on Mars," Mfume said.

"That's that insurance man talking."

"He would know. Besides, haven't there been a few too many mysterious ship 'disappearances' the past few years?"

"Maybe." Ed leaned over his desk and pointed at Mfume. "We're not a police force."

"Not yet."

"What gives us the right to be cops?" Ed held his hands out. "That's a government function."

"People asked the same thing when we started running rescue missions, Ed. It's the same question then as now. If we don't do it, who will?"

They both fell silent. Back when they'd founded Space Rescue, the United Nations had set up a Rescue Coordination Center, which relied on assets assigned by member nations. A number of those nations maintained military assets as well, but only a handful of them had ships even capable of getting to Mars, and none were stationed there. Not much had changed since then. The cavalry, the Chinese or even the US Air Force was not likely to show up.

"We don't have the capability," Ed said, breaking the silence. "And a lot of our people didn't sign up to be cops."

"We'll have to build the capability," Mfume said. He held up a hand to forestall Ed's objection. "I've found a funding source."

"This Yeargan fellow?"

"Yep. Pirates are getting into their pockets."

"Makes sense," Ed said. "You know, Spencer Pearce might also be able to help."

Mfume snorted. "That weirdo?"

"He's forming something he calls a 'Directorate of Settlements.' Basically, towns and stations pay in for services."

"Such as?"

"Commercial trade. For example, Port Lowell and Bradbury agree to a common set of laws to arbitrate commercial disputes."

"There's interest in this?"

Ed scowled across the desk at Mfume. "I didn't pick those names out of a hat, you know. Yes, there's interest."

Ed always was a good politician. Occasionally, that was just what you needed. "So, sounds like we're in agreement."

Ed sighed. "Yes, we're going to have to do something about piracy." He glanced at his wristwatch. "We've got a news conference in about five minutes."

"We?"

"We, as in 'you and me.'" Ed smiled. "Think I'm going to face the piranhas alone?" The smile faded. "But for God's sake, let's keep this 'anti-piracy program' vague. Especially since we don't really have one."

Mfume's cell phone went off, signaling a text alert. "Actually, Ed, you are going to have to handle this one solo."

"And why's that, Sam?"

Mfume smiled. "We've got a loose end on Phobos."

"You'll keep me in the loop on this 'loose end', yes?"

"Of course."

Sam glanced at the video display imbedded in the seat in front of him. To say that the news conference was the talk of Mars was an understatement. As he watched, Ed pointed out into the crowd of reporters.

"We've heard reports from Bensonville of up to fifteen dead," one of the reporters, a pale woman in a yellow dress, said.

"Yes, and Charles Benson Senior has said, just an hour ago, that there were no casualties in Bensonville. In fact, he denies having held the captives."

This got a chuckle from the hyenas—er, reporters. Ed was pretty good behind a podium. *Better him than me.*

"Based on our reports," Ed continued, "there were no more than eight killed. Everybody shot was an active combatant."

"Combatant?" another reporter asked. "These were civilians."

"If they're shooting at our Rescuemen," Ed said, "they're not a civilian anymore."

"What about this alleged pirate captured on the *Price*?" This from Yellow Dress.

"The man identified as Ian Lovitt will be handed to the police here in Port Lowell for prosecution," Ed said.

"Can you tell us about the decision to take this, I guess militaristic action is the word for it?" Yellow Dress again. "When was it made and what, if anything, are the long-term implications?"

"Well, the short answer to the first question is that Space Rescue doesn't leave our own people behind. Period. In the longer term, we've been aware that piracy is an increasingly serious threat to shipping, and we're working on plans to address it. This attack forced us to step up our timeline."

The hyenas erupted into barking, which Ed calmed by gracefully waving his hand. "If you'll excuse me, I have a number of pressing issues to attend to. Our press liaison will be announcing additional briefings when we have something new to add."

Chapter 43

**Tuesday 56 Virgo Year 52 19:45 local (March 28, 2074 13:25 GMT)
Yacht Randall Cranston, approaching Phobos, Mars.**

MINTY LOOKED DUBIOUSLY at the faded cardboard box labeled "Zero-Gee Sanitary Bags," thankful that her patches were still holding and she had pressure.

"This box is old enough to have shipped out with Armstrong," she said, using one of Bam Bam's sayings. She wondered, not for the first time, who 'Armstrong' was and when she'd shipped out.

Still, the contents of the box had saved her some wet pants. Some suits came with 'Dune rigs' or 'stillsuits,' which were basically rubber diapers that one could wear for days and pee in at will. Hers, like most suits, was designed for relatively short outings and only came with diapers.

Diapers that she hadn't had time to put on, instead putting the suit on over her jeans. That had been over twelve hours ago. So she'd had to strip down and pee in a crinkly plastic bag retrieved from the box. It worked, but Minty sincerely hoped she wouldn't need to do it again.

The computer beeped. Minty glanced at the screen. It had apparently found the beacon for the rental yard in Phobos, and it was calculating a course to the yard. Minty decided to get suited up.

She had just finished zipping everything up when the tug detached from the Cranston and headed off. The burn wasn't very forceful—maybe .25 Gee—but gravity after 12 hours without felt funny. Less funny was the wet splat of the pee-bag hitting the deck.

"Oh shit!" Minty said, scrambling around in the cramped compartment. If the damn bag came undone, she'd have pee floating everywhere!

The bag had in fact come undone, but Minty was able to pinch it shut and hold onto it when the burn quit. She used some of her suit-repair tape to seal it up and secure it out of the way. Only a little pee was floating around, and she was able to blot that up with some paper towels.

"We're probably not getting our deposit back," she said to herself. Assuming nobody's waiting for me at the rental dock, she added mentally.

Minty had found a news channel on the radio, and Space Rescue's raid on the *Cranston*, *Price* and Bensonville had been the lead story for hours. It had been a mix of repeating the same few facts and wild-ass speculation by pundits, although the news conference by Space Rescue had contained some actual information. The only good news had been a statement that there were only four 'pirates' on the Price, and all were 'accounted for.'

What was missing, and Minty felt her eyes water as she thought of that, was who'd been killed on Bensonville. Rachel had been supposed to grab up that Connor fellow. There'd been no news as to whether or not Space Rescue had had operatives in Bensonville prior to the assault team, but Minty was sure that they had to have had. And with Space Rescue reporting only one death, a woman, Connor, if he was an operative, was still alive.

The tug jerked as it made a lateral burn. Minty decided to strap herself into the seat.

The tug settled into a cradle on the surface of Phobos as gently as lying into bed. This side of Phobos was facing Mars, and the red planet loomed overhead, filling the sky out her top porthole. Minty started to depressurize the cabin.

She hadn't been actually on the ground on Phobos—that had been Rachel's job—but she hardly thought that walking around with a pink AR-15 would be inconspicuous. For about the fifteenth time, she wished she'd acquired a pistol, and for the fifteenth time she decided to make that a priority. For the meantime, the rifle would have to stay in the tug.

When pressure fell off to zero, she popped open the hatch and crawled out. Phobos' gravity was actually detectable, but very faint indeed. It was more like slowly sinking in water than anything else, and it would be difficult to walk in.

Fortunately, there was a metallic catwalk at the edge of the cradle. She clambered onto it, and was pleased to discover that it was magnetized. She followed the catwalk until it joined up with a larger one, and followed that one into a small building which loomed on the impossibly short horizon.

She locked in with somebody wearing a suit with the rental company's logo on it. Once inside the main area, a small lobby, she popped her helmet and turned to the person who'd locked in with her.

"Anyplace around here to make a call?"

The person she'd locked in with, a girl not much older than Minty, said, "dirtside or rockside?"

"If 'dirtside' means 'Mars,' then dirtside."

The girl smiled. "It does." She pointed at a door at the far end of the lobby. "Down one level there's a call center."

"Great, thanks," Minty replied. The instructions proved accurate, and Minty found herself in a small booth facing a video phone. Using one of Rachel's credit cards, she called the number Rachel had given her—Bryce and Associates.

A male face, unshaven and rumpled, popped up on the screen. "I'm..."

"I know who you are," the man said. "Don't say any more." The man turned away from the pickup, and returned with a piece of paper. He wrote on it "go to Sam's Bar," and tapped it.

Minty nodded. The man held up a second sheet. "Ask for Sam—go with him."

"Got it," Minty said.

The connection dropped. She walked outside and went up to the attendant. "Where's Sam's Bar?"

Phobos was honeycombed with tunnels and passageways, some of them, or so the guidebook said, cut by the ancient Martians. A series of such passageways, populated with people both in and out of spacesuits, had led to a small spinning centrifuge. Sam's Bar occupied about a fifth of the circumference of one level of the centrifuge, and proved to be a dark place with peeling plastic-laminate walls. Steeling her nerves, Minty walked in.

"I'm looking for Sam," she told the bartender, a battered woman of indeterminate race.

"Have a seat in his booth," she said, pointing to a booth near the door marked 'reserved.'

"Don't suppose y'all serve food?" Minty asked.

"Hot dogs," the woman replied.

"I'll have two. And a beer."

"We got a drinking age around here," she replied.

"Then a pop. Or ice tea or water or I don't care."

"Sit. I'll bring it."

Minty had just finished her overcooked dogs and weak lemonade when a tall black man with salt-and-pepper hair slid into the booth.

"I'm Sam," he said.

"I'm Minty."

He smiled wanly. "Some people looking for you."

"I'm looking for some people too."

"Follow me," he said, standing up. "I got a place."

Minty did as she was told. They walked maybe fifty meters until they came to a side passageway, which Sam ducked into. The side passageway led to a series of apartments or cabins. At the end of the passageway, Sam came to one and opened it.

"After you," he said.

Minty stepped into the dark room. The door closed behind her and the light popped on, revealing a man sitting in a chair pointing a gun at her. Minty tried to back out, but the door wouldn't open.

"Who are you?"

"My name is Sean Yeargan," he said. "Your sister killed my son." He gestured with the gun at a small couch opposite the room from him. Minty felt suddenly sick to her stomach, as if the hot dogs were trying to claw their way out. "Take your suit off and have a seat."

"What are you waiting for?" Minty asked. She'd been sitting now in her jeans and bra for almost half an hour. During that time, the man hadn't said a word to her. Although the gun had never wavered.

There was a knock on the door—two, then one. "The rest of the party is here," he said.

The door opened, and Rachel walked in, with Sam following her.

"What the fuck!" Rachel said, trying to push back. Sam had produced a gun which he had pressed to Rachel's back.

"Have a seat next to your sister," Sam said.

Rachel looked over, finally realizing that Minty was there. "You okay?"

"Yes," Minty said. "What happened to your nose?"

"Long story," Rachel said, her hand reflexively going to her face.

The door to the room opened again, and a white woman, brunette, slid in, a gun in her hand.

"Janet?" Rachel said.

"Long time no see," the woman replied. She looked at Minty. "I'm Janet Pilgrim, and J. R. and I had a chance to get caught up in Bensonville."

"Rachel," Sam said, "you should meet Sean Yeargan. I think you killed his son."

The white man, Sean, gestured with his free hand at Sam. "Captain Sam Mfume, new commander of the VSRS *Luidas Volodka*."

"How did you find us?" Rachel asked in a choked voice.

"Minty, there," Sam said, gesturing at her. "We knew she was hiding in the cargo tug."

"How?" Minty choked out.

"Infrared," Sam said. "So we monitored the calls coming out from the rental yard."

"I had an operative on the ground at Bensonville Under," Sean said. "To help get people out, if we needed to. When she saw Rachel at the terminal, she called me."

"But Bryce sent me..." Minty said.

"Once we told Bryce that we knew where you were going," Sean said. "he proved surprisingly willing to cooperate."

"I think he's allergic to jail," Sam said with a smirk.

The room fell silent for a moment. Minty finally broke it. "So, what's the deal?"

"The 'deal,' as you say," Sam said, "is this. You two work for Space Rescue, helping us identify and squash pirates."

"As spies?" Minty said.

"Yep," Sam said.

"And if we say no?" Minty said.

"I walk out of the room," Sam said.

And let Janet and Yeargan kill us like dogs. Minty tasted bile and swallowed hard. "Mister, you've got a deal."

"What about you, Red?" Janet asked.

"For fuck's sake yes, bitch!" Rachel said. Minty winced.

"That's, 'Aye aye, Ma'am," Sam said. He winked at Janet. "Lieutenant Pilgrim here will be running our new intelligence center." Any humor in his face vanished. "Now try it again."

"Aye, aye, Ma'am," Rachel said, looking at the floor.

"Better," Sam said. He holstered his gun. "We've got some other errands to attend to. Stay put here. There's a takeout menu on the computer, and some clothing in the other room. We'll come back for you."

"If we try to leave?" Rachel said.

"If either of you steps out of this room," Sean said, "One of my people will gun you both down like dogs."

"In other words," Janet said, "please feel free to take a stroll."

"We understand," Minty said. "Thank you, Ma'am, sirs."

The three of them left, the door closing with a click behind them.

"We're fucked," Rachel said.

"We're alive," Minty said, standing up. "Wonder if this dive has a shower in it?" Then her eyes filled with tears and she dropped to one knee. She felt Rachel's arms around her.

"We're alive," Rachel said, "and by God we're going to stay that way."

Epilogue

Rachel looked up from her tablet device to see Minty standing over her. The tiny cabin they were cooped up in was getting on Rachel's nerves.

"What's up?"

"One of my email accounts is still active," Rachel said from her seat on the couch.

"News?" Minty asked, planting herself in the room's other chair.

Rachel read the email from Tony Lords. "Eggman's shoulder is busted, but he'll live."

"They still in Roarke's Drift?"

"Eggman is," Rachel replied. "Tony and Bam Bam fueled up and got back to Bensonville."

"Good."

"Dolores Deschamps had her baby. A boy."

"Sammie would have loved to see him," Minty said. "Although she'd hate to be called 'Grandma.'"

"Wonder if they'll call him Sam," Rachel said.

"Probably," Minty said, looking away.

"She was dead before you could do anything about it," Rachel said.

"I still wonder—if I'd been faster getting there? Did I miss something on watch?"

"Who decided to keep the radars off?" Rachel asked.

"Russ."

"Then he's the one to blame for Sammie."

And the others. Christ, between the initial assault and this fiasco, there must be a dozen people dead. She looked at her sister. *Let's not add to the count.*

"What about the investors?" Minty asked.

"Tony said that their contact just disappeared."

"And we were all so scared of them," Minty said.

We still should be. The disappearing act was a mark of a professional. Amateurs stuck around.

The computer beeped, and a new email came in. Rachel opened it. "Senior's dead," she read aloud.

"Now it's Chuckle's town," Minty said.

"Thanks for coming," Kelly said. He gestured vaguely at the party going on in Dutchman's bar.

"Thanks for inviting," Penny Sharpe replied.

"Who's watching Mikey?"

"Sandra Kim's sister. Mikey's at a sleepover." Kelly felt her hand on his waist. "Have any plans for later?"

"Not really," Kelly said. She was an attractive woman. He glanced across the room. Janet was sitting in Peter's lap, the two of them cooing to each other. As he watched, Janet kissed Peter and untangled herself, then headed to the bar. Kelly drained the last gulp of his beer and gestured with it.

"I need a refill and you need a starter. What do you drink?" He asked.

"I'll do a wine," Penny said. "Cab if they have it."

"One cab and one beer, coming up," Kelly said. He gestured at a table towards the back. "I'm sitting at the table with the Air Force ball cap on it."

"I'll take that as an invitation," Penny said with a sly look. She walked over in that direction, giving Kelly a chance to check out her ass.

He started walking before she looked back, and slipped up to the bar next to Janet, who was also looking foxy in a tight black minidress.

"I hear you got a job offer, Janet," Kelly said.

"That's Lieutenant Pilgrim to you, Chief," she said, a big grin on her face.

"Yes, ma'am, aye aye three bags full," Kelly said. One of the bartenders came over and they both ordered, putting it on Sean Yeargan's tab.

"Can I ask you something?" Kelly said when the bartender left.

"I won't tell Peter if you don't," Janet replied. "About us. I already talked to Jack—he'll keep his mouth shut."

"That's nice, but that wasn't what I was going to ask you."

She looked up at him and smiled. "Fire away."

"Were you really going to kill Rachel? Back at Bensonville, I mean."

"Of course," Janet said. The smile faded. "I may get another opportunity."

"I thought she got away?"

Janet smiled. "That's the word on the street."

Kelly didn't quite know what that meant. He let that drop and said, "so you'd have just dropped her in cold blood."

"Dead bodies are easier than live ones," she said with a smile.

Kelly touched her arm. "I'm serious."

There was a pause as their drinks arrived.

"Morally I could go either way," Janet said when the bartender left. "But dead bodies are less risky then live ones."

"That's not an answer."

"Actually it is."

"So you're okay with people thinking you're a stone cold killer?"

"There's a real advantage in being perceived as a killer." She took a sip of her drink. "Especially if you can back it up."

She sashayed back to her table. It's going to be interesting working with her, Kelly thought.

About the Author

Chris Gerrib has always wanted to go to Mars. When he was a boy, one of his favorite escapes was devouring all the local library's books on space in the small Illinois town where he lived. He memorized a Werner Von Braun / Disney collaboration, which was full of cool pictures of cigar-shaped rockets.

He later went to the University of Illinois and ended up graduating with a degree in history. He had landed a scholarship via Navy ROTC and was then shipped off to the *USS Jack Williams* (FFG-24) in Mayport, Florida, in 1989, the year the Berlin Wall fell.

His service included a deployment to the Mediterranean Sea and Red Sea. Later, he earned an MBA at Southern Illinois University and is now a Senior Vice President of Technology at Republic Bank of Chicago. Chris currently lives in Villa Park, Illinois, a suburb of Chicago.

His first book, *The Mars Run*, was published in 2006. Visit his website privatemarsrocket.net.

CPSIA information can be obtained at www.ICGtesting.com
Printed in the USA
LVOW060234090412

276733LV00002B/7/P

9 780983 953135